the mozart maulers

Dorian Mode was born in 1966, on the day Arthur W. Falstaf revolutionised the culinary world by inventing the fork-and-spoon-in-one, known as the 'Spork'. He is a jazz musician and author of the comic novel *A Café in Venice*, also published by Penguin. His screenplay for *The Mozart Maulers* is currently in pre-production, and he writes features for several publications ranging from the *Sydney Morning Herald*'s 'Spectrum' to *Inside Sport*.

He lives on the New South Wales Central Coast with his wife and two children and enjoys fishing and playing snooker with anyone born between 24 July and 23 August.

Dorian's web site is www.dorianmode.com

THE mozart maulers

DORIAN MODE

PENGUIN BOOKS

To Peter

My biggest fan, my toughest critic, my best mate, my father

Penguin Books

Penguin Group (Australia)
250 Camberwell Road, Camberwell, Victoria 3124, Australia
Penguin Books Ltd
80 Strand, London WC2R 0RL, England
Penguin Group (USA) Inc.
375 Hudson Street, New York, New York 10014, USA
Penguin Books, a division of Pearson Canada
10 Alcorn Avenue, Toronto, Ontario, Canada M4V 3B2
Penguin Books (NZ) Ltd
Cnr Rosedale and Airborne Roads, Albany, Auckland, New Zealand
Penguin Books (South Africa) (Pty) Ltd
24 Sturdee Avenue, Rosebank, Johannesburg 2196, South Africa
Penguin Books India (P) Ltd
11, Community Centre, Panchsheel Park, New Delhi 110 017, India

First published by Penguin Group (Australia), a division of Pearson Australia Group Pty Ltd, 2004

1 3 5 7 9 10 8 6 4 2

Design by Louise Leffler © Penguin Group (Australia)
Cover photographs by Wides + Holl/Getty Images and Karin Kohlberg/photolibrary.com
Typeset in 10/14 pt Sabon by Post Pre-press Group, Brisbane, Queensland
Printed and bound in Australia by McPherson's Printing Group, Maryborough, Victoria

National Library of Australia
Cataloguing-in-Publication data:

Mode, Dorian.
The Mozart Maulers.

ISBN 0 14 100320 0.
I.Title.

A823.4

This project has been assisted by the Commonwealth Government through the Australia
Council, its arts funding and advisory body.

www.penguin.com.au

Acknowledgements

I'd like to thank: Richard Sutherlin for his comic tutelage; Frank van Putten for his advice and wisdom over the last year; my mother, for insisting I write the truth; Prof Jasper Griffin from the Classical Literature department of Oxford University; some folk from Penguin: Julie Gibbs and Bob Sessions, for never giving up on this book, Lindy and Heather, and Kirsten Abbott, for her creativity and lateral thinking; and my darling wife and soulmate, for her constant love and support, and for getting me through the stress of this book. (If it's not a bestseller, she's divorcing me.)

The Spartans, from their earliest boyhood, are submitted to the most laborious training in courage; we pass our lives without all these restrictions, and yet are just as ready to face the same dangers as they. Our love of what is beautiful does not lead to extravagance; our love of the things of the mind does not make us soft.

Pericles

Prelude

SOMERSET MAUGHAM described his novel *Of Human Bondage* as an autobiographical work of fiction. I describe this memoir as a fictional autobiography. Most of the characters in this book have been so gift-wrapped in the imagination that I have rendered them unrecognisable. I have subsequently created new creatures that live within its pages. Even the central characters (my father, my mother, Sol, Bernie, and my team-mates, for example) are comic facsimiles to a great extent. Then there are the composites, hazy recollections and inevitable reshufflings. A contrivance, I know, but to detail every event and character at that time of my life in fastidious chronological order would mean spreading this memoir over ten volumes – each more tedious than its predecessor. And, quite frankly, I'm not that fascinating.

Although this book is a comedy, you'll find dark pages. Nietzsche once wrote, 'In pain there is as much wisdom as in pleasure.' I've given this a great deal of thought and always draw the same conclusion: Nietzsche was a dickhead. In order to achieve 'the getting of wisdom' I would never have wished my mother to move to New York when I was a boy, or my father to marry three times. To repeatedly change schools. To be constantly bullied. I never found much wisdom in turning up at the letterbox on birthdays looking for that missing card from my mother, only to be perpetually disappointed.

Given the choice, I would have preferred to remain 'blissfully unwise'. But not wanting to bludgeon you with self-pity, I have marinated the darker pages in my usual brand of humour.

Aside from a confessional urge, I need to revisit some ghosts in order for you to understand why a promising young composer at the Conservatorium of Music would form a rugby league team and play other universities in order to have the living shit kicked out of him. So please indulge me a little.

Finally, within the confines of entertainment I have tried to bring you the truth. I know I failed miserably at times, such is the patina of memory, that and a whorish need to make you laugh. And like all memoirs, time morphs memory into nostalgia. Clive James wrote of his wonderful trilogy of memoirs, 'Nothing I have said is factual except the bits that sound like fiction.' The same applies here. And while I've put certain people under the microscope in order to bring perspicuity to the years of pain and loneliness I felt as a boy, I have, as usual, saved the toughest examination for myself.

⌒

Conductor, if you would kindly make your way to the stage . . .

Wriggletto

I'LL GIVE YOU A TIP: NEVER PISS off your shrink. Insult his receptionist and you're a misogynist. Accidentally step on his toe and you're a latent psychopath with a foot fetish. Scratch his car and you're a repressed homosexual with motoring issues. So, squirming in my new shrink's waiting room, I wriggled from one bony buttock to another. It was raining. Fat drops fell against the terracotta-tiled roof, the syncopated drumming an accompaniment to my thoughts. I was aching for a smoke. A sign on the wall said anyone caught smoking would be instantly beheaded (making it difficult to blow smoke rings). I didn't want to pop outside in case my name was called. I needed to make a good first impression.

Other medicos shared these rooms, so I sat facing several doors not knowing which one offered a glimpse of sanity. A receptionist spoke on the phone in muffled tones (something about 'Barry's rash') as patients feigned reading year-old magazines and peeked at watches. I leafed through the good old waiting-room staple: *National Geographic*.

A doctor walked out, eyes in a folder. Neatly dressed in a sky-blue linen shirt and knitted tie, he looked like my man. I sat to attention like an eager schoolboy. He nodded across the waiting room. A fiftyish woman with a spherical bottom waddled into his surgery. I slouched back into my seat, perusing a riveting article on the fossilised turds of Neanderthal man.

This was my seventh shrink in as many years. I was counting on this one offering a ticket to normalcy because he was the only one in the country to take Medicare. It's why a glut of writers, poets, musicians and a motley collection of deadbeat bohemians sought him out. He was free. You could bludgeon him with 'penis envy' or 'vagina dentata' till the cows came home and it cost you zip!

A tremulous, gaunt man in his late thirties was sitting at the end of the room masked in sunglasses. He was a local jazz musician but I couldn't place him. He eschewed my gaze, glued to some yachting magazine – like jazz musicians are big yacht owners.

A door opened and a grey-templed man in shining brogues scanned the room. Balancing a pair of half-moon spectacles on the end of his nose, he peered into a manila folder. This *must* be the guy, I thought. Looks like a Jungian to me.

He looked at me; I looked at him. He looked at me; I looked at him. He looked annoyed. I stretched my eyelids and smiled. He signalled with a nod.

Closing the door, he asked me to remove my shirt. He felt my arms, measured my chest. He asked me to lift small weights. (This was different, I thought.) He made notes. He then asked how long I had suffered from an eating disorder! Now, although I possessed the stunning physique of a concentration-camp victim on a low-carb diet, I was offended. I said I didn't *have* an eating disorder. I was merely watching my weight. He said he treated people with anorexia. I said I was here to see 'the shrink who took Medicare'. We quickly realised our mistake. He gave me some McDonald's vouchers and I left in high dudgeon.

I returned to my *National Geographic*. More muted conversation about 'Barry's boils' from reception. Dr Food re-emerged, red-faced, and called out a name in private-school vowels. An anorexic teenager got to her feet. This took about a week. She stumbled into his office as I continued reading about artificially inseminating the Himalayan yak.

Another door opened and a dishevelled man staggered out, puffing a cigarette. A light snow of ash covered his tan polyester suit. With his matted brown hair, baggy trousers and shirt dotted with cigarette burns, he was obviously in need of urgent psychiatric care. He stood in a daze, rambling to himself. Then he called my name.

I trailed him into his office, which was blue with cigarette smoke. There was no leather couch. No shelves of golfing trophies, medical degrees or cairns of middle-class mags on cigars, antique sports cars or European retreats, just a couple of chairs that he'd picked up off the street and some lame pictures of dolphins. You remember those ghastly prints from the 1980s, don't you?

A leaning sign on the wall read: 'The Dolphin Clinic'.

Great. A bloody hippie! I thought.

He asked me to take a seat in the gutless chair that was a patchwork of gaffer tape.

'My name's Sol,' he said. 'Dr Solomon Goldworm.'

'Hi, I'm Dorian.'

'Dorian Mode? That's a jazz scale, isn't it?'

'Yes.'

'How did the name change come about?' he asked, through a veil of smoke. 'I'm interested in people who change their names.'

'Do you think I'm trying to reinvent myself? Trying to reconstruct my childhood? Trying to hide behind a musical pun? Cowering beneath an aegis of levity? Trying to . . .'

He furiously took notes.

'. . . oh, well, actually, I didn't think I'd be accepted into the Conservatorium, so at the audition I signed up as "Dorian Mode" and got in. You a musician, too? Can I smoke?'

'Have one of mine.' He offered me a cigarette from a blond pine box that contained enough cigarettes to sustain the troops during the invasion of Normandy. 'Yeah, I play the saxophone,' he said. 'Rather badly. What do you play?'

'The piano. And I sing a little.'

'So you're studying the piano?'

'I'm a Composition major, actually. Though I'm taking a lot of jazz subjects. I'm studying jazz piano with Mike Nock.'

'Can't say I've heard of him,' he said, balancing a totem of ash before dropping it in a coffee cup. He shuffled papers. 'Now . . . you were seeing Dr Carpenter . . . at outpatients . . . Prince of Wales . . . how long?'

'Not long.'

'Why?'

'The first question he asked was: "How many times a day do you masturbate?"'

'What did you say?'

'"The only wanker in this room is the one wearing the tie." Things went downhill from there.'

He nibbled his pencil before putting a line through something. Wanking questions out.

'So what's on your mind?'

'Mainly insanity.'

'Well, you've come to the right place. We do insanity in three different shades: mania, phobia, schizophrenia. What's yours?'

'What's in this year? I believe schizophrenia is the "new black".'

'Is that what you think you have? Schizophrenia?'

There was a silence.

I cried.

Between a thousand cigarettes and bad jokes, I spoke on the Freudian bread-and-butter subject of my childhood. Here it is in a nutshell (a somewhat apt noun).

⌒

Before I was eight years old my father had married three times – common today, unusual in the late sixties, early seventies. My parents separated when I was a toddler and my father quickly remarried. My stepmother resented being fettered to me while my real mother enjoyed the liberty of single life. My father exacerbated the situation by being either at work or at the pub for long hours. So my step-mother took it out on me. My memories of her are most unpleasant.

In the custody battle for my person, she told the judge that she would happily bring me up as her own son. But my stepmother was soon pregnant. The arrival of my brother ensured the imbalance of love was palpable. I soon began to have trouble at school and con-stantly ran away from home. However, by some divine intervention, my father and Mommie Dearest were heading for the divorce courts. But the seed of neurosis had taken root. They say, 'Give me the boy until he is seven, and I'll give you the man.' By the time I was seven, I was a burgeoning basket case in a Spiderman costume.

My stepmother remarried and moved out west with her new hus-band and his children from a previous marriage. She took my (half-) brother with her. He was a macho kid who dreamed of joining the army. He seemed, unlike me, to take his share of childhood trauma in his stride. His psyche was the Rock of Gibraltar.

While my father was between wives, I was shuffled off to my paternal grandmother, who had regular electric-shock treatment for depression. (I believe this therapy has since been superseded. They now have alternative treatments: large doses of country and western music.) I lived with her for a year in the beige stain that was the housing-commission belt in the outer western suburbs of Sydney.

Meanwhile, Mother was on her peregrination of self-discovery. I'd receive random postcards festooned with stamps from France and Italy and other exotic places.

My father soon remarried and I moved in with Dad and stepmother #2, Patsy. (They are still married today.) My mother eventually returned and I stayed with her on odd weekends.

However, as my stepmother experience was tainted, I didn't make it easy for my father's new bride to adjust to instant motherhood. We got on like fire and water. I still have many issues with her, but she did bring me up and never sent me away. For that I am grateful.

I am also reminded of Strindberg, who was so bitter about his step-mother he entitled his autobiography *The Son of a Servant*. Petty.

I emerged from childhood feeling worthless, unwanted and replete with self-loathing. The residuum of which still lines the soul. My escape was my imagination. But this sanctuary was turning on me. Becoming a dark friend. Someone not to be trusted. By the time I was twenty, I was suffering from crippling anxiety attacks. Being hypersensitive, I shouldered the blame for my father's failed relationships and my mother's periodic abandonment until it ultimately consumed me. My father prefers not to recall this period of my life, but you didn't have to be Carl Jung's bartender to realise that my mangled psyche was headed for a meltdown.

That day, my childhood poured into Sol's office as from a broken sewerage pipe. During my adolescence I had seen a procession of school counsellors, therapists and shrinks, so sitting in Sol's rooms felt like home. And I spoke with ease and an emerging sense of relief.

After the smoke cleared from his pencil, Sol put down his notes, shook his head and sighed. He sat staring at me for a while. He finally said that he was amazed I wasn't addicted to heroin or institutionalised or hadn't attempted suicide. He confessed he'd seen others with less childhood trauma fare worse and seemed genuinely astonished that I'd managed to survive at all. (This cheered me up. Perhaps I'd be presented with a psychiatric blue ribbon!)

Sol told me not to panic. I wasn't losing my mind. I wasn't, he said, suffering from a psychosis but a neurosis. He defined neurosis as old-fashioned behaviour. Anxiety attacks on the surface resemble schizophrenia but I wasn't a schizophrenic as had been thought. He declared anxiety was not a real feeling but a flag. A signal that something within requires resolution. A short circuit between thinking and feeling. The wider the gap between thinking and feeling, the higher the level of anxiety. He said my anxiety was repressed hostility, adding something about 'parental causations'. And the closer the feelings of rage bubbled to the surface, the more acute the anxiety.

However, what alarmed him (which I found out only recently when I tracked him down for the purposes of this book) was my 'unconscious death wish'. (Something that I still have but only after watching 'Big Brother' on television.) Obviously, he kept this to himself at the time.

To further assuage me, Sol said I would grow out of these attacks – eventually. I asked him to define 'eventually'. This was where he became vague and started humming the 'Marseillaise'. However, I was elated. Up until then, I had seen my life as an inexorable, terrifying descent into madness. No one had ever offered the slightest glimpse of recovery. I wasn't a psychotic but simply a neurotic. Sounded like good news.

Sol was a lateral thinker. He didn't see himself as a glorified chemist. So he devised a radical new therapy. Rather than prescribe my usual cocktail of pills, he asked me to 'externalise my anger'. I immediately walked over, violently snapped his pencil and swore at him.

This was not exactly what he had in mind. He was thinking more along 'sporting lines'. After much beating around the bush till the bush was well and truly beat, he asked me to take up *boxing*! I remember the time exactly. It was three twenty-five. I know this because Sol never replaced the battery in his clock. After being brought around with smelling salts, a framed portrait of the Queen Mother's teeth and a rubber chicken, I asked him if he wasn't sucking on his own medication. However, I listened to his pugilistic reasoning.

Sol had suffered from mild anxiety himself and while at university he had taken up boxing as a kind of stress management. It had been of enormous benefit to him and he had written a paper on it. (These days much has been written on the benefits of exercise in treating clinical depression.) Sol spoke glowingly of ringcraft. Of sparring and confrontation. It was hard for me to imagine him boxing. A diminutive, gentle person, he reminded me of a dishevelled pixie with a nicotine patch.

Problem was, I simply *loathed* sports. I spent the rest of the session trying to wriggle out of the boxing and obtain my regular prescription for tranquillisers and be happily on my way. But it was Sol's anger therapy or no therapy. Pills, he said, were now to be viewed as a safety net.

So I had to find somewhere to, God forbid, 'box'. But where? We had no sporting programs at the Conservatorium outside ascending and descending in minor thirds. I then discovered that the Con was affiliated with the University of Sydney. I made a couple of calls and got myself on the University boxing team.

Putting down the phone, I immediately took a Valium and prayed to the ghost of Percy Grainger.

2

The ring cycle

GYMNASIUMS ALL HAVE THAT same smell about them, don't they? A dusty, sweaty, hemp-like smell. The lighting is spartan and they are immersed in a long echo. It's a sound that reminds one of school PE classes with the teacher who was an ex-footballer and struggled through teachers' college in order to exercise the privilege of screaming at and belittling teenagers like me who had no inclination for sport whatsoever.

That autumn evening at Sydney University gymnasium, I was about to be reacquainted with my athletic shortcomings.

As you drive through Australia's oldest university, you step into the pages of a Colin Dexter novel. An Anglophile's dream. Modelled on the archetypal English university, it is different from the intimate atmosphere of the Conservatorium. In dimension and population, it is a veritable suburb unto itself. Everywhere you look, squads of students are training for something. Hockey, athletics, rugby, soccer, army cadets, fencing, rowing, debating, patronising blue-collar workers; you name it, they're training for it. For this working-class boy it was a middle-class metropolis.

I yanked my 1960s bubblegum-purple Vespa onto its stand. Fallen maple leaves became coloured flagstones as I neurotically hop-scotched to the booming hall. (I defined obsessive-compulsive.)

I stood at the entrance for an age. A squadron of powdery moths orbited a bare globe that drooped above the doorway. I finally stepped into a reverb of squealing sneakers, basketballs banging against backboards, muffled instructions from coaches and the clinking motif of free weights: an etude by Steve Reich.

I found the locker room, changed into my gym clothes and looked at my reflection in the greening, mould-speckled mirror. I felt depressed.

Limping into the main hall, I felt acid undulating in my gut. The (inappropriately named) 'ring' stood like a gallows in the corner. Long leather bags swung like pendulums around it. Students punched bags, punched mitts, punched the air or punched each other. This was accompanied by the 'boxer's grunt' (a sound like air being beaten out of a tyre with a baseball bat) and the slap of leather against leather. The smell of BO was overpowering. A man I guessed to be the coach leaned over sagging ropes, hooting instructions at his panting warriors. He was a short, stocky, beetroot-faced man who had a punch that would break concrete (I had the privilege to later discover).

I approached apprehensively. He spoke without taking his eyes from his fledgling pugilists. He was enthusiastic about my inclusion in the squad.

'You're from the Conservatorium of fucking *what*?'

'. . . of . . . um . . . music.'

'Keep your left up, for Christ's sake!'

'. . . eh . . . we're affiliated with Sydney Uni, actually,' I said.

'Really? Don't just stand there waiting for him to hit you! Take the fight up to him, Nancy. Boxed before?' he asked, watching his boxers, head rocking like a puppet with each punch.

'I've seen *Rocky* on video.'

'Huh? He's a southpaw, for Christ's sake! What *are* you doing in there? Jesus, these blokes, fair dinkum. Oh, well, can you take a punch?'

'I played the piano in high school.'

'So you're quite experienced then? Footwork . . . footwork!'

'In an inverse fashion.'

'Break!' My interlocutor opened the intestine of ropes and stepped between them. 'Like this!' He hit one of the students in the shoulder, knocking him to the canvas. 'Got it?' He stepped between the springy ropes and resumed his gaze.

'Look, have you ever done any *real* boxing before?'

'I've done yoga.'

'How much do you weigh, you reckon?'

'It varies. I'm a vegetarian. If I eat a lot of dairy I can be grossly overweight.'

He stole a glance at me before fixing his eyes on his boxers. 'Seem like a lightweight to me.'

'You've been reading my critics.'

He lifted my arms. 'Nah, middleweight.'

He asked me to step into the ring to 'see what I had' – which was nothing, excluding a penchant for French cinema and a lifetime aversion to being punched in the face.

In the time I trained there, Lou (the coach), being the gentleman he was, never hit me in the face. Perhaps he didn't like to see a grown man cry, but when he hit me in the body (which he did constantly), it felt like being skittled by a compact four-wheel drive. He would then ask *me* to hit *him*.

'Bloody hit me, Stravinsky!' he'd yell.

Now, anyone who steps into the ring with someone infinitely better than oneself thinks: If I hit this guy, he'll get rather annoyed and start hitting me back and I'll bleed all over this nice clean ring. So I hit him with diffidence.

On my first night, after an exhausting two-minute round in which I assailed Lou with everything from wild aeroplane swings to slaps, chops, and lyrics by Leonard Cohen, I was spent. If you've never boxed before, you can't *imagine* how exhausting it is. We only ever sparred for three two-minute rounds, but it had to be equivalent to three Rach Four concertos wearing a leather helmet and a jockstrap (as worn by the composer on opening night).

At the end of the evening, Lou was rather taken with my natural ability as a boxer because he pulled me aside and said: 'Why don't you piss off and play the bassoon?' I then had to go through the embarrassing explanation of the anger therapy bit. Being the big-hearted soul he was, he relented – as long as I boxed anonymously, wearing a fake nose and glasses.

Over the next couple of months I was punching bags and mitts and things, but at the end of each training session I was forced to step into the ring and punch fellow human beings. God forbid! For some reason most of the boxers were engineering students. Perhaps they were studying the reconstruction of the skull. I recall being forever pitted against a German guy whose name was Gunter Rhinegold. If it wasn't Gunter Rhinegold it was Helmut Hindenburg.

The Germans are a handsome race on the whole, but with a face that would make Socrates seem fetching, Gunter was boxing to improve his looks. Needless to say, he was no oil painting. And if he was, it was a dark portrait by Max Ernst. We were roughly the same height and weight (yes, Gunter needed to eat more) so we were thrown in the ring together. The best thing about Gunter was his asthma. After half a round I'd hear him wheezing through his puffy leather helmet. Some friendly banter would wear him out a little more.

'Can you breathe in there, Darth Vader?' I'd ask, bobbing from his tired jabs.

'I'm [*wheeze*] okay. Just worry about yourself, ya?'

'You're turning blue. Can I get your puffer out of your bag, Gunter?'

'Put your [*cough*] hands up, you irritable man!' he'd say, cross-eyed and gasping.

We'd wheel, pathetically jabbing each other. I'd chat away.

'Do you eat a lot of cheese, Gunter? Cheese is deadly for asthmatics, you know.'

Even with lungs, Gunter was no Max Schmeling. He would usually pepper me with weary jabs till someone called for an iron lung.

I survived quite nicely till Gunter suddenly left (no doubt to have a lung transplant). Alarmingly, there were no students who shared my skeletal physique. So I was pitted against heavier opponents. Like one Malcolm Slater.

Malcolm must have eaten a lot of meat as a child because he looked like he'd swallowed three small cows. He was roughly my height but had to be fourteen stone around the neck. When he hit me, my eyeballs spun like marbles. I guess Malcolm felt he wasn't punching me very hard, but somehow me dropping to the canvas like a stone, drooling and speaking Dutch didn't give him a hint. The only time I ever got knocked out was sparring with Malcolm. (I even saw stars – just like in the cartoons.)

Another pugilistic impediment was that I could never see a left hook. Even if my opponent held up a sign saying, 'Attention: about to throw a left hook!', followed by a polite announcement over the intercom, 'Left hook arriving in five seconds: stand clear!', I couldn't see it coming. It wasn't long before word got around and all and sundry had me smelling their boots on a regular basis. In the end, I spent so much time on the canvas, I thought about a career as a model for a crime-scene artist.

I eventually broke the news to Lou that I was sacrificing my career as a boxer to concentrate on music.

He took it well. But I thought the high five to his assistant was a little unnecessary.

3

Just godunov to get in

WALKING INTO THE CONSERVATORIUM with my final black eye felt like defeat. My boxing therapy had come to an ignominious end. The good news was that the blinding headaches and spontaneous nosebleeds passed. The bad news was that I was really back at square one re Sol's anger therapy. Sol was bitterly disappointed. After all, for him I was a psychiatric guinea pig with mild internal bleeding. My abandoning boxing was hindering his objective of curing me through 'death by violent sport'. So as I shuffled out of orchestration class, I felt lower than Tom Cruise in flat-heeled shoes. Sol's anger therapy had at least given me hope.

⌢

I should tell you how I came to be a student at the Conservatorium. At eighteen, and obviously needing more trauma in my life, I went to live with my mother in Manhattan. The positive about this was coming to the realisation that I was never meant to live with my mother in Manhattan and that growing up with my father, as turbulent as it was, was less traumatic than being consumed by my mother's neuroses.

However, the nice thing about having a mother in the arts and living in New York is being dragged to art-house cinema, fabulous theatre, jazz gigs and opera. One evening, she took me to a jazz club called Sweet Basil. There we met a wonderful old black trombone player by the name of Al Grey. Seeing my enthusiasm for the music, he sat at our table and spoke with me at length. He even gave me one of his records. Finding out I was a budding jazz musician, he asked me to 'sit in'. Although I'd played the piano since I was a boy, I *so* didn't have the chops to cut it with them, so declined. However, I determined to one day return. (Sadly, Sweet Basil, one of the few remaining jazz clubs in New York, closed. Al Grey died the same year.)

I eventually made my way back to Oz and auditioned for the Sydney Conservatorium of Music. At the time, I was primarily interested in twentieth-century classical composition and writing modern opera. I discovered I could also incorporate jazz studies into a Composition degree – if I was lucky enough to get in.

They take merely a handful of Composition majors into the Conservatorium each year. People auditioned from across the country and as far away as Asia. At the audition the line of candidates stretched around the block. Being accepted was a long shot. I rocked up on the day with my lame orchestrations and would-be sonatas with nonchalance. I also had a written exam to pass. So convinced was I that I would not get in, I filled in my name on the application as Dorian Mode. The musical equivalent of Luke Warmwater. Unbeknown to me, my best friend from school, Phil, had also auditioned.

Months passed and I'd forgotten about the audition, until one day I received a letter to say I was in! I read it and reread it. I asked friends to read it to me. I made strangers read it aloud in funny accents. I simply couldn't believe it. Neither could my family. Until then I had excelled in failure. My father – in an overwhelming display of belief in his son's talents – made me ring the Conservatorium to ensure it wasn't a clerical error. It wasn't. The fools had accepted me. Better still, they had accepted Phil. A dazzling fluke!

I can still see my first day at the Con. I was with my father and Patsy being herded around the studios and surrounding Botanic Gardens in a state of bewildered delight. You see, almost all students at the Con were private-school types; few came from 'lowbrow' public schools like mine. The world of classical music is a middle-class one. Working-class children seldom choose to play the oboe for a living. In fact I became the first person in my family tree to be accepted into a university.

The Sydney Conservatorium of Music – designed by the young colony's brilliant architect, Francis Greenway – is a spectacular music school. Originally commissioned in 1817 by Lachlan Macquarie, it was the ostentatious stables for the then colonial governor's horses. When it was pointed out to his nibs that his horses were better housed than his citizens, it was a horse shed no more. It became a school of music in 1915, intended to 'provide tuition of a standard at least equal to that of the leading European conservatoriums'. Founded by the Belgian conductor and violinist Henri Verbrugghen, its honour roll of former students is mind-blowing. Under the leadership of Sir Eugene Goossens – who was director from the late 1940s to the mid-1950s – it became a leading school in the world of opera. Its orchestra was the principal orchestra in the country until the emergence of the ABC Orchestra, which became the Sydney Symphony Orchestra in the 1940s. Even the legendary violinist Jascha Heifetz, who donated money to the Con, played with the orchestra in the 1920s.

Part of the Conservatorium's unique charm is its breathtaking location. With views to die for, the castellated building stands on the edge of the Botanic Gardens like a gigantic chess piece.

Some of my most tranquil memories of that time are of lunchtimes spent drinking my thermos tea and eating sandwiches in the Harbour-flanked gardens, with their potpourri of floral perfumes, green ponds cradling mosaics of waterlilies and bowing swans. I can still hear the students practising their instruments on the rolling, sunlit lawns. Scales, arpeggios and sequenced motifs melding with the songs of birds – each one a study by Messiaen – played over and over until mastered.

⌒

With lectures finished for the day, I was lying on the lawn catching some rays when Phil walked over, making acerbic remarks about my swollen eye. Phil possessed the driest wit since Wilde. When he wasn't welding sarcasm like a scythe, he was practising. He was an excellent violinist. (Composition majors each had to play an instrument.) Phil had been an anomaly at school. He played the violin and was openly gay. I think Phil first realised he was gay while travelling through the birth canal. No doubt thinking: *I'm never going up there again!* What I mean is, Phil was 'out' at school; audacious in the late seventies. What I liked about him most was, unlike the flock of bleating yobs at school, Phil was never afraid to be himself. He was also a great listener and never sermonised. Not wishing to be judged, he seldom judged others.

Recumbent in autumn sunlight, I explained that I had finished with boxing but was still suffering from anxiety attacks and was shopping for some other kind of contact sport that wouldn't affect my speech in later life. Phil could never come to terms with the anger therapy and suggested that if I was hell-bent on being bludgeoned to death, why not consider becoming a clown at children's parties?

We agreed to discuss this over a glass of white at the Oyster Bar. The Oyster Bar was our local. It is a pocket bar on the rim of Circular Quay, formerly Port Jackson, the place where Arthur Phillip set foot and established this remote continent for the English, but not before saying, 'What *is* it with these fucking flies?'

Phil, me and some other students played jazz at the Oyster Bar for drinking money as ferries bobbed at their jetties and seabirds cried in an unrelenting chorus. What I liked best about the Oyster Bar was that you always found a drinking partner there. One of my favourite drinking partners (and fellow band members) was Big Marty. I spotted him holding up the bar with his bulbous belly. Marty was a fine jazz trumpet player, in the throes of a never-ending teaching degree (I recall once accompanying him on the piano for his trumpet exam). Originally from the north of England, and with a schooner permanently super-glued to his hand, Marty was the biggest drinker I knew at the Con. Whether we were discussing Skryabin's mystic chord or Nietzsche's idea of alcohol being a crutch for the masses, Marty would always say, 'Let's discuss it over a beer.' I suppose I was drawn to Marty because he was a working-class lad like myself. His old man captained one of the Sydney ferries, tooting us on occasion as he sailed past the Oyster Bar.

Marty was partial to Sol's anger therapy and opposed Phil's relentless sniping. As Phil savoured a crisp sauv blanc, he accused Marty of being a 'brass-playing oaf' (in the way string players think they're more civilised than brass players) and said what I *really* needed was meditation and calming crystals. (I'd tried that, by the way. Never worked. I'd ended up throwing the fucking calming crystals against the goddamn wall.) Marty, being the testosterone-laden individual that he was, said I should step back into the ring. It was with some embarrassment that I had to explain that they didn't actually want me back.

I left Phil and Marty slugging out the next stage in my anger therapy to meet my father.

⌒

At that time, my relationship with my father was strained to say the least. Yasser Arafat and Ariel Sharon got on better. Forever seeking his approval and never getting it, I found my father a constant source of frustration and despair. And a veritable stranger. The only thing we had in common was a gene pool and, oddly enough, music. Jazz was an unspoken, spiritual connection between us. In his early days, Dad had been a professional musician. He had (and still has) a passion for modern jazz and, in particular, piano players. He had loads of records and cassettes, and no family barbecue would be complete without Dad's Oscar Peterson anthology. (Although not in vogue these days, you've never heard anything swing like the Oscar Peterson Trio.) He taught me how to appreciate jazz, what to listen for: hidden magic buried within the music. He would heap superlatives on the brilliance of Oscar's technique, the Gibraltar-like time of Ray Brown, the electricity of Ed Thigpen. Sometimes he would play a selection of pianists and I'd have to guess who it was. Was it Bill Evans? Was it George Shearing? He dragged me to local jazz gigs. His favourite venue was the Soup Plus jazz cellar in the city (where I would eventually play with my quartet for years). So music was our only common ground.

⌢

Dad is what Australians of his generation call 'a man's man'. Although artistic, he derides people in the arts as 'soft-cocks and try-hards'. His family immigrated to Australia from the slate-grey north of England in the 1950s (when Dad was ten). They lived in sunny poverty in one of the migrant hostel's hive of half-circle corrugated-iron army huts in the western Sydney suburb of Cabramatta (now a small province of Vietnam). In a cruel irony, post-war Britain seemed opulent compared to the dirt-floor poverty that awaited them in the 'Lucky Country' (if they'd only known Horne was being sarcastic). Most immigrants – the Brits, Yugoslavs, Italians, Greeks – moved on after a month or so, but since Dad's father walked out on them on arrival, his family lived in the migrant hostel for ten long, hot years. My grandfather was an alcoholic (he was never the same after Dunkirk). My grandmother had talked him into migrating to Australia because he was drinking too much. The equivalent of moving to the Sahara to get away from the heat. As soon as the old boy stepped off the boat he discovered a veritable drunks' Valhalla – consequently I never knew my paternal grandfather.

After leaving the navy, and in between bands, Dad floated from job to job until he ended up as a sales rep for a multinational electronics corporation. It wasn't long before his natural talents were recognised and he ascended the classless corporate ladder (a ladder of merit that would not have existed in the country of his birth) to become general manager of the entire corporation by age thirty. (One of the first non-Japanese employees to do so.) From the tin huts of Cabramatta to the mahogany boardrooms of corporate Australia in less than ten years was an achievement.

When I was a student at the Con, Dad had left the corporate world and was running his own importing business. With the business failing, Dad was under a lot of strain and drank a lot more than he should – but he always seemed to cope. That was a certainty. Unlike me, Dad always coped, beer a gassy respite. Therefore he enjoyed pubs. For as long as I can remember Dad had surrounded himself with a pod of purple-nosed, hard-drinking boozers, who all thought I was from another planet. It was a fair call. At times I looked like David Bowie's slightly eccentric cousin.

Dad has always been more comfortable around groups of men. He explained only recently that the hostel experience perhaps shaped this. His family ate in the hostel canteen every day. From the age of ten, he ate with his mates at the far end of the canteen. His pals became a surrogate family. I guess this is why he feels so at home in pubs.

One of Dad's favourite haunts was a cramped, olive-tiled pub called the DA Hotel in Surry Hills. It's been tarted up since, but it was quite the workingman's pub at the time. These days most pubs in Surry Hills seem more like gourmet cheese shops, but entering one of my father's drinking holes back then was to step directly into a Hogarth canvas. The smell of one of his taverns was always pleasant: a bouquet of urinal vapours, sour beer and stale cigarette smoke.

Sighting Dad's boozy posse holding up the bar that night, I leaned against the heavy glass door. A television flickered blue in the corner.

The tipplers looked dishevelled in the way alcohol makes you look more slovenly by the hour. Their conversation was a protracted, unintelligible slur. One of Dad's cronies was in the throes of telling a salacious joke. Another lifted a leg to fart. When Odysseus landed at the island of Aeaea, the enchanting temptress Circe gave his friends a drink that turned them into swine. Rumour has it that when she left the island she got a job behind the bar at the DA Hotel.

Dad was with his best mate, Bernie Johns, an ex-football hero with no neck. 'More neck than brains,' I used to tell my father. We pretended not to see one another in the bar. I never liked Bernie much. He brilliantly encapsulated everything I hated about growing up in Australia. The dislike was happily reciprocated. He once told me that they needed to drop nerve gas on Surry Hills in order to kill off all the 'freaks and geeks' who now made the inner-city suburb their home, implying I was one of them.

The room was fat with smoke so there was no oxygen. By the time my drink arrived I was breathing neat carbon. Dad and his mates were cheering and yelling at the nicotine-stained television. It was the Friday-night football match: a moronic game of rugby league. Bernie turned his back to me.

Those of you not familiar with the game of rugby league will assume I mean *rugby*. Not so. Up until recently, rugby was an amateur game. The aristocratic powers that ran the game around the turn of the century thought, say, a miner asking for match payments – because he had inconveniently ruptured his spleen playing rugby and therefore couldn't feed his family – was terribly undignified. So a rival professional code for the working classes formed to compensate players for their gladiatorial efforts. *Ergo* the best players gravitated to the big money. Rule changes saw the game become faster and more brutal. Think gridiron without the armour and you'll get the picture. It's certainly the toughest contact team sport in the world, rivalled only by shopping for children's toys on Christmas Eve. And, it must be said, it was the sport I most loathed.

Not to look out of place, I feigned some weak cheers at the flashing screen.

Dad sipped his ale in ecstasy. He held the glass of beer to the light and studied it as if it were a vase from the Tang Dynasty. He was moved. 'How do they make it so cheap?' he said, with a loving smile, shaking his head. Beers at the DA were a dollar a schooner (at the time). He drained his glass and licked his lips. 'You know, at these prices, the more you drink the more you save!'

Without taking his eyes from the screen, he asked how things were going. As he only ever solicited a filtered response, I said, 'Fine.' Dad never asked about Sol. He knew I was seeing a shrink, but he preferred not to talk about it. Seeing a psychiatrist was weak. (Even though his mother had been in and out of mental institutions all her life.) In his book, you simply coped without burdening others. That was the 'manly way'. Talking about it didn't help. It was self-indulgent. Middle-class. Unfortunately, this strategy of sweeping it under the carpet till it became an Everest of Axminster didn't work for yours truly. The more I tried to bury the pain, the more the anxiety attacks increased.

My mother wasn't much help either. Since she always seemed to be deserting me, her counsel rang hollow. The antithesis of my pragmatic father, she was vague and flighty. I'd called her in New York only that week, distressed.

'You need to find the real You,' she'd said. 'And the real you needs to find the You that the real You needs in order to survive. The You that will become the ultimate You after finding the real You. And vice versa.'

This is exactly what Clytemnestra said to her son Orestes before he strangled her. (Then Orestes was chased by the Furies, until he realised that they were nothing but a folk band from Dublin and could be destroyed by simply puncturing their bagpipes.)

However, Mum always supported my seeing Sol and asked about progress.

Let me fill you in about Mum. Mum, too, was from a dirt-poor background. Her father, a cab driver and fabulous dancer, was an artistic man devoid of ambition. He had a gift for belittling people. This toughened Mum's hide, but made her feel worthless and ugly. My mother and her two brothers lived in a fibro in Cabramatta – where she met my father. From birth, my mother has had a love affair with the arts. She also had theatrical talent and was one of the first women to win a scholarship to a renowned acting school in New York (where she now teaches). Her students marvel at her gift for accents. She has the ear of a musician (which she carries around in a small case). If you ask her to do an Irish accent, she virtually asks, 'Which County?'

Mum says that when she met my father he was a completely different person. A working-class anomaly, he could draw, sculpt, craft furniture, play music, write funny stories: he was the Renaissance man of Cabramatta. The two were soon drawn to each other – both interested in the arts and consumed by an insatiable desire to escape the prison of their class. They were ambitious, self-motivated, hungry. Problem was, Dad was a little too fond of the pub and Mum too determined to be subjugated by it. The marriage was over before it started.

It's hard to imagine them together today. They are anathema to one another. Mum's a non-drinking, health-food-eating New York feminist. Dad's a hard-drinking, pie-munching Aussie chauvinist. I can't for the life of me imagine them at a fiftieth wedding anniversary. Who would do the catering?

So over the long cheer of the football game that melded with the sour melodies of poker machines, I invited Dad to the first-year student concert. With eyes fixed to the telly, he grunted he'd be there. I downed my wine and left him with his slurring mates and their rugby league.

I remember looking at them, thinking: morons watching morons play morons.

4

Rodolfo woos Mimi
with his vegetarian cuisine

WITH ANXIETY ATTACKS unrelenting, Sol and I agreed on a new strategy that, funnily enough, placed me back at Sydney University. This time it was decided that I externalise my anger by means of the more genteel sport of fencing.

Now, let it be said that had I been born in the Middle Ages, I'd have been stabbed. I was crap at fencing. Having an overactive imagination, I walked into the gym like Errol Flynn. The reality was markedly different. I found fencing frustrating. If you've never fenced before you won't understand. What they conveniently omit telling you is that it's not like the old films. I'd fantasised that I'd be swinging from chandeliers, upturning tables and fighting around them with a princess swooning in the corner. *Au contraire!* Fencing is on the tedious side of boring. Especially if you are as crap at it as I was. You see, like men's tennis, it's all over in a nanosecond. Anyone who has watched fencing at the Olympics can attest to this. Since the ancient Greeks held their Olympics in the nude, no doubt fencing was once a riveting spectator sport (we won't mention the wrestling!), but these days it's on the dreary side of dull. And another thing, fencers are excruciatingly prissy.

As in all sports, there was a clique of skilled veterans, who had the best accoutrements and could alter your trousers with a whistling swish of their foil. I remember one such person: Rupert Carrington-Jones.

Rupert was from money. Old money. And he let you know it. Unlike the others, who were all aspiring accountants and such, Rupert was studying Medicine. He had an oily wisp of black hair and a pencil moustache. He was Basil Rathbone in a platinum Rolex. And he had the full dress-up. His was imported from Italy (he informed all who would listen). Unlike Rupert, I never had any gear. I said I'd reward myself when I got better. I never got better. In my jeans, moth-eaten sneakers and dented mask that looked like the eye of a neglected fly, I fenced like Zorro's retarded nephew. In a supercilious tone, Rupert would ask me to fence early in the evening (to get it out of the way). With his mask neatly tucked under his arm, he would draw his foil to his lips and recite some asinine poem in French. (The French being rather good at that sort of thing.) I'd reply, 'Yeah, yeah, let's get on with it, D'Artagnan.' In a microsecond, he would stab me like Vlad the Impaler on caffeine tablets and move on to his next victim.

What really bugged me about Rupert was that, whenever he'd score against you, he'd yell a short, sharp 'Hah!' So the hall was filled with the sound of clinking foils and shrieking gym shoes, punctuated by Rupert's diaphragmatic 'Hah!' Sometimes, in a difficult bout (lasting three seconds longer than the normal two seconds) he would yell 'Hoo–ah!' If you fenced really well (sadly, I never did), he would honour the vanquished foe with another tedious poem in French about being a 'worthy opponent' or something. The recital took longer than the bout.

Sometimes we'd fence electronically – an anachronism, I know, but it was fun. Essentially, you fenced in special suits that were wired so when your opponent touched you with his foil, thereby completing the circuit, a buzzer sounded. My buzzer went off so many times it started to blow smoke. In the end they asked me to stop using the suit.

The finale of the night was the sabres. Sabre fighting is different from fencing with foils. The sabre is a short, hard sword. You kind of whack your opponent with it. I'd liken it to a giant spanking.

Rupert and his crusaders would engage in dazzling duels of sabre fighting – stretching it out and impressing the hell out of the girls. One night a funny thing happened. As Rupert was spanking the living bejesus out of some poor aspiring accountant, I yelled, 'Rupert, your fly's open!' He looked down and got whacked occipitally for his trouble. He let out a high-pitched shriek. The girls giggled. I smirked. It was a Pyrrhic victory, I know, but savoured nonetheless. I believe today that Rupert is one of the country's leading neurosurgeons. Hey, don't let him near you with a scalpel!

So the fencing was pretty cruisy. Problem was, it didn't much help with the anxiety attacks. It was all over too quickly to be in any way confrontational. In the end, I handed back my foil and mask and moved on to new cures.

On my final night, as I said my goodbyes, Rupert said something belittling to me in French. His friends sniggered. I walked up to him and replied, '*Ne fumer jamais une Gauloise dans un café; ça sent les crottes brûlantes*,' which in English means: Never smoke Gauloise in a café as they smell like burning turds.

‿

Like a downtrodden character from a Dumas novel, I camped at the Oyster Bar behind a tall glass of white, fencing mask flanking the glass, foil speared into a nearby pot plant. In a corner, I spied an attractive brunette with a certain *soignée* charm. She stole glances at me as she chatted with her friends, who all looked like dancers. I don't know if it was the fencing mask, the sword in the pot plant, or me striking a series of forlorn attitudes at the bar like the protagonist in a film by Jean-Luc Godard, but she eventually made her way over. If she was pretty at a distance, she was seraphic in close-up and, it must be said, way out of my league. Her pre-Raphaelite face was framed with a shock of curly chestnut hair cut into a neat bob. A figure sculpted by years of dance. She introduced herself as Lydia. Alcohol being the liquid arrows of Cupid, I informed her (at length) that Lydia (or the Lydian) is a jazz scale two up from the Dorian. Therefore, we were in fact a match made in heaven! This must have impressed her because she looked at her watch. I quickly danced on my feet and cranked up the charm-meter. Like most of us who don't look like Brad Pitt, I tried to dazzle her with wit and personality. Less inclined to hide my light under a bushel back then, I nearly blinded her with it, as if trying to illuminate a Henkel bomber. My unashamed, rampant id ensured that Lydia didn't get a word in edgeways. I then bludgeoned her with artistic and political credos and (the student staple) conspiracy theories. There was no subject upon which I was not an expert. I was an authority on everything. And, like most first-year students, I knew an enormous amount of very little.

When I came up for air, she managed to squeeze in a little about herself. It transpired that the 'tattooed lady' (as I christened her, after Groucho's famous song) and I had a lot in common. A dancer, she was passionate about the arts. She grew up in a working-class family that had emigrated from England in the 1960s – a mutual family history of sorts. She also liked jazz and old films. Anyway, she must have had a penchant for insecure lunatics who were crap at fencing because she agreed to go with me on a date.

This became my new anxiety.

When you are a student you have no money. So rather than take my glamorous date to dinner and a show, I invited her to my house to cook for her instead (this appeased budgetary concerns). However, one of the problems with asking girls to my house was, in fact, my house. A turn-of-the-century, rat-infested weatherboard shack in Moorehead Street, Redfern, it virtually leaned in the wind. One positive is that it had great ventilation: no rear windows.

Although Lydia was a fellow bohemian, I didn't think she was quite prepared for Château de Redfern. Another problem was my flatmate, Duncan. Duncan was a poet and, let's face it, poets never make great company. If he wasn't miserable, he was moody; if he wasn't moody, he was down; if he wasn't down, he was flat; sometimes he was simply unhappy. Duncan would write reams of tedious, angst-ridden poetry and then assail me with it over cornflakes at breakfast. His poems were always terrible. I remember one about fleas.

⌒

Having got rid of Duncan for the evening, I dragged Lydia back to 'the palace'. I gave her a drink to steady her nerves. After the initial shock, she pulled up a milk crate and sat down. I had prepared a magnificent vegetarian feast. That was when I found out Lydia hated vegetarian food. It was also a bad sign when she mumbled something about Hitler being a vegetarian. I was in a panic. I had no meat in the house. Since high school I had been a vegetarian and, consequently, a pleasant shade of green. I never looked healthy. I was the kind of vegetarian who would chide you about the dangers of red meat while downing a greasy Chiko-roll before lighting a French cigarette. (Lydia was not shy about pointing out this inconsistency in my diet, I might add.)

I placed the meal gingerly on the dining table. Placement of the meal was paramount. Not because the meal warranted such affectation, but because I'd handcrafted the table myself. (My father still talks about this table!) You see, I couldn't afford a dining table so, in a move that would make my paternal grandfather (a fitter and turner) roll in his grave, I found an old door and attached poles (as legs) to it with ten-inch nails. It collapsed if you put anything heavier than a letter on it. (When Lydia first tossed her handbag on the table, I held my breath and clenched my teeth.) I had this bloody table for years. God knows why. It was the source of much family humour. (I never did inherit my father's handyman gene.) So Lydia's meal shimmied on the table with each careful stab of the fork.

My gorgeous date gallantly ate my 'chickpea surprise' through a forced smile. (The surprise being that the chickpeas weren't cooked properly, with one nearly breaking a molar.) Then we drank cheap red and smoked cigarettes. She was *so* easy to talk to. We clicked. By the fifth glass of petrol-matured red wine I determined that she was just tipsy enough to forget her surroundings, the chickpea surprise, and my nervous babbling monologue and agree to another date, when I heard the rotund Duncan, fumbling for his keys. I sank. We waited for what seemed like an age before he managed to open the door. With a flagon of cheap sherry under his arm, his greasy hair mane-like across his frayed duffel coat, he staggered in reciting T.S. Eliot. A heavy drinker even then, he had the purple beginnings of the 'RSL Club tan'.

It seemed Duncan had forgotten about our 'arrangement' somewhere after the twelfth schooner and not before the fifth whisky but, we'd be pleased to know, he had a poem for us. We sat through a slurring piece about Nicaragua (a word drunks should avoid), scrawled over a series of fifteen damp beer coasters. He then proceeded to talk nonsense all night. On the bright side, he made me look like a catch.

Discovering the beautiful Lydia was a dancer, Duncan suggested we put on a show. 'A conceptual piece,' he said. He would recite his poetry, Lydia would dance, I would compose the music. Seizing the opportunity to see more of this goddess, I wholly supported the idea. I don't know if it was the wine (which if held too close to the face made your eyes run), the effusive company, or the antarctic draught that steadily howled through the pane-free windows, but for some mad reason she agreed. Later that night I had downed too many wines to offer her a lift on the scooter so I called her a cab. As Lydia made for the door, shivering, we arranged to rehearse.

We stood in the darkness of the doorway, alone again at last. A light rain fell in a mist. We chatted until the taxi flashed its headlights. I motioned to shake her hand. She kissed me goodnight. I could taste the cheap claret on her full lips. Was it more than a friendly peck? Had to be. Part cheek, part lip, but only because I had turned in surprise. What could it possibly mean? Did it mean she saw me as more than just a casual date with multiple neuroses? Did she want a small wedding? Was she good with children? The cab's horn tromboned. She bolted through the thin rain, holding her purse overhead.

Stunned with delight, I stayed like a Cretan frieze on the verandah till morning.

5

Cosi reckons you're a poof!

TRUDGING THROUGH MY ENORMOUS workload and keeping the anxiety attacks at bay was taxing. (We had approximately thirty-eight hours of lectures, tutorials and individual lessons a week. Not to mention time needed for composing, researching and writing papers and, that good old chestnut, practising.) I wasn't sleeping. I was stressed. I was subjected to night after night of irrational terror, forcing me to pull out of gigs, thereby letting friends down. (Big Marty was forced to replace me for the Oyster Bar gig.) I fell further behind in my studies. I became a nervous wreck in class. Eventually, the inevitable happened: I lost it. Judy Bailey, who took us for improvisation, would no doubt recall the day, vividly.

For Judy's class, each student was required to present a conceptual piece using whatever came to hand. With weeks of no sleep, and on the edge of a nervous breakdown, I had nothing prepared. She was furious – and rightly so. She insisted I do *something*. I refused. She *demanded* her conceptual improvisation. I gave her one. It was titled 'Christmas in May'. Tearing a fire extinguisher from the wall, I painted the class in white foam, running around, screaming and in tears. I was subsequently thrown out of her class.

I went back on medication.

That was how I got to see the Dean of the Conservatorium, always a terrifying experience. Sir Richard, silver hair and tweeds, had the ability to inflict exquisite terror with his soft voice and intimidating pauses. I sat in his oak-panelled office, crossing and uncrossing my legs. He leaned back in his leather-studded chair, made a pyramid of his long fingers and smiled. His manicured fingernails glinted in the pockets of sunlight that bounced off the harbour and into his dark chamber. After an age, he finally said that my card was 'marked' and if I stepped out of line again I would be hanged, shot, beheaded, sent to the electric chair and then severely reprimanded. I was officially on notice.

⌢

For the first-year composition concert, I was teamed with a young pianist who would later become one of the leading concert pianists in the country. His name was Michael Kieran Harvey. I could trawl through the superlatives that described Mike, but one thing I liked best about him was his easygoing and unpretentious manner (rare in a concert pianist). Another was his enthusiasm for new music. He didn't think life ended with the death of Brahms, as everyone else seemed to. He revelled in twentieth-century classical music. The more ear-bending, the better. As a student I was obsessed with composers such as Cage, Ligeti, Nono, Penderecki, Stockhausen et al and was trying to incorporate jazz elements into my music – nothing startlingly new, but at the time I thought it terribly experimental. My ultimate goal was to write avant-gard operas that no one would perform. At the Con, all of us, in fact, were trying to be more experimental than the next. Silly. As Mingus once said, 'Anyone can be weird.' We were being weird for the sake of it. Desperate to alienate the listener. No one wanted his or her music to be thought of as 'simple'. But 'simple' would have been at least a starting point.

Anyway, Michael and I spent the afternoon rehearsing before I left for the Oyster Bar to meet Phil. I desperately needed a drink. It had been my most stressful week at the Con, what with the carpeting by the Dean and the preparations for the concert (part of our annual assessment). I was so strung out I could have drunk the wine out of the barman's shoe (which would have been a false economy as he wore innersoles).

Phil, too, showed the strain. However, his stress was uniquely manifested. Ever since I'd known him he became masochistic when stressed. This was evident in his approach to dating. I satirically called it 'Extreme Dating'. That is, he would try to pick up straight guys – the blokier the better. (He never liked 'queens', he said.) It was a complicated affair that I never really understood. You see, he was beaten up so much at school for being openly gay that I half-wondered if he wasn't locked into a game of sexual brinkmanship. This bruising paradigm emerged at high school.

Phil had fallen in love with Jonno, the captain of our high-school rugby team. His panting ardour was violently unrequited. However, the attraction was obvious. Jonno was everything Phil and I were not. Wheat-blond hair, gas-blue eyes and a Chesty Bonds dimple in his chin, Jonno was the all-Australian hero. Before the ubiquity of gymnasiums, he had a body that was chiselled by a lifetime of surf-ing. He was a sculptor's ideal; a Michelangelo's *David*. And the school hero. Phil virtually swooned when he walked past. He'd get the vapours.

Phil's pining after Jonno was hazardous because everyone knew Phil was gay, since he'd told them so. (I was thoughtfully referred to as his 'poofter mate'.)

Phil never denied he was gay. His feeling was: why should he? But there were times when I saw boys come up to Phil and smash him in the face, totally unprovoked (in a pressing need to showcase their overt heterosexuality). Phil would crouch, wipe the blood from his nose and hold back the tears. They'd snigger while onlookers slapped the fist-happy heroes on the back as they stood over Phil and spat on him. The rueful irony was that the guy (not Jonno) who caused Phil the most grief was a closet homosexual. I know this for a *fact* because he tried it on with me one day and I had to set him straight. He then wanted to punch me in the head for intimating he was a homosexual. Rather confusing. To punch me he would first have had to remove his hand from my crotch.

So Phil showed incredible gall at times.

Like the school dance.

⌒

The end-of-year dance was a stressful time in all our lives. Going to a boy's school never made things easy when it came to matters of the opposite sex. Bastardisation, mental cruelty and repressed homosexuality we understood. Girls terrified us. That year, the dance was being held in the basketball dome of the neighbouring girls high school. This 1970s architectural fad was an acoustic idiocy. A whispered conversation could be heard still reverberating a week later. For a school dance, however, the building's design seemed apt. The low, flat dome with its nippled summit was the exact shape of a fourteen-year-old girl's breast. It could have been designed by Freud.

As the Bee Gees' strangled falsetto echoed around the concrete cupola in an attenuated incomprehensible drone, we danced like chickens under the science teacher's homemade coloured lights. I collected the prize for best dancing that year. Mrs Nixon, the music teacher, announced over the mike: 'And the winner is . . . Bones!' (My nickname at school – hard to imagine now when I see myself in bathers. Even the teachers called me by that horrid name, thinking it gave them 'cred'. *Welcome Back Kotter* has a lot to answer for.) To be frank, it wasn't hard to win the dancing prize. The Greek and Italian kids did okay, but the rugby boys had no sense of rhythm. They made Prince Charles at a James Brown concert look groovy. They thought dancing was effeminate (despite the phenomenal success of *Saturday Night Fever*).

At the time, I felt an affinity for the movie, since feverish was what I felt like as I trembled to the school disco, sweating and coughing. Aside from the horror of having to ask girls to dance and face the inevitable rejection in front of your classmates (in my teens I was more insecure than Kafka), you never knew which little prick would turn on you next.

Without the teachers and the UN (aka the school library) around your frail person, you were safer in Johannesburg at midnight in a suit made of diamonds. So I wasn't thrilled to win the dancing prize. I turned pale when they called out my name. That night I was trying to keep a low profile. To blend in, what I really needed was a flared, brown-and-yellow corduroy camouflage suit with purple platform-shoes and a matching velvet waistcoat.

As I gingerly climbed the stage to collect my prize, to the charming accompaniment of raspberries, cat calls and the discordant chant of 'Bones is a wanker' (an unimaginative three-quaver–two-crotchet motif), I scanned the hall for Phil. We'd planned to meet after his violin exam.

(Now I don't expect you to believe this next episode but it *did* happen.) This heart-warming mantra was interrupted by some Scandinavian musical finger-painting known as ABBA. It was Phil's favourite song, 'Dancing Queen'. As I examined the audience, I saw Jonno dancing with an ugly girl with enormous breasts. Suddenly Dolly Parton's teenage daughter winked at me in a series of stills in the strobe lighting. With a sense of emerging horror I opened my mouth and held my hands to my cheek in the manner of Edvard Munch's *The Scream*.

It was Phil in drag.

Not *only* was it Phil in drag, but it was Phil in drag, dancing with the captain of the school rugby team. Not only was it Phil in drag dancing with the captain of the school rugby team, it was Phil in drag humiliating the captain of the school rugby team in front of all his fist-happy chums. If detected, Phil would end up in intensive care in lip-gloss and sequins, drinking through a straw for a month. Phil was simply 'dead girl walking'. I *had* to get him out of there.

I hovered around the punch bowl (a turbid pool of dried orange peels and a lone cigarette butt) in a panic. Then I spotted the handball nerds. I cornered Andy and the Twins and asked for ideas. It was decided to get Phil out while he still had teeth. I was grateful for their help. While they didn't really hang out with Phil per se, they never judged him – probably because we were all different. In the same way chicks will peck to death a chick with a spot on it, so too will children brutalise anyone who is different. Andy was South African and the only black boy at the school. The Twins were 'freaks' because they looked like each other. Mark had ears that stuck out. Brian sweated a lot. Gabe was bastardised because he was a Hassidic Jew. It was cruel. It was unjust. But it was our lot in life. We accepted it.

What was my role in this colony of teenage lepers? I had the double misfortune of being nerdy (by virtue of the fact that I was into the arts and loathed sports) and being in possession of a smart mouth. Might have got away with it in a grammar school. It was nothing short of heresy in a public school.

While Beaumarchais' cutting satire sowed the seeds of the French Revolution, mine earned me a kick up the bollocks and glue in my hair. I'd interrupt a lesson so often, the teacher would glare at me with the subtlety of Fred Nile handcuffed to a float at the Sydney Gay and Lesbian Mardi Gras, then decree in SS tones that we were being kept back this afternoon 'because of one disruptive individual'.

Inevitably the class would wait for the bell to ring to beat the shit out of me – forming an orderly cue and taking turns. Sometimes they'd beat me up en mass. Occasionally they'd feel fatigued and break for a cigarette. I'd briefly get back to my book, then reassume the position and they'd start beating me again. It was a working system. They seemed happy. I never retaliated – wasn't in my nature.

Ironically, the thing that often saved me was the thing that placed me in continual peril: humour. It's tricky to kick someone in the kidneys while you are shaking with laughter. In rare moments of clemency, when I had them laughing hard enough (doing silly voices, impressions of teachers etc.), they'd simply end up yelling, 'Arr, stacks on Bones.' They'd all flop on me in a tediously homo-erotic manner (hey, at least Phil was honest about it!) and then leave me the fuck alone.

But sometimes humour would fail. They'd find more imaginative ways to demoralise me: lock me in cupboards, rub dog shit in my hair, pants me. It was humiliating, horrible. Sometimes I cried. Sometimes I stayed away from school for days on end, lying by the ponds in Centennial Park writing reams of awful teenage poetry. I don't know what dark impulse compels me to tell you this. But if you are to understand me, and this journey, I must. Write it all out. Every shitty, ugly, detail.

So we hatched a plan. I was to cut in on Jonno and whisk away the fair Rapunzel with the ginger bollocks, while the Twins created a diversion outside by letting off bungers. For those of you not old enough to remember, a bunger is a small red firework. If you had tied enough of them together you could have taken out the Arnhem Bridge and stopped the German counter-offensive. For some inane reason, children over the age of seven months were allowed to purchase fireworks from milk bars. So each year we loyal children of the Empire celebrated the Queen's birthday by blowing off our fingers. This made it tricky to salute her ever-youthful portrait.

After standing at the bellying sub-woofer for an age, I attempted to cut in. But there was a problem. Phil, besotted, thought Jonno was finally 'coming out'. By the delirious smile on Phil's face, I could see the movie that was playing in his West Coast Cooler-affected brain. Phil would dramatically yank off his Marilyn Monroe wig, the crowd would gasp, glitter would rain from the roof, and Jonno and Phil would slow dance to Mark Holden's 'I Wanna Make You My Lady'. This was similar to my own reel, except that the final scene involved plaster, bandages and copious amounts of blood, some of which was my own.

Now (and I've had this argument with Phil since) there is no way on *earth* Jonno knew that it was Phil in drag and was in fact coming out. The only things coming out that night were Phil's front teeth.

As I tried to cut in, Phil kept turning his back on me, coquettishly dancing with his dashing prince.

Sweating, I anxiously waited for the explosion like a boogying David Niven in *The Guns of Navarone*. Problem was, it had started to rain so the bloody fuses kept getting wet. This meant I was cutting in on the captain's 'hot date' without the aforementioned bang. Jonno turned on me, swearing and promising to 'see me at school'. But at that moment the (pardon the alliteration) fucking fireworks finally went off. Everyone rushed outside. Andy and I managed to drag Phil away, we all lived to tell the tale.

6

Faust night nerves

THE NIGHT OF THE STUDENT concert had arrived. Backstage was a pastiche of sound: musicians tuning up, playing scales, cracking knuckles, rosining bows, pacing up and down, singers clearing throats and gargling, lecturers metronomically looking at watches, checking program times, tutting at musicians arriving late.

This was my moment of truth. My music would be unveiled to an adoring public. It would be considered daring, new, brave. Bouquets would be hurled at my feet against a backdrop of thunderous applause and shouts of 'Bravo!' I'd blush, leaving the Verbruggen Hall in a fireworks of flashing bulbs. I would be hailed a genius and a modest, but not insignificant, plaque would be erected in my honour in the foyer.

As I peeked through the voluminous curtains, my fantasies were dashed. This audience of thousands consisted of thirty parents and bored siblings. Not quite the glittering debut I had imagined. It was the tertiary equivalent of the school pantomime.

I forlornly took my place in the audience with Dad and Patsy. Dad was reading a newspaper. He nudged me. 'Psst! Phil's dad's put on some pudding.'

I looked at him. 'Who are you? Twiggy?'

The house lights dimmed with a badly earthed buzz. The first composition, Prue's solo piece for flute, was a vapid, Schoenberg-inspired twelve-tone piece. Twelve tones too many. It finished with muted applause and glances at watches. I should point out that none of the students were remotely interested in each other's work. We (and our relos) were there to hear our own compositions. Who cared about anyone else's?

As Geoffrey's piece for cello and short-wave radio drew to an inexorable, running-a-fingernail-down-the-blackboard-for-twenty-minutes-style cadenza, I glanced at my father. He looked as excited as a eunuch in a brothel on a cold night. At one stage he was surreptitiously reading the sports section of his newspaper. Something about 'Panic over Blocker's groin strain'. In his defence, all of the student compositions (including mine) were utterly tuneless. For most laymen, Boulez is tedious enough, let alone an apprentice facsimile. No doubt being in the audience that evening was 'hard yakka', as Dad was apt to say.

☉

At last, my piano sonata was unveiled to an eager public. Mike did a splendid job. It was quite difficult to play but Mike threw himself into every note with his usual verve. It was thrilling to hear it come to life. However, it received yawning applause. No flowers. No telegram from the Prime Minister. No plaque. No Bravos.

Dad couldn't get out of the concert hall fast enough. As he bolted for the exit with my stepmother and the other relieved parents, I foolishly asked him what he thought. He shrugged and said, 'Well, you can't tap ya foot to it. (The same thing Prokofiev's old man said to him, only in Russian.) Look, why don't you stick to jazz?' he said. 'Least you can make a living playing the goanna. I made a good quid playing music. Who's gonna cough up their hard-earned to listen to that crap?'

With slumped shoulders, I watched them run to the car.

In my early twenties, I was convinced my father was from another planet. Or at best a space station with an all-night bar and

Sky Channel. Dad never really got where I was coming from. Nor I he. But if we hadn't connected in the past, this was the winter solstice of our relationship. It seemed we would never understand one another.

However, there was a pearl of wisdom in Dad's comment. The concert was a turning point in my life. When I enrolled at the Conservatorium, although I was scratching a living playing jazz piano, I wanted to write opera. I was hoping to combine an emerging aptitude for narrative with a fledgling talent for composition. (Hitherto, Wagner, Massenet, Sondheim are the only composers to have ever achieved it in my opinion.) After the concert, the whole thing seemed horribly middle-class. Elitist. In truth, it was everything I would come to hate about the arts. I couldn't imagine Dad and his drinking buddies paying money to see opera. Unless it was performed in the nude. And possibly with supermodels involved.

So I had to ask myself some serious questions. Had I become an artist to connect with people or alienate them? I decided that if I wanted to plumb the depths of my father's universe, I had to create something other than a tedious cerebral concept funded by government grants.

⌒

It wasn't long after the student concert that I found myself back in St Vincent's Psychiatric Unit.

A pal of mine, Ben (now a producer at SBS Television), invited me to a dinner party. He lived in an inner city warehouse with the customary matching set of moody art students. I invited Lydia, hoping to impress her with my dazzling dinner conversation. (It was our official second date.)

The meal was one of Ben's infamous curries. Ben was one of those people who made curries so ridiculously hot that if you dropped some of the saffron-yellow gumbo onto the floor, it burned a hole right through to the bohemian chalet below. If you called for a glass of water to mollify the Dante's inferno that was now your mouth, you were a redneck (which is what you indeed were if the curry inadvertently became lodged in your oesophagus). So we ate it with a red-faced smile.

Lydia began to notice something was wrong when, during the dessert, I moved the conversation pleasantly along and began talking with myself – never a hallmark of sanity. I was making an interesting point with myself about Picasso and his role (or lack thereof) during the Spanish Civil War when she ushered me outside. This annoyed me, as I hadn't finished my argument with myself and was gaining ground. I then became slightly hysterical in the style of Lady Macbeth. The only thing that calmed me was my mantra, which I repeated over and over: *Holy fuck!* Panicked, Lydia raced me to St Vincent's.

Until then, I had managed to hide my cerebral malady from my friends and startled date. (What Lydia didn't know was that I had been in the psych unit before.) Now the cat was well and truly out of the straitjacket.

In the psych ward, with the emerging nightshift of lunatics, I was made to fill out forms – never easy when you're losing your mind. One guy made a paper hat with his. Another was eating his. He called for salt. I asked for a pen. Answer me this. Why do they only have one space where it says 'Name'? For schizophrenics, it should be multiple choice, surely.

To calm me, they gave me a shot of something pleasant, but not before I argued with the nurse for an hour, convinced she was injecting me with the soul of Gladys Fife, a canteen-lady from Greystanes. It was then suggested Lydia leave, but she hung on for another couple of hours.

In my Valium-induced haze I finally saw a callow psychiatrist in frayed white coat, black jeans, Doc Martin boots and earring, who treated me with a professional indifference. His office had that Public Health feeling of impermanence about it. No part of the surgery was an extension of his personality, although, in a half-hearted attempt at verisimilitude, it was made to look that way. There was a Cinzano lamp and some mental-health pamphlets with cartoons of people cheerfully losing their minds. A droll sign on a peeling wall read: 'Smile if you're insane.' There were the obligatory calming Monet prints.

Dr Disco asked questions while eating hot chips. I recall him blowing on them as he spoke.

'Have you taken [*blow*] any illegal drugs or medication this evening?'

'No.' I said.

He ticked a box. 'Are you [*blow*] feeling suicidal? Chip?'

'Daily. No thanks.'

'Wyatt Erp fargo seuz dial?' He said, open-mouthed and balancing a burning chip on his tongue.

'Huh?'

'Sorry,' he gulped, 'these chips are hot. I said, why are you feeling suicidal?'

'Voices in my head.'

'What are they saying to you now?'

'Those chips will go straight to your hips.'

He made notes.

My young doctor sounds heartless. But in his defence, St Vincent's Hospital stands symbolically at the midden of Sydney's damaged: Kings Cross, the city's red-light district. That evening he would have seen a cross-dressed procession of drug addicts, hookers, crazies, pimps and hobos. I was simply another lunatic in the queue.

You are beyond help at that point, anyway. When in the midst of an unbridled attack, you have a solipsistic view of the universe. There's not much they can do but wait for you to float back to terra firma. In your delirium you are convinced you are talking to an alien, the CIA, an agent of the devil or some other dark incubus of your imagination. The awful pain of it all is that you're there for help, but can't be helped. So after filling in the usual forms, he gave me the usual pills and I had the usual gut-wrenching tarry until stumbling into the safe passage of sleep.

After a period of time, armed with a missive scribbled by my potato-munching medico to give to Sol the following day, I was released. Lydia met me at the entrance with a posy of flowers and an idling taxi.

⌒

Later that week (in what was to be one of the blackest weeks of my life) I was sitting in Music History class when a bespectacled student with a twitching mouth interrupted the lecture with a note. I was summoned to the front office.

I picked up the phone and, in an unsteady voice, my stepmother delivered the news.

My brother had committed suicide. He was fifteen.

7

The Sorrows of Young Werther

I HAVE BEEN PUTTING OFF THIS chapter for a year. But something compels me to write it today. Perhaps it's the stifling heat, bringing it all back.

My father is reading this and he is angry. We have never spoken of my brother's death. Like certain Aboriginal tribes in the Western Desert who never allow the name of a loved one to be mentioned after death, it is a taboo subject in our clan. (Even at the time-honoured Aussie confessional: the pub.) This is anathema to me. I am someone who needs to talk about pain – to try to understand it, confront it, head on. Perhaps I have some sort of perverse survival instinct that forces me to tap away at the keys, that forces me to describe every grubby detail. I've always been this way. I am someone who has survived by catharsis.

After my father's divorce from stepmother #1, I seldom saw my brother. Usually for a couple of weeks on school holidays – if that. For a large part of my childhood he lived in Alice Springs.

My brother and I vied like Brutus and Cassius for our father's attention. Since his visits were infrequent, naturally Dad showered him with attention and outings that were drip-fed to me throughout the year. Already feeling disenfranchised by my newly arrived half-sisters, I saw this sibling inequity as another blight on my happiness.

When I left home I began to understand the situation. My brother and I started calling each other and became friends of sorts. Objectivity being something that usually emerges with maturity. This, I like to think, would have bloomed in later years, away from the crucible of divorce. Too little too late. One Christmas, his mother bought him the gift he had been nagging for: a rifle.

⌒

As Dad, Patsy and I pulled through the over-sized cemetery gates in our dark, air-conditioned cocoon, the car crunched along the gravel, stopping with reverential slowness. I saw a black cloud in the middle distance. As we drew closer, the inky fug separated into the funeral party. The dark assembly turned their heads in a collective movement. I looked for relatives, for familiar faces among the gloomy strangers and tailored schoolboys.

We stepped out of the frigid biosphere with the torpor of grief. The breathless heat of western Sydney greeted us like a hot blanket. You can't *imagine* how hot it was. The heat pierced the shoulder-blades of my black, moth-eaten 1960s St Vincent de Paul suit. You don't expect funerals to be hot. In your mind they are a garland of black umbrellas on a wet Tuesday. This had to be the hottest day of the year and it was autumn! And there was no wind.

A trendy priest, garbed in a white cassock and earring, greeted my father, who furtively wept behind his sunglasses – my step-mother a crutch as he walked to the open grave. I could smell the freshly dug earth as I trailed them. Clods of orange clay sat in an undignified heap beside the deep trench. Beneath a shimmering eucalypt, two gravediggers leaned on spades. They reminded me of roadside workers waiting for traffic to pass in order to finish kerbing a sidewalk. This reinforced the terrible sense of waste we all felt. It was the first funeral I'd attended, and it seemed that, in the end, you are buried like garbage.

The priest offered the usual Christian ramblings that none of us would remember. This was accompanied by my brother's mother's howling. Most Australian women have the Anglophile propensity for reserve. The stiff upper lipstick. But wife #2 wailed with a latin intensity. This shocked everyone. After a while her moaning became a snug, low-pitched threnody – like the melancholy drone of a bag-pipe. To me, this unabridged outpouring of emotion seemed the only real thing on the day, the only authentic, human response to the relentless sea of grief that engulfed us.

It was strange seeing wife #2 again. I hadn't laid eyes on her since she'd stood in the doorway with her hastily packed vinyl suitcases, festooned with P&O stickers, arms and legs of clothing dangling from them like cobras. I still see her in her Morris Major, disappearing at the end of our street in a cloud of blue smoke.

My brother had been in the army cadets, so he had a sort of pubescent honour-guard on the day. As boys stood in army fatigues in the choking heat, waiting to play 'The Last Post' or something equally ridiculous, one of them actually fainted. As you may have gathered, I have an inappropriate sense of the absurd, so as the agitated priest kept the show rolling, looking frantically from left to right, something shameful happened. I started giggling – something I feel guilty about today. And once I started, I couldn't stop. With #2 howling, the pop-star priest stuttering, the bubblegum soldiers dropping like flies, it all seemed like a bad Ealing comedy. Until I felt the (oddly named) 'funeral party' scowling at me through dark sunglasses. I desperately tried to think about something else. Anything! Anything but the absurd and horrible ritual that was being played out before us. As I mutely giggled, they scowled. Problem was, I was whacked. I had swallowed so many pills I rattled like a maraca with each teetering step.

Patsy (famous in the family for peddling her medicine chest – a chest that rivalled the collective warehouses of Glaxo) actually gave me tranquillisers! She had never done this before. She must have anticipated a scene. What luck! You see, I was already fully medicated when I arrived at Dad's house. She should have guessed this when she found me dribbling at the doorway, asking if this was the home of Honoré de Balzac. She gave me more pills at Uncle Doug's house, then more in the car. By the time we reached the cemetery, I was pinned to the eyeballs.

I regained my composure when one of the gravediggers lit a cigarette. Another snuck a look at his watch. Seemed we were holding them up.

The coffin was lowered into the hollow and we looked down upon it. We were drunk with heat. The sweating priest threw a gob of clay onto the polished rosewood lid. It made an undignified thud. I'll never forget that woody note. Then we all threw handfuls of clay onto the glossy sarcophagus. It felt awful. I imagined him down there, his head a mess, looking up at a group of people in dark glasses throwing dirt at him. When in life do you throw dirt at people? Flowers I understand. But dirt? Felt awful.

The diggers seemed pleased. I suppose they knew it was a downhill run from there.

As the priest said his goodbyes to immediate family members with a measured amount of gravitas, the diggers moved in like seagulls onto a hot chip. Before we even reached the gates, they were filling in the grave, cigarettes dangling from sweating lips.

The divorced parties made their separate turns at the cemetery gates. My father and #2 never layed eyes on each other again. There was no need. A chapter of their lives had drawn to an undignified close.

I pressed my face against the cooling breath of the car's airconditioning. Then I looked over my shoulder to watch the diggers fill in his grave. In the end, my brother was left with two people who viewed him as an inconvenience. They never saw him as the little boy who bravely bottled all the years of hurt and loneliness inside until it imploded. He was the 'three-thirty'. Another long box at the bottom of their feet.

⌒

The wake was held at Uncle Doug's palatial 'McMansion' on the southern beaches. A wake seemed inappropriate for a fifteen-year-old. No speeches were made over raised glasses. No family snaps were passed around. In that time-honoured Australian tradition, everybody simply washed away the hurt by getting pissed – including yours truly. We should have all gone home.

Nevertheless, it was fitting that Doug held the wake. Like a procession of avuncular figures in my life, Doug Chambers represented a part of Dad's life when Dad was shacked up with #2, and the two raffish chums lived in each other's pockets.

A professional photographer and one-time president of the district's rugby league club, Dougy was the quintessential Aussie bloke. Everyone liked Dougy. Handsome (in that Bryan Brown in *A Town like Alice* kind of way), self-assured and flirtatious, he was what Australian men of my father's generation called a 'ladies' man'. And his larrikin blue eyes sparkled as ebulliently as his Blue Haven pool. His glory days were the 1970s. So, all through the eighties, in his faded Boz Scaggs denim ensemble and high-heeled cowboy boots, he never failed to look like he'd stepped off the set of an Alpine commercial. When I was a kid, he'd always ask me, 'How's ya sheila?' It was difficult to offer an objective assessment at the age of five. But this was to keep me sexually on track. You see Dougy (and Dad) despised 'poofs'.

I was downing Scotch and listening to them talking about the weather and next week's football scores in funereal tones when I thought it timely to make an arse of myself. I unexpectedly broke down and started screaming. Nobody knew quite what to do. (To this day, it is the only time my father has ever witnessed an anxiety attack.) Tricky talking about next week's football scores with someone screaming on the floor. Dougy decided it was a good time to check the filter on his new Creepy Crawly Automatic Pool Cleaner. My stepmother quickly rushed in with pills. I must have blacked out because I remember coming to on the sofa in my crapulous clothing, wondering where I was. I asked my stepmother what had happened. She said, in hushed tones, that there had been an 'episode'. I take it not a rerun of *Cheers*.

I had once again let my father down with my inherent weakness. I was flawed. Less of a man. At the wake, like all upstanding Australian men, my father remained the picture of emotional sobriety. I did not. As I lay cataleptic on the sofa, cradling a freshly filled Scotch and balancing a tranquilliser on the apex of my tongue, out of the corner of my bloodshot eye I could see him staring at me.

What on earth was he thinking?

8

Tackling will only Salome down

AFTER MY BROTHER'S SUICIDE, the attacks grew steadily worse. With alarming regularity I was back in Sol's office, my eyes twin black moons. He was always there for me, chain-smoking, taking notes, thinking. Through a pall of smoke I could just make out his form via the glowing red beacon that was the ember of his perpetually burning cigarette. The Olympic flame never burned so constantly. He looked worried. My brother's death had rattled him. Rattled all of us. And it infused my own plight with a sense of urgency.

To get me off my medication, we were back on the anger-therapy horse again. I was thrilled. Boxing had been a disaster. Fencing had been a complete waste of time – although it did improve my French. I was behind in my studies. But I was taking more pills than Elvis. So Sol came up with an idea that had me suspecting he was dipping into his own medicine cabinet.

He suggested I play football.

After momentary shock, I explained that my childhood experiences with rugby were simply *too* traumatic to revisit. That I *despised* rugby. And people who played rugby. That rugby brilliantly encapsulated everything I hated about Australian culture. Everything I hated about school, about my father's machismo universe, about my childhood. Sol furiously took notes. Pausing to ash his cigarette, he then explained that he wasn't actually referring to the gentleman's game of rugby union: 'the game they play in heaven'. He was, in fact, referring to 'the game they play in hell': rugby *league*.

I removed my shoe and threw it at him.

⌢

Needless to say, at school I was dreadful at sport. I could just manage soccer. (I played it on weekends for a while. Dad was the manager of the team and used to drive carloads of kids all over Sydney.) I liked soccer but, if you were an Anglo and played soccer at school, you were an outcast. Johnny Warren, the face of Australian soccer, entitled his memoir *Sheilas, Wogs and Poofters*. Because, according to Johnny, that's what you were if you played soccer at school. Real blokes played footy (i.e. rugby, rugby league or, in southern states, Aussie Rules).

My high-school years were mostly spent at a no-frills school in the south-eastern suburbs of Sydney. The suburb is a proud rugby district. If you were an Anglo and had at least one lung, you were expected to play rugby. To this day, the school has one of the finest schoolboy rugby teams in the world. So you either played rugby or perished. My English teacher would one day coach the national team, so you even got rugby mixed with your poetry. And I *hated* it. (Later that year Phil and I would have a new English teacher, a wonderful man who introduced us to the comedy of Spike Milligan and James Thurber and made Shakespeare seem exciting. Then it was Goodbye Mr Chip-kick!) Under duress, and wanting to advance in English, Phil and I finally joined the school rugby team. Dad was ecstatic.

At the tryouts, we were beyond tragic. However, by some divine intervention we made the D team. (I was later told they were short of numbers.) Since they took Phil and me, Andy, Gabe and the Twins joined too.

It must be said that the best thing about joining the rugby team was the prized myrtle-green jersey. That and the fact that the D team was presented with the same jersey as the A team. It didn't have 'fourth rate' plastered all over it. I remember when I got mine. It was an absolute chick magnet. The thing to do was to swagger around the shopping mall with it lassoed around your waist. Girls were impressed. Boys treated you with respect. It veiled unwanted erections.

For boys as inept as Phil and me, playing in a schoolboy competition that spawned the Ella brothers, several future South Sydney and Eastern Suburbs rugby league stars, and a pantheon of Randwick rugby legends, it was an uphill battle. In the end, it boiled down to a case of physics. The other boys all ate copious amounts of red meat and surfed. On weekends, as I combed the beach for shells, I'd see them drifting on their surfboards like seabirds, waiting for the perfect wave, their 'moles' shiny with oil, baking themselves like chickens till their heroes returned. Shaped by the sea, they were mini Sherman tanks with acne. Tackling them was perilous. Whenever I tried it, I was felled like a sapling. In the end, I undermined the confidence of the entire team. There is nothing worse than someone trembling at the back of the scrum. Makes everybody nervous. Luckily, none of the D team that year was much good. We got a regular shellacking. (This didn't sit well with the rugby-proud coaching staff.) Certain teams we simply dreaded playing. We hated playing Maroubra. They were mostly Polynesians. They all looked like pocket nightclub bouncers. Even the girls could whip you.

We played mid-week so Dad couldn't make every game. When he did watch us play, he'd be screaming from the sideline like a half-starved sailor sighting land. To please him, I'd attempt some sort of feeble tackle, only to be mowed down by a rolling maul of Maori teenagers. As the whirly-whirly of flesh moved down field I'd lie prostrate, till our coach – Mr Diamond the metalwork teacher – ran onto the field with his comprehensive medical kit: a bucket and sponge. If you broke your nose, snapped a tendon, punctured a lung or ruptured a kidney, the treatment was the same: slapped about the head with a wet sponge and told to get off your arse and join the fray. It was horrid.

Phil was smart. He was on the wing. The only way he was going to get the ball was by Zeppelin. I was in the forwards. Stupid. I remember the most terrifying part of being a forward was being caught under the ruck. My position was flanker, or what they used to call 'breakaway' (aptly named in my case). I unfortunately discovered that the flanker is the suicide bomber of the team. It is the flanker's mission to dive on any loose ball and recycle it to the rest of the forwards. After doing this a couple of times I never made the mistake of doing it again. You see, if you were caught on the wrong side of the ruck, the opposing coach would instruct his players to give you what is known in the parlance of rugby as 'a little shoe'. Essentially, this gave the team – in their screw-in metal-studded boots – carte blanche to re-enact the final dance sequence from Gene Kelly's *An American in Paris* upon your fragile skull. This was your cue to cover your head and get the hell out of there. Tricky when your arm is pinned to the turf by some fat teenage prop-forward. I quickly grasped the situation. So with thespian athleticism I would arrive at the ball a fraction after someone else had. In the end, it became superb pantomime. Worthy of a BAFTA.

The school we most dreaded playing was at La Perouse – so named after the ill-fated French explorer who arrived at Botany Bay a week after dear Cook, thereby saving us from a lifetime of Charles Aznavor records but abandoning us to the delights of that ultimate oxymoron: 'English cuisine'. Fittingly, La Perouse was an endless, sandy expanse of bleakness. For the hapless D-team, it was a racial battleground.

We would sit trembling as the 394 bus snaked along Anzac Parade to its destination: the end of our terracotta-tiled universe. When you stepped off the bus you could hear the wind whistling through the place. Arrival was always signalled by the anxious look on the driver's face. Why? Because La Perouse was full of very angry Kooris. And they were never angrier than when they met you on the football field. It was time for some cultural payback, meted out mercilessly.

To add to this tableau of despair, we played our indigenous neighbours on a field that was beside a maximum-security prison. We would have preferred playing the prisoners. Before sledging became fashionable in world sport, the Kooris were true innovators of the craft. They would begin a corroboree of sweet-nothings, defeating us before we even took the field. 'I'm gunna fucken kill you, Whitey.' Or, 'What are you starin at, Honky? Haven't ya seen a blackfella before?' Or, 'I'm gunna spear-tackle ya, white trash!'

A spear-tackle (since outlawed) is a two-man tackle where someone drives you back, while another player grabs you kindly by the testicles, lifts you arse over apex and drives you head-first into the turf like a javelin. If, after the tackle, you still have feeling in your arms and legs, you are seriously concussed and, in later life, unable to hail a cab without involuntarily sticking out your tongue. In the end, we'd resort to our familiar strategy: get the ball to Trevor.

Trevor Applebottom would run up the ball with the courage of a lion and the brain of a lobster. The team would watch with cringing bemusement as he was positively creamed (making us wince at times). This was our cue to make a lot of noise, form a ruck over his corpse, perform the 'River Dance', retrieve the ball, cradle it in the maul, wait for him to get to his feet, shove it to him, watch him charge it up, be poleaxed, wince, form the ruck etc. It was a good system. Everybody was happy. At thirty-two, Trevor probably lapsed into a mysterious coma while watching *Sale of the Century*.

I was a passive participant to say the least. I hardly touched the ball in the whole three months I played school rugby. It is possible. I discovered that with the glut of players on the field, as long as I created an atmosphere of competency and made a lot of noise, I fooled a lot of people. So I looked busy and ran around the field randomly shouting. I looked great. In the end, I made more noise than the entire team. I bellowed a monologue of nonsense. Eventually I exhausted my repertoire of shrieks. So I started screaming out the names of the impressionists.

'Go! Go! Go! Goooooooo—gan!' (I realise some consider Gauguin a *post*-impressionist, but, hey, I was fourteen!)

So no one was the wiser. That is, until my English teacher, Mr Chip-kick, fronted our training session to fathom why the D-team was such a disaster that year. We were playing a friendly against the Cs for all of ten minutes when I heard a long, terrifying cry that emanated from the pit of the diaphragm and finished in a high-pitched shriek.

'*Yeeeeeeeeeew!*'

He was pointing in the direction of Phil and me. I ran over. Phil trailed, sheepishly. Chip-kick was furious. Cranberry-red, he began screaming, an inch from my face. He said that he had been watching me for the last ten minutes and all I was doing was running around the field yelling like a bloody lunatic. And that Phil was playing like an old poofter (which Phil deemed insightful).

The game was up.

He told Phil to walk away and not look back for fear of suffering the fate of Lot's wife, and told me that I was to see him in his office. After much quizzing, I finally confessed that tackling only slowed me down and removed me from my primary role: motivator and team-crier. I added that I hadn't really touched the ball since joining but enjoyed wearing the jersey in shopping centres. He wasn't impressed. He insisted I leave the team. So I was forced to hand back the prized myrtle-green jersey – a pity because it offset my complexion so nicely.

⌢

After taking some deep breaths and doing knee-bends for five minutes, I pointed out to my clearly mentally disturbed medical adviser that tapping a few bags and running around the ring from an asthmatic

German engineering student or locking swords with a haughty Franco-phile was markedly different from playing an entire game of full-contact football. Rugby league would be eighty minutes of sheer terror. At the word 'terror', Sol's eyes lit up (as did another cigarette). I felt a sickly foreboding. I was *convinced* he was dipping his Dunhills in hashish at home. I reminded Dr Death Wish that a game of rugby league, with a squad of heavily built thugs, would be unlike schoolboy rugby. I wouldn't be able to attach myself, limpet fashion, to the back of the maul and scream out the names of the impressionists. In rugby league there is nowhere to hide.

Sol gave me an ultimatum: a lifetime of drugs, or rugby league.

So, with nothing to lose except the use of my limbs and vital organs, I agreed. But there was a problem; an enigma that even the oracle at Delphi would struggle with. I hated football. I was bohemian thin. My complexion was acid-green. And I ran like Iris Murdoch in her later years. What rugby league team would want me?

9

Aida lot of meat

AFTER HOURS OF PACING, picking up the phone, putting it down again, picking it up, putting it down again, I finally plucked up the courage to call Lydia for a third date. She reluctantly agreed, but only after I promised not to lose my mind after the dessert.

With no expense spared, I decided on a fancy restaurant: No Names in little Italy, favoured by students and tightwads alike. Nothing was over $5. No Names – so named after the Sydney Godfather's dying words to the police – still provides the best-value meals in town. For a few bucks you can glut on an enormous bowl of pasta and more free bread than Judas at the Last Supper. They even provide free drinks, albeit orange cordial. As you pull up a vinyl chair at the laminated table, a genuine Italian waiter from Taiwan takes your order.

I wanted the date to be a success so I got there early to secure a table. (I had a tool kit in the Vespa.) Then I waited. And waited. And waited. Cuing diners hovered over my table like birds. Waiters clubbed me with angry looks. The manager was called. I was just about to leave when Lydia ascended the stairs like Joan Fontaine in *Rebecca*, resplendent in a vintage white silk dress. Waiters clapped and sighed. She sat at the table like a princess. Her beauty was breathless. The scent of her perfume, an angel's breath. I clumsily gave her a posy of flowers.

After quizzing the waiter about whether they cooked with olive oil or animal oil, and being reassured by a grinning shrug, I ordered my usual vegetarian fare: the Neapolitana, always fabulous! Lydia ordered the veal. Taking a political stand, but keen to win another date, I tactfully voiced my concerns about gorging on the flesh of a fellow sentient being, gingerly suggesting that she was perhaps a tad heartless, and immoral, eating an infant one at that. She coolly thanked me for this information, as she had forgotten that veal was in fact 'baby cow' but was relieved that the meat wouldn't be tough. This is when I suspected I would not easily convert Lydia to the fashionable yet flavourless world of vegetarianism.

Impressing her by grandly breaking the seal on the cask wine, I waxed lyrical about art and music and the meaning of life with the tedious conviction of all first-year students. Eventually the conversation moved to sport and its omnipresence in Australian culture. This was a pet topic of hers. Lydia hated sport with venom. And being an artist, she despised the inequity of arts funding vis-à-vis sports funding in this jockstrap-obsessed continent. This grew from a seed in her youth. She grew up in a sports-mad family and weekends were spent freezing on sidelines at winter football games or, on long hot summer drives, accompanied by the unabridged nasal soliloquy that is cricket on ABC radio. So it was with some apprehension that I broached the subject of my glittering rugby league debut. I was unnerved by her silence but concluded by telling her that I was in the process of auditioning for teams.

She dropped her fork and screwed up her face. 'Auditioning?'

(Apparently one doesn't 'audition' for football.) I further explained that, as in school, my immediate challenge was one of physics. In a nutshell, I was a skinny weak bastard. Not the footballer's corporeal ideal. It was obvious that my skeletal frame wouldn't stop Kylie Minogue let alone a rampaging prop-forward, so I had to quickly bulk up. On the words 'bulk up' she stuffed some 'baby cow' into my mouth.

I was in a state of shock. I couldn't believe it. It tasted so damn good! A divine ambrosia. I'd been a vegetarian for so many years I'd forgotten just how good meat tasted. As I masticated (that is masticated), I thought, where have these infants been hiding all my life? The crib? That was the last day of eating bean sprouts and fucking lentils, let me tell you.

I signalled my Mediterranean waiter. 'Chan, bring me flesh!'

I was now officially 'bulking up'. As I finished my third T-bone Sicilian, with Lydia wiping a purple shoelace of blood from my chin, I heard a clank in my belly. It was my bowels, locking up shop for the next few months. At meals end, Chan and some of the other waiters helped me out of my chair and downstairs into the café. It was hard work. I'd put on three kilos at the table.

The café was chiming with the sound of pinballs and the rumbling surf of coffee machines, punctuated by the thud of spent coffee-patties being jolted into a timber drawer. After some fabulous coffee (I tell you, Jesus drinks coffee at No Names!), we left. But as I straddled the Vespa, trying to kick-start it, the meat must have moved to one side (upsetting the ballast), subsequently tipping me over. I jumped up and down till the meat repositioned itself, picked up the scooter, and gave my carnivorous date a lift home.

᭢

I became fatalistic about football. I bought a pair of boots and it wasn't long before I had my first 'audition'. I set it up with the coach over the phone – although the conversation didn't quite go to plan. When he asked what my position was on the field, I panicked.

'West,' I said.

There was a silence.

He asked how much I weighed. I explained it was difficult to ascertain as I was on a new weight-gaining program that involved adding meat to my diet. Therefore my weight fluctuated with each meal.

Silence.

'How fast are ya over a hundred metres, you reckon?' he finally asked.

'Uphill or on flat ground?'

'Flat,' he said. (Rather sharply, I thought.)

I confessed that running wasn't my strong point.

More silence. In fact, for a moment I thought we'd been cut off.

I must have impressed him in the end because he said, 'Arr, ya midaswel turn up, anyway.'

The team was one of the local ones in my area. Problem was, I was an impoverished student. My area was Redfern, a tough neighbourhood to say the least. I met the coach (muscles and smudgy tattoos) and his broken-nosed assistant, who wore faded football jerseys cut off at the sleeves. They looked uncomfortably at each other as they shook my hand. Don't know why. I looked every bit the athlete in my lycra bike pants, sixties-style Converse sneakers, and an old T-shirt that read *Meat-eaters are Murderers*. Also, something I haven't pointed out to you before, dear reader, is that I wear glasses. At the time I was sporting a pair of petite, vintage specs as worn by Igor Stravinsky when he lived in Paris in the 1920s. I cut a menacing figure on the blight-mottled oval and was more than ready to 'kick ass'.

Under the moth-encrusted flood-lit lights of Redfern Oval, I trained with various hopefuls 'auditioning' for the team. I noticed the other contestants looked like they'd played before. They also looked like they'd eaten before. Next to them, I was a corpse in sneakers.

Redfern Oval is one of the few remaining inner-city ovals. A veritable Hadrian's Wall of housing commission flats encircle it. As I hovered on the sideline, two slurring hobos argued in the street beyond, reprimanded by the yap of a small dog. This melded with the drone of a car alarm: a nagging motif by Philip Glass. Looking up, I saw the sky, thick with fruit bats, each flock a volley of shrapnel in the thinning orange of twilight.

The assistant threw me the ball (which I instantly dropped) and asked me to run to the posts and back. I was cut before I made it back. In hindsight, leaning against the posts for a quick breather wasn't a good look. I explained that I run faster when not actually carrying the ball but apparently that scene wasn't in the production.

At Sol's insistence, I tried again. The next audition took place in the neighbouring suburb. I didn't impress the coach as much over the phone this time, particularly when I mentioned that I had now 'learned to run while carrying the ball'. He insisted on meeting me in the flesh before making a decision about my footballing future with the Alexandria Spartans (I chose the team by name alone). I met him at the team's watering hole: a crumbling pub on Botany Road. Back then it was a hard-nosed tavern frequented by local gangsters and standover men.

I stood for an age outside the hotel, pacing. I really wanted to impress. There was a spaghetti-western silence when I finally entered. I heard a gravelly voice from the back of bar.

'You're not fucken Darien, are ya?' (They never got the name right.)

I removed my beret. 'Ah, yes. I believe I am. You must be my new coach?' (Presumptuous, I know.)

The lanky barman, who was cleaning a glass while chewing a toothpick, detonated with muted laughter. The coach, cauliflower ears and a crooked row of false teeth, sighed as he flagged me over to his table. He lazily put away the manual he was studying, *Penthouse Couples*, and asked what I was drinking. Asking for a glass of dry white was poor theatre. I should have spat, ordered a yard-glass of whisky, decked the barman and groped his wife. The coach looked at me, closing one eye like a sleeping cattle dog.

'The Spartans *are* shorta players this year. Second-rower broke his collarbone. Our prop done his Achilles. Winger broke his leg. If they was horses, you'd shoot the bastards. So yeah, I spose . . . we could use a winger. Used to play a bit at school, you said over the phone. You did say . . . what position were ya on the field?'

'On my side, curled in a ball, screaming,' I said but it came out as, 'Wing.'

He eyed me up and down, shook his head and screwed up his face like a mechanic about to tell you that the cost of repairs to your car exceeds its value. 'Son, there isn't much of ya.'

'I'm gaining a pound a week!'

Silence.

'Well . . . I dunno, can ya tackle orright?' he asked through an upturned beer glass.

Tackle? I panicked. No one had asked me before. I said that there were certain deficiencies in my overall footballing armoury; however, I was actively engaged in addressing those deficiencies, but had to confess that tackling constituted a greater part of that aforementioned armoury – as did catching and kicking the ball in general play – but he would no doubt be pleased to know that I had read Thucydides' complete *History of the Peloponnesian War* and was fully versed in Spartan culture; and that the name 'Dorian' in fact *comes* from the ancient Dorians, the rather prosaic ancestors of the Spartans, who invaded from the north and usurped the original inhabitants, the Mycenaeans, which was a travesty since the Mycenaeans, descendants of the Minoans, a sensuous, artistic people, had a flourishing culture that is now largely lost, and this subsequently plunged Greece into a dark age for about four hundred and fifty years, from which it didn't emerge until the resurgence of the Ionians, the descendants of the Mycenaeans, who then became the Athenians, and established a flourishing culture of art, philosophy and science and forged one of the most awe-inspiring epochs in world history.

He stared at me like I had three eyes.

Dostoevsky wrote a book about someone who habitually tells the truth. He titled it, *The Idiot*. He took out his watch and asked me to run around the block. I leapt from my seat and bolted out the door. I ran like a madman, gasping.

He was gone by the time I got back.

10

He's Callas enough to knock your Bloch off!

I FELT DEFEATED, SLUMPED IN Sol's newly painted mellow-yellow office. With the anger therapy in abeyance, I was tormented by nightly anxiety attacks.

Sol and I had hoped that at least *one* team would have given me a chance. He wanted me to try out for other teams but I had a mass of study to get on with and compositions to finish. Besides, I simply couldn't take any more rejection. At the last 'audition' I was running up and down sandhills at Kurnell. It was embarrassing when the team had to dig me out of the final dune. I had come to the conclusion that I wasn't going to play football. But I still had the problem of the anxiety attacks and a swelling bathroom cabinet of coloured pills.

At the time I was plagued by an unrelenting playhouse of dreams. Sol, Jungian enthusiast, asked me to keep a 'Dream Diary'. Each morning I would wake up, record my dreams and we would discuss them at the session.

'This one is really mysterious,' I said. 'I'm standing on the edge of a diving board about to plunge into a swimming pool. I'm wearing football boots. There is a sign above the pool that reads *Hope*. I dive into the pool. It's empty. I crack my head on the bottom. What could that possibly mean?'

Sol rolled his eyes behind the clipboard.

I moped around the Con all week. Relieved we had abandoned the football idea but depressed at the thought of taking more pills, I didn't know what to do. Phil wasn't much support. He could never come to terms with football therapy. He reminded me that I had once declared that 'molluscs and certain species of shellfish have a greater intellectual capacity than footballers'. But this was said in a moment of crisis: the nadir of our high-school years.

⌒

Sport, sport, freakin goddamn sport. It's all they talked about at school. Like death and taxes, it was unavoidable. But Phil and I happened upon something wonderful: 'mixed sport'. Mixed sport comprised a twenty-minute, half-arsed game of soccer with the art teacher at the reserve above the Clovelly Baths, then some serious sunbathing. For Phil and me, it was sport made to order.

Clovelly is one of those concealed pockets of Sydney splendour. The Baths are a natural shard of the Pacific, fashioned into a majestic sea pool. Swimming there in your trusty sluggos and goggles with flipper-clad undulating feet, you are plunged into a powdery netherworld. Once the eyes adjust, you are dazzled by sea life: silver sheets of baitfish; belly-dancing membranes of jellyfish; crimson fingers of sea urchins; and, if Poseidon is smiling, the electric-blue of the resident, giant groper (which some fool recently speared and tossed into the boot of his car).

Phil and I would perfunctorily kick the ball around the browning grass in the heat, then dive into the green water, parting curtains of baitfish like seals.

It was the final year of school when things turned ugly for Phil and me. 'A Year of Living Dangerously.' The school rugby team had by then placed a fatwa on Phil. It was decided to celebrate the team's rampant heterosexuality by that time-honoured school tradition of punching Phil in the head. An etching would be commissioned. A plaque erected at the site.

One day in the bountiful Australian sunshine we lay sunning our honey-brown bodies. Phil's cossie was outrageous. To maximise his tan, it was high-cut. Next to my boxy 1970s cossie his was high camp.

Phil was on his pet topic: shoes. Phil could talk about shoes for hours. And he had more shoes than Imelda Marcos' cross-dressing teenage son.

Suddenly, amidst the pale saltbush that kowtowed in the sea breezes, a hedge of mullet cuts appeared. I watched in horror as the entire rugby team came over the reserve in an adolescent, sweating mass. Phil remained composed. He said the team wouldn't be bothered with us.

Things didn't look promising when the A-team's half-back screamed in a pubescent yodel, 'There's the faggots!'

On the other side of the pool stood the relative safety of the idling blue Leyland 339 bus. It sat blowing staccato puffs of black smoke, beckoning. It was only a few lazy breaststrokes away. However, Phil was determined to stand his ground. What can I say? Phil had the courage of Socrates.

I looked over the string of banksias that had grown into grotesque shapes from the relentless ocean winds, embodying the tortured spirits of Clovelly's original inhabitants. Apt.

Then suddenly, the pack of salivating hounds was upon us. They circled, close enough for us to smell cigarettes on them, or as Tim Winton elegantly describes it, there was a 'tobacco closeness', The captain of the first fifteen, Jonno, stood looking from side to side like a seagull, urged on by his team-mates. Phil and I were frightened.

It wasn't Jonno's style to be a bully. He was a soft boy in a spiky carapace. His mother, a single parent, raised him on a widow's pension in the no-go-zone that was the housing commission strip in South Maroubra. Jonno was often left to clean up and make dinner when his mother was catatonic from booze. He'd buy her cigarettes and liquor. So he had an aura of independence that made him seem old for his years. As his home life was as fractured as ours, I felt an unspoken kinship between us. Perhaps it was this resonating sadness that so attracted Phil to Jonno. As he stood over Phil, I could see no hatred in his liquid-blue eyes, which twinkled with the baths below. Then I panicked. Had he suddenly found out that it was Phil he was touching up on the dance-floor? God, we had all sworn each other to secrecy. How could he?

Jonno looked around, from side to side, over the hill, down to the ribbon of beach and up at the cancerous apartment blocks. This wasn't good. I've noticed that when someone is going to hit you they repeatedly survey the scene for incriminating witnesses.

There was no doubt in my mind: he was going to deck Phil. This surprised me. I'd never seen Jonno pick on anyone. With little to prove in the school's machismo pantomime, he mostly defended weaker boys. I stepped forward. I didn't want to fight Jonno but would at least do better than Phil. If I was hopeless, Phil was pathetic. Perhaps I'd break the tension with humour. I'd pulled one or two gags out of my pocket in the past before impending doom. We'd all laugh and go home. I turned over the engine. I walked up to Jonno and said, 'Look, this is silly. I don't know what ahh fuck, Jesus *Christ*!' Jonno punched me flush on the chin. He was a solid boy, so it felt like being hit by an adult. I stood numb from shock. The pack moved in to put the boot in. However, providence was smiling. It came in the form of an angel in a hairnet, with emphysema. An old lady stuck her curlers through an apartment window overhead. With a cigarette dangling from the corner of her mouth, she shouted a phlegmy, 'Boys!' and coughed.

Teenagers are like schools of fish. One panics and takes flight, they all follow in a pimply current of spontaneous erections. Jonno took off. The pack followed and disappeared over the reserve in a covey of Leif Garrett haircuts.

Already the school punching bag, I screamed at Phil, nursing my chin, trembling with shock. 'Are you familiar with the phrase "guilt by association", for Christ's sake?'

'Shut up and start swimming, nancy boy!' he said.

Diving into the burnished water, we swam for the south bank like frightened seals.

So you can see why Phil was so caustic about me playing football. The irony was never lost on him. We saw jocks as the enemy. And as an artist in this country, you can't help but feel resentment for our sports stars. Pen a prize-winning novel, compose a groundbreaking opera, write a hilarious play, you move one rung up the dole queue. Run one hundred metres in under ten seconds, you have a new car, a sports-shoe sponsorship, a series of mobile phone commercials, and you're dating a goddamn supermodel! Phil and I talked about this inequity ad nauseam. So he saw me as selling out – betraying him, a Trotsky in shoulder pads. I argued that I was simply trying to get off medication. But that supercilious tone was always in his voice. Couldn't blame him. We hated footballers.

Later that week I met Lydia in the gardens for lunch. As I ambled down the sandstone steps and into the gardens, which were twitching with insects in the midday heat, I saw her. She was reading a book in a yellow pool of sunlight, a study in concentration. A Vermeer portrait. Her face was an artist's model. Her every feature perfectly proportioned. An amalgam of 1950s movie stars, her smile was Grace Kelly; her eyes Katherine Hepburn; her poise Audrey Hepburn; her voice Robert Mitchum. (Lydia had a deep voice.)

I watched her as she read before a breathtaking display of bird of paradise, acutely aware of my good fortune. A minimalist triumph, the bird of paradise's conical orange and purple petals are pure origami. When sunlight reaches them they glow an intense, Mars-orange. Lydia suddenly looked up to catch me staring. She smiled and opened her mouth like a Dutch tulip.

'What am I? The goddamn *Mona Lisa*? I've been waiting for

nearly twenty minutes, for Christ's sake!' she said in her booming baritone.

Beneath a sky that could have been a ceiling by Correggio, we sat in the bright wintry sunlight, washing down thick roast-beef sandwiches (I was trying to eat as much meat as possible) with a thermos of tea that tasted faintly of boiled plastic. I had asked Lydia to meet me in order to get some feedback on my radical new footballing strategy. I'd devised a cunning plan to force a team to allow me to play. I knew she was keen to find out all about it because on the word 'football' she rolled her eyes. (She may well have mumbled the word 'Jesus'.) What Lydia didn't realise was that I needed to play at least *one* game before moving to new cures.

Framed by an early bloom of pink camellias, Phil passed by, violin tucked under his arm. I was keen to introduce them to each other so I motioned him over.

'Lydia, this is the fabulous Phil.'

Lydia offered her hand. 'So this is Phil. I've heard a lot about you.'

'And I you, Miss Sharpened Fourth.'

She looked askance at me.

'It's a musical thing,' I said.

She sighed.

'Have you told her yet?'

'Eh . . . no. I'm just coming to it now, Phil.'

'Told me *what* exactly?'

'Go on "Blocker", tell her.'

I pulled a face at him. 'Ahem . . . well as you know my football career has been impeded by the trifling fact that no team will actually allow me to join . . . so . . .'

'We're waiting . . .' she said.

'So . . . I'm forming my own team.'

'You're *what*? With whom exactly?' she asked, looking at Phil, who was grinning like a Cheshire cat.

'With students from eh . . . school.'

'I don't understand. Which school?' she said.

'Um . . . well . . . this one.'

'The *Conservatorium*? You're not serious, *surely*.'

After her last comment I began to think she didn't support the idea in its entirety.

'Yes.'

'Sir Richard will have a fit,' Phil said, turning to Lydia.

'He'll never find out,' I said.

'And how do propose to keep a little thing like the Conservatorium's new rugby league team quiet?' Lydia asked.

'I'm still working out the details.'

Phil and Lydia looked at each other and exploded with laughter, frightening the flock of pigeons pecking crumbs at our feet. Eyes glazed with tears, she quizzed me on plans to recruit this mysterious team. I asked them to follow me.

I marched them across the manicured lawn and into the main foyer of the Conservatorium. The student noticeboard was festooned with the usual selection of handwritten advertisements.

For sale: Selmer Mark 6 Tenor Saxophone (with roadcase) $4500.
Cellist urgently needed for quartet specialising in the music of Bartok – no time-wasters!
Wanted: Flatmate to share large house in Annandale. Must like the sound of the tuba late at night – $85 p.w. + bond.

From my sheet-music folder I produced a magazine entitled *Rugby League Week*. I can still see their expressions. It was as if I had held up *Turd Weekly*. I removed the page marked by a fluoro Post-it note. It revealed the terrifying face of a renowned Cronulla Sharks forward. His face looked as if it had been run over by a steamroller driven by a group of fat people. In fact, it was hard to determine where the nose ended and the cheeks began. It reminded me of a particular cubist painting by Georges Braque that was either a man's face or a small Parisian village. Beneath this beatific countenance I had pasted the cryptic legend: *'If this really turns you on, be at the Botanic Gardens reserve Thursday the 14th at 1 p.m.!'*

As I secured the sign to the noticeboard – recycling someone's pin, forcing an ad for Haydn scores to cartwheel – a bass clarinetist walked past. Squinting at the note through thick lenses, he turned to me. 'Looking for musicians for a new work?'

'I'm recruiting for the Conservatorium's new rugby league team.'

Phil and Lydia looked at each other.

'Sorry,' he chuckled. 'I thought you said rugby league team.'

'You heard right.'

He had a look on his face as if someone had told him a recent paternity test proved his father was an orang-outang living in Venezuela under the assumed name of Mr Champs. He wandered off, dazed.

I threw my hands in the air. 'Come on. What about you, Phil? You were the fastest guy in school!'

'Yeah, from a lifetime of running away from homophobic bullies. Forget it, Rambo. You're on your own.'

Lydia shot a deadpan look at me.

Big Marty walked past, spotting us quibbling. He dropped his trumpet at our feet.

'What's oop?'

Phil, in dry tones, informed Marty of my 'quaint' pig-skinned plan. His eyes widened. He wanted to know more. Dancing on my feet, I explained that a football team meant drinking copious amounts of beer after matches, and in that role I saw him as an obvious leader. His face broke into a watermelon smile.

I had my first recruit.

11

I Figaro way to build the team

WITH MY NEWLY PURCHASED Steeden football that smelled of cheap tennis shoes, and my rugby league rulebook, I was now an 'expert' on the game. On Thursday Marty, Phil and I made our way to the Botanic Gardens. We didn't know *what* to expect. Would anyone at the Con be remotely interested in football? I was sweating on at least a *couple* of students turning up. I reasoned that with a nucleus of five or so players I could build a team. Phil cajoled me with dry remarks, preparing me for the worst as we walked in and out of the attenuated shadows of the figs. Feeling an emerging anxiety attack, I took a zen-like breath.

Imagine our astonishment to find sixty or so students, running around, kicking footballs and playing games of touch. We stood stunned. Even my housemate, Duncan, had turned up (later crafting a poem to mark the auspicious occasion).

I addressed the students with the pomp and ceremony of Cicero addressing the Roman Senate.

'Okay everybody, who is here to play football and who is here to belittle us with satirical remarks?'

Phil put his hand up and said, 'Satirical remarks.'

With Charles' French horn case and Harriet's music stand as one set of corner posts, Marty's trumpet case and the azalea bush as the other posts, we had our field. Phil argued that our far post was not azaleas, but rhododendrons. Squinting at them, I argued that they were, in fact, azaleas, as they were clearly perennials. Phil argued that while they were *obviously* perennials, an azalea is in fact a shrub from the genus *Rhododendron*, a member of the heath family. Jane argued that they were winter roses, as it was a little early for azaleas.

Marty, in his no-nonsense on-the-road-to-Wigan-Pier accent, grabbed the ball and yelled at us. 'We're not on *Burke's* fookin' *Backyard* but here to play a game of football for fook's sake.'

With his fine nose in the air, Phil walked to the sideline.

I picked the teams. This was to spare me the embarrassment of being picked last. At school, I was forever the kid picked last, then argued heatedly over. 'You take him! No, it's your turn this time! We took him last time . . .' etc. The two sides took their positions.

Big Marty punted the ball high overhead. It was beautifully taken by a young cellist with a long neck worthy of Modigliani. He ran the ball back up field, whippet-like. Marty broke into a sinister smile. He lined up the skeletal string player and belted ten shades of shite out of him in a ball-and-all tackle. A hush fell over the reserve. A crow released a long cry that sounded like 'fuuuck!'. Our cellist didn't move. In fact, we thought he had stopped breathing at one stage. His friend, Margaret, a first-class harpist, rushed onto the field, screaming at Marty, breaking the silence.

'You've half-killed him, you fat oaf!'

'Ah, for fook's sake, he'll live,' Marty said, lighting a crooked cigarette.

The cellist wobbled to his feet. We all asked if he was okay. Things didn't seem right when he replied by reciting the monologue from Ibsen's *A Doll's House*.

Duncan theatrically carried the concussed musician from the field like Byron as if he'd found a drowned Shelley at the seashore.

'It's supposed to be *touch* football, not *real* football, you big ape,' Elizabeth, a baroque flautist, screeched from the sideline.

Phil nudged me. 'Go on . . . tell them, Tarzan.'

I cleared my throat. 'There seems to be a misunderstanding. Um . . . we are here, in fact, to play *real* football. Not touch football.'

On that note, the entire group of students turned on their heels. I faintly heard my name and the words 'lunatic' and 'arsehole' coupled together as, one by one, they were swallowed by the shadows of the Morton Bay figs. One of them yelled, 'This is what happens when you play too much Thelonious Monk!'

Phil shrugged. 'No one can say you didn't try, Dorian.'

'At least *Phil's* having a go!' I yelled back.

Phil looked askance at me. Duncan was impressed. Marty slapped Phil on the back, causing him to cough.

At the camellias, three boys stopped dead in their tracks. They conferred among themselves and there was much finger-pointing at Phil. They meekly approached. Preston Pemberton, a tall French-horn player with mouse-brown curls, Nicholas Herringbone, a handsome, preppy tenor (an opera singer with a divine voice), floppy blond hair cut into a shiny bob, and Meyer Moscowitz, a short, dark-eyed, gifted Jewish violinist on a Jascha Heifetz scholarship. They asked if I was serious about playing *real* football. I said that I had never been more serious in my life – even *more* serious than the time I walked into the bank and demanded a million dollars for the production of a new opera I was writing.

'What did he say?'

'Huh?'

'The bank manager?' Moscowitz said.

'Oh, he said, "What have you as collateral?" To which I replied, "Nothing but my genius and ten shares in a man from Toongabbie called Eric."'

The new recruits looked at each other uncomfortably.

Moscowitz asked why I wanted to play football. I replied, 'For medical reasons.' (Which they assumed to be of body not mind.) Marty quickly took the floor, declaring that football was part of his overall fitness strategy and he was already seeing its many benefits. They looked at his sagging gut, unconvinced.

Phil could see I was stressed. So in a moment of brilliance, Phil spat, John-Wayne style (inadvertently splashing Duncan's slippers – Duncan never owned a pair of shoes in the whole time I knew him), grabbed the football and started jogging around the manicured quadrangle of lawn. He looked fantastic. He was Alf Langer in cherry-red sandals. The recruits looked impressed as Phil kicked the ball around, spitting. Much finger-pointing was directed at the 'footballer' in the oversized T-shirt and candy-cane-striped leg warmers. Eventually the bantam violinist returned with a look of consternation.

'Who will we be playing?' he asked.

'Um . . . er . . . other colleges like our own,' I said (making it up as I went along).

They again had a conference for what seemed an age before returning with smiles. 'We're in!'

We all excitedly shook hands.

'Where do you play?' I asked the diminutive spokesman.

He seemed offended. 'First violin, of course.'

'Violin? He doesn't play the violin!' Phil said. 'God plays it while he holds it.'

Moscowitz blushed.

'No, I mean where do you play on the field? What position?'

'Well . . . at Kings I was a rather decent half-back till my mother came to a game. Then it was back to violin practice.'

The others nodded.

This seemed to be the general theme. Like Moscowitz, who hadn't played football since God made his covenant with Abraham, Herringbone and Pemberton couldn't recall the last time they'd even touched a football. All had attended elite private schools and would have certainly played rugby but for making the fatal error of revealing a musical gift and subsequently being wrapped in cotton wool for the remainder of their schooling.

Marty suggested we go back to the 'footballer's fitness centre' (the pub) to talk tactics.

Marty, the Conservatorium's elected party animal, always got the first round in. He whistled as he arranged the table with drinks. Inspired to write a poem, Duncan drifted off somewhere after one sip, brimming with similes. The new boys were not really drinkers but soon learned. I had abandoned chardonnay for stout to gain weight. Marty switched to Scotch to lose some.

Marty dropped coins into the gut of a poker machine while we sat around a circular table in the dank Ship Inn (then an old merchant sailor's pub) talking all things football. It was exciting. Seditious. Between the bass note of city trains rumbling overhead and the crooning horns of the ferries, I neurotically arranged the team's coasters into an orderly pattern for them, as was my custom (in my twenties, I *defined* anal-retentive). Herringbone kept nudging his east. This caused me some consternation. I quietly nudged it west, into my makeshift compass. He nudged it east. I nudged it west. He looked askance at the others. He placed the coaster in my shirt pocket (a little embarrassing). After a few more ales, it was decided that if a team was going to get off the ground, we needed (a) more players and (b) a coach.

Phil was quite friendly with Pamela, who was in charge of the student funds, and suggested that for the price of a new Kronos Quartet recording and a posy of orchids, Pam could be persuaded to designate a few lazy shillings for the Conservatorium 'Fitness Program'. (It all had to be hush-hush from an official point of view. With no sporting programs whatsoever, the Conservatorium absolutely forbade contact sports.) As a result of this suggestion, it was decreed that Phil be team manager.

From the poker machine, Marty said we should elect a captain. Naturally, it was deemed that, as it had been my idea to form the team, I should be captain. I argued that it is customary for the best player to be elected captain and, it had to be said, I ran up the ball like a pensioner with clubbed feet. I further argued that we had already elected a team manager and did not need another. (The reason I dodged the captaincy was the trifling fact that when the shit hit the fan with the Sir Richard, I didn't want to be the guy left standing with the brown umbrella as my card was already 'marked'.) The captaincy was put to the vote.

We ripped up sodden beer coasters and wrote a name on the back of each shard. Glued to the one-armed bandit, Marty called for a pen. I placed my beret on the table. Phil tossed in the chips of damp cardboard.

The first name drawn was mine. The second was mine. The third said – in Marty's distinct hand – *You're all a pack of losers*. The fourth vote (mine) was for Marty. The final vote (Phil's penmanship) was for *Wolfgang Amadeus Mozart*.

Marty had one vote, Mozart was dead, so guess who won the lucky dip?

12

Dante's (portable gas) inferno

SMOKE STINGS MY EYES AS MY father stands over the rusting hot-plate, beer in one hand, over-sized spatula in the other. Our eyes water in the brown smoke. As Caesar once said to Brutus, '*Animad-vertistine, ubicumque stes, fumum recta in faciem ferri?*' ('Ever noticed that wherever you stand, the smoke goes right into your face?') In his umbrella-like sombrero, plastic apron with half-naked stripper motif, and golf-shirt so loud it comes with a set of its own tweeters, my father is the portrait of alfresco elegance. In the kitchen, I see my stepmother dissecting onions. In order to avoid unsolicited displays of emotion she is wearing a pair of swimming goggles. She arranges the onions into a white tower of hoops, the discarded brown skins brushed to one side like the husks of dead insects. Lydia, framed in the next window, is separating lettuce.

My father never actually barbecues food. He cremates it. So we stand, hypnotically staring at the hotplate, which blurs with heat, metronomically sipping beer, and watching the meal slowly become the final act of Joan of Arc.

It is ritualistic.

Dad begins by scraping off the rust for a brain-jarring twenty minutes: a sound not unlike someone dragging a Fiat Bambino on its roof down the Hume Highway. Then he pours the remnants of his beer over the remaining rust to 'give the food flavour'. Cue the hissing

onions. Cue the onion gag. ('These'll make ya fart tonight, son!')
Next, sausages are lobbed on and impaled with a fork to let the sur-
plus fat escape and make a sizzling dash for freedom. One splits
open, disembowelling itself onto the hotplate. Eventually the rest of
the abattoir arrives: steaks, always thick, always huge; a necklace of
lamb chops; chicken satay; marinated pork spare-ribs. The hotplate
buckles under the weight. Then Dad pours a bottle of 'cooking
lager' over the lot. I tell him DA (Dinner Ale) is not for cooking but
drinking. After our copious amounts of beer and red-eyed conversation, the onions begin to resemble black beetles. They taste like
onion in the exact way debris from an airline crash tastes like onion.
As we gaze indifferently at our blackening cuisine, Oscar Peterson
tinkles from Dad's primer-speckled tape deck, which is perched
above the humming beer fridge. In a primeval stupor we watch the
fat inexorably leach from the meat and dribble into the netherworld
of volcanic rock below: Dante's inferno.

In a time-honoured Australian rite that is handed from father to
son, Dad passes me the hallowed, over-sized tongs to allow me
to poke one of the charcoaled sausages, which by this stage has the
consistency of an ember from the Great Fire of London – an honour
reserved for immediate family and visiting dignitaries.

'Need a bit more, you reckon?' he says, squinting through the
brown smoke.

'Yeah, I see a speck of meat that isn't quite incinerated.'

I return the sacred tongs like an Olympic torchbearer.

He pokes a shrivelled sausage. 'Really?'

'Third sausage from the right. Although, it could be a flake of rust.'

'Nah, just rust,' he says, poking the sausage and chugging down
his beer, squeezing the can and tossing it into the recycling bin for a
phantom two points.

'Um, do you think it might be time for a new hotplate, Dad?'

'Mate, any doctor will tell ya that a bitta iron in your diet's good
for you.'

'Who? Dr Kevorkian?'

He opens another can of VB with a swish. He always makes a cunning dent with his thumb in the side of his can so he knows which is his. This seems superfluous as the can is never out of his hand. I can never keep up with the drinking. This irritates him.

'Am I drinking with the sheilas today?'

'Just pacing myself, Dad.'

With the efficiency of Rommel, he has installed his beer fridge less than one metre from the crematorium. This means, with an outstretched arm, he can grab a fresh beer and nuke meat simultaneously.

However, Dad is not himself. Naturally, he has taken my brother's death badly and it weighs on him. So he scrapes the hotplate a little forlornly that day, if truth be known.

As he cooks and scrapes and marinates meat with DA (or Dirty Annie, as he calls it), Lydia helps my stepmother prepare the rest of the salads in the kitchen. 'Secret women's business,' Dad calls it. She had agreed to come on another date with me if I promised not to talk about football. As Dad mechanically turns long pieces of coal that he calls sirloin, he slaps a lentil patty onto the hotplate. It falls silently, like a war victim: not springy like meat, but flaccid like clay. The rival offerings of flesh hiss at it.

'Can I skip the vegie burger today, Dad? I think I'll have um . . . a steak.'

Dear reader, you must pause to take in the magnitude of this moment. I have been a vegetarian since the age of fourteen (as my father says, thanks to my 'wacky mother'), so Dad takes a while to absorb this. He falls to a chair. I fan him with a tea towel. Then, he asks me to carefully repeat the sentence. On the word 'steak' he feels my pulse.

This becomes one of the happiest days of his fatherhood. (He talks of it to this day.) Rapture is written across his face. His son is consuming the meat of another living creature. (Dad has always declared that we didn't work our way up to the top of the food chain to eat bean sprouts.) He runs into the house and returns with a steak, almost tripping down the stairs. I look at the bloodied slab with apprehension. It is the size of a small calf.

Dad tosses it on the barbecue. The hotplate vibrates for three full minutes. Dad quickly seals the steak on both sides and then waits for the blood to leach from the browning flesh, a trick he learned from Nick the Greek. He doesn't ask why I'm surrendering my vegetarianism, for fear of changing my mind. He cooks silently, avoiding eye contact.

He yells to my stepmother, 'This is ready, Patsy! Can you bring a plate?'

I have never understood why my father serves his barbecue on a plate. Surely an urn would be more practical.

The women emerge with the salads and bread, holding the food before them like sacred offerings to Athena.

Meat, stacked on a plastic plate, steams in the exact way blackened magma steams. My father places the 'calf' on my plate with some sausages that resemble the swollen fingers of a torched corpse.

'Onions?' he asks, scattering a confetti of burnt match heads.

Setting cutlery in front of me, my stepmother asks why I am suddenly eating meat. My father muzzles her with a look. He quickly makes nervous small talk as I cut into the flesh with my buckling knife.

As I loosen my trousers for the final sausage, my father creeps off for his Polaroid camera. He wants to capture the moment and place the proof beside his pillow. He wants it to be the first thing he sees upon waking. His happy thought.

Blinded by the flash, Lydia blinks rapidly. Her long black lashes, two butterflies.

'Well, I never thought I'd see the bloody day . . .' Dad finally says, pouring himself a generous glass of shiraz.

'Are you not well?' my stepmother asks. 'Do you have an iron deficiency?'

I try to talk but I have to wait for a globular, fatty piece of meat to pass through my oesophagus. It takes about a week. 'Well, if you must know,' I say, swallowing, 'red meat is part of my new training program.'

'Your what?' says Dad, spitting red.

'My training program.'

'Bought yourself a piano accordion?' he sniggers.

'No, I'm playing football.'

'Bull. Shit,' he says, sitting bolt upright.

'Sad but true,' says Lydia.

My father looks around and into the bushes. 'Is there a hidden camera out here or something?'

'No, straight up. Look.' I reef my Miles Davis T-shirt to reveal plum-coloured bruises.

My father looks dazed. 'Steak . . . football . . . this is like a dream I had once . . .'

'Ridiculous, isn't it?' Lydia says.

'Ridiculous? *Ridiculous*? It's bloody *fantastic*!' he says, snapping photos of my bruises.

Lydia frowns.

'This is what he's needed all his life, luv. A bit of biffo and the old tough stuff.'

Lydia rolls her eyes.

'Who's coaching?' he asks, with Gestapo speed.

'That's just it. We don't have a coach.'

That afternoon we talk football and football and more football, interrupted only by talk of football.

Lydia is thrilled.

As the sun slips behind the wind-tickled trees, a flock of rosellas stretches overhead. A feathered paintbox. My father looks up to the chorus of squawks, and into the heavens, raises his glass and smiles. 'What an end to a perfect day.'

13

The rake's progress

WORD GOT AROUND AND IT wasn't long before we had more players (although, still not enough to field a team). We mostly had brass players in the forwards (they always seemed beefier) and strings and woodwinds in the backs. At that stage, I was the rake (the hooker).

Our training sessions were unique. They never failed to become a stunning re-enactment of Napoleon's defeat at Waterloo on cough medicine. We were beyond tragic. Even the gardeners laughed at us. Problem was there were too many cooks. Everybody was bitching with everybody else, yelling at each other for dropping balls and missing tackles. What we really needed was a coach.

Dad would sometimes drop by after work and bugle a few words of encouragement from the magnolias – but to little effect. He was clearly frustrated by our ineptitude but urged us to stick with it, saying we'd improve with training. We never improved with training. And all we ever seemed to do was train. Cicero was right when he said, '*Assiduus usus uni rei deditus et ingenium et artem saepe vincit.*' ('Constant practice devoted to one subject often undoes both intelligence and skill.')

When the Composition Department brought over Richard Mills from Perth, we walked into the lecture immediately after training, sweating like wrestlers. A disciple of Mills' stunning opera *Summer of the Seventeenth Doll* (based on Ray Lawler's wonderful play), I was eager to hear him discuss his work. You can imagine the composer's horror as we sat impregnating the air with the sour odour of sport – much to the chagrin of poor Trevor Pearce, our composition lecturer. No doubt that was an *annus horribilis* for many of the lecturers as we sat stinking out their classes for some mysterious reason.

However, the best part about training was the pub. Dad was in his element. Sometimes he'd drag us all to the pub, then 'get the taste' and we'd all end up at his favourite haunt at three in the morning: the Bourbon and Beefsteak Bar at Kings Cross (where they knew him by name). The resident jazz trio (there for nigh on twenty years) sometimes invited Dad up to sing. Out of practice as a muso, he could still belt out a tune and was a decent crooner in his day. Unfortunately, by that stage of the night 'Girl from Ipanema' sounded like 'Pearl from Hiroshima' (a quarter-tone flat) as he would slur his way through the modulated bridge – leaving one string player with perfect pitch to squeeze his glass and gnash his teeth. Dad couldn't care less. And as all of us were ridiculously pissed by that stage, he was cheered from the bandstand like a conquering Caesar. He was funny to watch – my anxiety attacks momentarily pickled in alcohol – and I began to see another side to him. Not as a father but a friend.

One evening, Dad said something at the Beefsteak that changed everything. He said what the team *really* needed was a goal! Something to work towards, like, God forbid, a game! This shocked us. A game? We hadn't really thought about a game at that stage. We were in training. What we were training for was in question but we were training nonetheless. We felt we weren't ready for a game and therefore needed more training. In the end, it became a kind of Penelope's Tapestry.

Seizing the moment, Dad stood on a chair and talked about JFK's goal to reach the moon, Cook's quest to discover the Great Southern Land. Dad stood with raised glass and spoke sombrely about Scott of the Antarctic, about Matthew Flinders, about Colonel Sanders (it was late and we were hungry). I must say, it was all very inspiring at 3 a.m. We agreed to play a game! We then went looking for fried chicken.

I don't know if it was the hangover, the partially digested chicken or the man tapping a hammer inside my skull, but it still made sense the next morning. So I got on the phone and organised our first match! After all, wasn't that the reason for forming the team in the first place? The opposing team seemed delighted. As luck would have it, they had a bye the weekend I suggested. So a game was arranged to be played in twelve weeks. Plenty of time for us to find more players and get into shape.

⌒

When I informed the team that our first game would be against Sydney University, they seemed a tad displeased. I gleaned this from the way they chased me down the street and threw stones at me.

'You said we'd be playing other colleges, like our own,' Moscowitz said.

'Yeah, like Sydney College of the Arts or something,' Pemberton said, taking aim with a bottle.

'And in what competition would that be?' I screamed over my shoulder, 'The Jackson *Pollock* league?'

You see, the only colleges that had rugby league teams were major universities. Gang tackling isn't offered as a course alternative at NIDA, for example. So we had to play one of the universities sooner or later. Unbeknown to me – and with the luck of Pete Best – I had picked the leading side.

I returned to the angry throng and explained that I'd organised the match for their own good, that what we needed was a goal to bring us all together, and that this game would bring out the best in each and every one of us.

The team looked unimpressed.

In the hysteria that ensued it was brought to my attention that we were still short of players and without a couple of extra forwards couldn't even think of fielding a team. In the midst of this heated debate, in his crisp white Panama and Italian linen suit, Sir Richard came bounding through the camellias.

'Hide the ball!' someone hissed.

'Ah, what have we here? The dirty dozen?' Sir Richard said, smiling.

'Just practising, Sir Richard,' said Moscowitz.

'Eh . . . for the Mozart,' Phil said.

'On the lawn? In the open air? Without your instruments? How richly innovative. You really are a most talented group.'

We turned red.

'No doubt you couldn't maul poor Mozart – may he rest in peace – any more than you do with your instruments.' Tucking his soft leather satchel under his arm, he walked off. 'Keep practising. It's the best you've sounded in months!'

'Smug bastard,' said Phil.

'What a perfect name for the team!' I said.

Phil shrugged. 'Huh?'

'*The Mozart Maulers!*' I said.

Marty nodded. 'I like it.'

Moscowitz shot a deadpan look at me. 'Since our first game is against Sydney Uni why not call us Mozart's *Requiem.*'

The mood grew dark. I detected a little hostility towards the captain. I thought of Julius Caesar's last words to his waiter: '*Sentio aliquos togatos contra me conspirare.*' ('I think some people in togas are plotting against me.')

We went back to the Oyster Bar to have a crisis meeting. I bought everybody drinks and showcased my repertoire of smiles.

⌒

I don't know whether it was the stress of the team's animosity to the game but I had a very bad turn that evening. Too fragile to attend lectures, I was camped in Sol's office all week.

Sol was giddy with delight about a team of musicians playing football. It was beyond his wildest Jungian dreams. I think he saw it as a living, breathing thesis. He was forever pressing me for team details. Who was playing in what position and why? Up until then I wasn't sure if the whole thing wasn't some kind of pig-skinned placebo. But Sol was thrilled that our first game was against Sydney University. He also seemed interested in my new relationship with my father. His pencil smoked whenever I mentioned his name. (It would ignite if I mentioned my mother.)

Needless to say, calling my mother in New York and telling her I was focusing all my energies on rugby league wasn't easy. She would have preferred a conversion to Islam and my subsequent recruitment into the Ayatollah Khomeini Comedy Dancers. She was furious. Her unwavering religion was Art. And if you had talent, you defied the gods by neglecting it.

Naturally, she suspected this 'footballing madness' was my father's idea. I argued otherwise. But she always saw Dad in the same negative way. Like all divorced couples, Mum and Dad blamed each other for my neuroses.

Mum dragged Frank to the phone. Frank is my stepfather and couldn't be more antithetical to my real father if he tried. In the 1970s, he arrived in New York on a Dutch government scholarship to study acting. This is how he met Mum. Tall, svelte, softly spoken, clad in designer suits and handmade shoes, Frankie speaks seven languages and is extremely well read. To this day, we are close and haven't had an argument since we've known one another.

When Mum put Frank on the phone, she was pulling out the big guns. Frank could talk me into anything. His strategy was to say nothing. Like Sol, Frankie is an expert listener. With Buddhist hustle, his technique largely consists of allowing me to talk myself into a corner till I undermine my own argument. He should work at the UN.

In his mellifluous, hybrid Dutch/American baritone, he asked me to tell him all about this 'football madness'.

Luckily for me, Frankie had never seen a game of Sydney-style football and no doubt thought it to be a facsimile of the armour-clad American version of the game. He was further reassured when I said we were merely playing other colleges like our own in 'friendlies'. Had Frankie been born on the western side of the North Sea, I wouldn't have got off so lightly. Unless it's a game of touch, in full-contact rugby league there is no such thing as a 'friendly'. In the same way that there is no such thing as a rodeo friendly. The only thing that renders more brutish physical contact is going up to a pianist at a gig and asking if they know 'Piano Man'.

Frankie put the phone down promising to mollify my mother.

14

Titus a fish's arsehole

I WASN'T PRESENT FOR THIS next scene, so I can only imagine the way it played out. With scantily clad facts, mortared with imagination, I present it for you as the following.

⌢

Dad is hunkered over a newspaper, quietly sipping a middy of what he calls 'mother's milk' (Victoria Bitter) in his usual nook at the end of the bar of The D.O.G. (aka the Duke of Gloucester Hotel, so named after some visiting minor royal that Australians slobbered over in the 1930s). He holds up his glass to the light.

'So much beer, so little time,' he says quietly.

Between sips, he peaks at the polaroids of his son's battle scars and forays into the gastronomic nirvana that is otherwise known as the mixed grill. They are jumbled with betting slips. (Dad places a lazy dollar on the 'dish lickers' on occasion.) Ultimately, they are spread across the sodden bar-towel. Rubbing his fingers through his salt-and-pepper hair, he smiles, comforted by the nasal drone of Sky-Television: a continuous monologue of racing updates, the monody of Dionysius.

The Saturday afternoon quietude is broken by his best mate, Bernie, holding up the back bar with tales of pig-skinned triumphs and calamities.

Bernie waves Dad over like ground crew. Dad waves him away. Bernie is insistent.

Bernie, *sans* neck, whispers to the others. 'Poor ol' Pete. I take it ya heard about his son passing away . . .'

Hiding the polaroids, Dad begrudgingly squeezes his gut into the circle of bulbous bellies.

'G'day, Pedro, whaddya know, chief?' Mulberry Cheeks asks.

'Yeah, haven't seen ya for yonks. How ya been?' Rugby Nose says.

'Ah, fair to middley, mate. Fair to middley. And how are you, Bern?'

'Fit as a trout, Pete. Hey, did ya see my boy score that try in Saturday's game?' Bernie says.

Someone nudges Bernie with a don't-mention-sons-type elbow.

'No, I missed it, mate, how'd he go?' Dad says.

'Mate, he went unreal. The Broncos have offered him a contract.'

'League?'

'Yeah, he'll stay with Randwick but. There's dollars in union, these days. Not like when I played. If a bloke wanted to buy a house, he played league.'

'Not everyday ya get an offer from the Broncos. You must be happy,' Dad says, flatly.

'Mate, I'm happier than a dog with two pricks.'

Dad drains his glass. 'How are the Lions going this year, Bernie?' (Bernie is the coach of local rugby league team the Maroubra Lions.)

'Mate, pretty ordinary to be honest.'

'Shame,' says Mulberry Cheeks into an upturned glass.

'There's no work ethic. I mean, one or two of em go okay, but summer them are dead-set lazy bastards.'

'Really? They seem to train hard,' says Dad.

'Yeah, but that's not enough these days, Pete. Not at an elite level. If they want to go all the way like I did, play rep footy an that, ya need that liddle bit more. That liddle bitter magic that you only find with hard yakka, an that,' Bernie says, eating a peanut.

Mulberry Cheeks raises an empty glass. 'Your shout, Bernie. Ya mouth must be pretty dry by now.'

'Bernie wouldn't shout if a shark bit him on the prick,' Rugby Nose says.

'He's as tight as a fish's arsehole,' Mulberry Cheeks says.

Bernie, cigarette dangling from bottom lip, heads to the bar. 'Arr, bullshit. Same again, fellas?' (A 'drinking smoker', Bernie never sticks to the one brand – he'll smoke whatever's in your top pocket.)

Dad makes his excuses and returns to his paper at the end of the bar. After a few more 'cleansing ales,' Bernie makes his way over.

'You know, Pete, I was sorry to hear . . . I mean, I got a sunner me own and . . .'

Dad, never one to indulge in the Californianism of sharing, cuts him off.

'Don't worry about it, mate.'

'Pete, if there's anything I can do for ya. Ever. Just let me know, mate.'

'Thanks, Bern.'

'I mean that. Anything. You name it. And, mate, when I give me word, it's bloody etched in granite. You know that, Pete, don't ya? I mean, everyone knows that. Me word is me bond, mate.'

My father, a sudden twinkle in his eye, places a brown arm around Bernie's hulking shoulders.

'Well, Bernie, as a matter of fact there is a little something you can do for me, mate . . .'

15

Madam Butterfingers

DAD COLLECTED BERNIE FROM The Dog, and they made their way through the snaking peak-hour traffic to our hard-nosed training arena (aka the Botanic Gardens). It seems Dad wasn't completely straight with Bernie about the coaching position and had omitted minor details (e.g. we were a group of musicians who had never played football before). The coaching position was shrouded in mystery. The only thing Bernie knew was that the position of head coach for a major college team had suddenly become available. No doubt Bernie saw himself surrounded by strapping collegians in striped blazers and house ties. Perhaps a modest oak-lined office in the bowels of an old university, with gilded lettering reading *Coach* across the door that had survived one hundred years of gentlemanly knocks.

The Maulers were ecstatic to finally have a coach. (The student body had even coughed up a few shillings for his services.) That afternoon we ran through our paces with anticipation. We were tossing the ball around with our usual flair – or lack thereof – when we heard a terrifying howl from behind the rhododendrons.

'The Conservatorium of fucking *what*?' the voice said. A shrieking flock of parrots became a white cloud overhead.

Suddenly Bernie and Dad cornered the rhododendrons. We continued to run our drills as they watched. Our new coach seemed impressed because I heard him turn to Dad and say, 'Ah, Pete, I don't fucken believe this!'

'That's my boy over there. In the purple cardigan,' Dad said, pointing.

At that moment, someone threw a high pass, knocking my glasses to the ground. Everyone rushed over to see if I was okay.

Dad called us over. 'Men, I'd like to introduce you to your new coach, Mr. Bernie Johns. For those of you not familiar with football – um, which is most of you – Bernie Johns is a legend of the game. A former Wallaby and South Sydney first-grade rugby league star for over ten years. So there's not much this bloke doesn't know about football. Even met her worship, the Queen. So consider yerselves honoured to have him as ya coach.'

The team applauded.

Clad in a lime-green tank top and matching winklepickers, Phil ran up and introduced himself.

'Hello Mr Johns. I'm Philip, the team's manager. We'll be working closely together.'

Bernie stood dumbfounded. Then Duncan, pissed, stumbled over and introduced himself as the team's poet laureate. He cleared his throat, sounding like a wino at daybreak. Then with vowels rounder than Noel Coward, Duncan recited his football poem. (I still have a copy.)

Football
A game of triumphs and tears,
A game of laughter and beers.
It's a little boy running on the field with a bucket of sand.
It's an old man cheering from his favourite seat.
It's a girl with a pompom and a high-kick.
It's a man eating a bun filled with rancid meat.
It's a coach swearing on the sidelines.
It's a blessed game for a privileged few.

You can play it too –
Football!

The Maulers cheered. Making a present of it, Duncan placed the verse in our coach's shirt pocket and belched. Duncan grandly bowed and walked off, like Byron emerging from the Hellespont after swimming it. Dad smiled uneasily. What can I say? Bernie had a look on his face as if someone had told him he'd accidentally drunk a litre of cat's urine.

We awaited instructions from our new coach, who remained speechless. We waited. And waited. And waited. Bernie suddenly called Dad over to the rhododendrons. We couldn't hear what was said but it looked like Bernie needed to wash his hair because he kept frantically pointing to his head and waving his arms about. Bernie walked off, waving Dad away.

'I understand, Bernie, ' Dad yelled. 'No worries, mate. I mean, ya word doesn't have to be etched in granite or anything . . .'

Bernie stopped in his tracks. He dropped his shoulders. Turning on his heels, he returned.

'Orright, let's see what youse miserable packer noise-makers can do,' he said.

We stood to attention.

'Mate, they'll surprise you. They're quite fit,' Dad said.

'*Fit?* They don't look fit enough for lawn bowls!' Bernie threw out a lazy arm. 'Arr, run up to that bush an back,' he said, gobbing on the lawn as a full stop.

'What? Through the magnolias?' Herringbone said.

Bernie became red in the face. 'It could be a field of turds for all I care! Just bloody run round the joint for ten minutes for Chrissake!'

We took off in a flap. Moscowitz was still tying his boots. Bernie screamed at him. He bolted, laces flapping like stock whips.

⌒

That night we ran and ran and ran. We ran till we thought our lungs would explode. Cathy Freeman never ran so much.

As we stood buckled and gasping, Bernie spoke of either the benefits of gang tackling or the benediction of Glen Campbell. Who knows? By the end I was flat on my back, siphoning air.

Bernie scorned the supine among us. 'Get off ya bony arses, for Chrissake! This is football not fucking.'

'That's what they need, Bern. Bitter the old tough stuff,' Dad said.

'Tough stuff? Pete, these blokes need the laying on of hands.'

We struggled to our feet like war victims.

'Now. Let's put this gang-tackling into practice. I wanna see one round the legs. One over the top. And another bloke coming in from the side. Orright?'

'Won't we get injured doing that?' asked Moscowitz, sucking on his Ventolin spray.

'Injured? You *are* joking? Listen, sonny, I broke me ribs, me collarbone, me shoulder, me jaw courtesy of Crusher Keith one day. I fractured me eye socket. I gotta titanium pin in me wrist. Done all me ligaments. Done me knees.' He turned to me menacingly. 'And I won't *tell* ya how many fingers I've broken.'

'Good, cause I don't want to know,' I said, looking around, wide-eyed.

'Don't worry, cause I wouldn't tell ya!' he nodded.

'Good, because I don't want to know.'

'Hey, don't worry, I wouldn't tell ya.'

'Good, cause I *really* don't want to know.'

'Five.'

'Oh. Fair enough.'

The Maulers drew a collective gasp. It seemed the only bone Bernie hadn't broken in nigh on twenty years of professional football was the stirrup bone, a small bone in the base of the ear.

Bernie smiled unctuously. 'Hey, why don't ya try netball? Now that's a rough game. I'll get me wife, Anne, to coach youse.'

Moscowitz hid his face.

'Now let's see ya tackle them bags.'

A grove of padded vinyl trunks appeared on the edge of the lawn. (Dad had collected them from the car while we were re-enacting Alexander's march from Macedonia to India.)

We didn't quite know what to do. So he screamed at us in despotic tones to 'hit em'. Like startled wildebeest, we began to tackle the coloured bags. Bernie roared, 'Tackle em! Don't fuck em. They're not ya blow-up sheilas, for Chrissake!'

Bernie demonstrated. He asked a gaunt flautist to hold the bag while he 'hit it'. Cantering up to it, Bernie drove his yoke-like shoulder into the bag. The wispy flautist tried to cushion the impact of Bernie's seasoned tackle. The winded musician had to be dug from the earth with a shovel.

'See? Put ya bloody shoulder into it, for Chrissake!'

We tackled bags in counterpoint, Bernie shouting at us like a terrorist.

If our new coach was to stick around we needed to impress. So we hammered the bags with zeal. No musician slackened off the pace. I know he appreciated our efforts because he turned to Dad and mumbled, 'I'm only here for the extra cash.'

The *sine qua non* for any footballer is what is collectively known as 'ball skills'. So Bernie had us weaving in and out of each other, passing balls, kicking balls, lobbing balls. Confused, we stuffed it up completely. I was the biggest culprit. To instil much-needed confidence in his captain, Bernie christened me 'Madam Butterfingers'.

As we ran around like drunken ballerinas, Bernie looked stressed. I noticed he slapped a nicotine patch on his arm. One of several. In fact, by training's end, it seemed the only place he didn't have a nicotine patch was on the sole of his foot.

With the onset of twilight, he put an end to proceedings and asked us to gather around. He studied his notes. We stood patiently. He said it was clear we couldn't run, kick, tackle, or pass, had no fitness and were bereft of hand–eye co-ordination. But it wasn't all bad news. Our major strengths would lie in singing the team song – an area, he felt with confidence, in which we would excel. To spare our feelings, he summed the team up as 'weak as piss'. And said that there was only one thing left to do that evening: go to the pub and get completely rat-arsed. We agreed.

The Oyster Bar was a little up-market for Bernie. He said he didn't like the bartender's nose-ring. So we galloped down to a seedy pub at The Rocks. If it wasn't The Captain's Bollocks or The Captain's Bollocking, it was The Captain's Rollicking Bollocks – anyway, something nautical and nineteenth-century Sydney. Marty's eyes lit up at the tinkling hedge of poker machines. Dad got the first round in. As usual, Duncan wandered off quoting Yeats.

We sat around the Dickensian bar feeling defeated. Feeling sorry for us, Bernie said that we at least needed one 'really big mean bastard' on our team to gain some metres for us. We again spoke of that really tall guy with the thin hair. A fellow Composition student, we could never remember his name, so we simply dubbed him, That-really-tall-guy-with-the-thin-hair. Our lofty friend went on to become an actor of sorts. You may recall him in those Energy Australia ads where a really tall guy with thin hair comes to the door to change a light globe for a really little guy with no hair. Sadly, TRTGWTTH refused to join the Maulers.

'Bloody tall guys!' Bernie said.

'Yeah, bloody tall guys,' we said.

With an evil smirk, Phil nominated the one person we dared not speak of. The one person who could instil more terror in his fellow students than Sir Richard after a bad review. A student as tall as he was wide. We mumbled in chorus, 'THE MINOTAUR!'

'The fucken what?' Bernie said, setting his beer on the table.

A favoured motif of Picasso, The Minotaur was the mythical monster of ancient Crete who was half-bull, half-man. Ours was an ex-army-band tuba player, built like the proverbial brick shithouse.

He was a contrabass with eyes. And so stand-offish that none dared approach. The Minotaur always greeted you in the corridor with a bellicose stare that said 'Fuck off or I'll gore you.' If he wasn't in such a good mood, he'd gore you.

Bernie's face broke into a sinister smile. He said that wanton violence was football's raison d'être and that rugby league was built on the foundations of just such aforementioned lunatics and it's to those deranged pioneers of immense bulk and depleted grey matter with a penchant for violence that the game is, in fact, indebted. (Perhaps I'm paraphrasing.) He ordered another round and spoke movingly of his old adversary, Crusher Keith. 'Now when the big fella would run at ya, he'd be out to hurt ya every time. You knew that. That's why you respected him.'

We looked confused. Moscowitz interjected. 'So, Bernie, are you saying you liked him because he tried to put you into hospital?'

He raised his slopping ale and closed one eye. 'Exactly!'

Moscowitz shook his head. This credo was hard for our Jewish half-back to fathom. Imagine Isaac Stern saying, 'Whenever we walked past him, he tried to gas us. That's why we admired Hitler so much.'

Dad put down his glass. 'Boys, what Bernie is trying to say is that Crusher gave one hundred per cent every time he played. He respected him.'

'It's like this,' Bernie said. 'If your orchestra was playin Beethoven's *Four Seasons* –'

'Vivaldi,' Herringbone said through the froth of his beer.

'Orright, Valbi. Whatever. What I'm sayin is that you'd want every bloke in the orchestra givin a hundred and ten per cent, right?'

'But the second violin isn't trying to break the leg of the first violin,' Moscowitz said.

'But you respect the people dedicated to giving it their all?' Dad said.

We agreed.

'So ask him, Dorian.' Big Marty said, without taking his eyes from the poker machine.

Bernie looked askance at Dad. 'Ask me what?'

'Well, I know you haven't seen us play much . . . and we are a bit rusty . . . and I know . . . but . . . well . . .'

'What chance do we have against them?' Marty said, pushing fat flashing buttons.

'Just who is this little team you're playing?' Bernie said.

'Sydney University,' Phil said through his wine spritzer.

Colour drained from our coach's face. 'Bullshit!'

'Straight up,' I said. 'Didn't Dad tell you?'

Dad hid.

'Please tell me it's not Sydney Uni! Jesus, they're coached by a mate of mine! A bloke I played with at Souths!'

Dad decided it was his shout again and ran for the bar.

Bernie looked to the heavens. 'I'll have to move to Perth.'

In flat Yorkshire vowels, Marty reiterated, 'So what chance do you give uz?'

'Honestly?'

'Yeah,' Marty said, dropping his last coin into the niggardly machine.

'I'd say somewhere between Buckley's and fuck all.'

My eyes lit up. 'So you're saying there's a chance?'

'Tell us what you really think, Bernie,' Phil said.

Bernie was the Schopenhauer of coaching. 'If it's a University Shield team –' Bernie said.

'They're leading the comp, actually,' Moscowitz said.

Bernie downed the surf of swill in his glass. 'Boys, what can I say? They'll give you such a touch up you won't walk for a month. And I won't be able to show me face at Souths Leagues Club for the rest of me life.'

Imbibing treacle-coloured spirits at the Bourbon and Beefsteak – or 'filling up the cracks' as Dad called it – Bernie insisted we watch as many games of football as time permitted. As many of us had never watched a game of football before, it wasn't a bad idea. Herring-bone likened it to *listening* to lots of Wagner if you wanted to *sing* Wagner. Bernie rolled his eyes. It was also suggested that we all go to a game together sometime. This wasn't a bad idea.

This turned out to be a bad idea. The match we chose to go to was the brutish State of Origin final. We decided on this one because Sydney University happened to be playing England Combined Universities as the 'opening act'.

In an atmosphere reminiscent of Caesarian Rome, and with forty thousand salivating fans cheering the home team to victory, it became a mini test match, with both teams belting the stuffing out of each other.

The Maulers left the ground scowling at me. I decided it was an opportune time for an anxiety attack, instilling much confidence in the troops.

16

Porky and Beast

AS CAPTAIN, I WAS LEFT WITH the task of speaking to the-thing-with-the-tuba. I'd been putting it off for weeks. When Phil and I were in the library one afternoon researching the twelve-tone composers (Schoenberg, Webern, Berg, Manilow – including the major works: 'Copacabana' and 'Mandy') the Minotaur walked past, ploughing through people for the elevator. Phil nudged me, then hid behind the Puccini scores. It was time.

I sidled over to the lift doors, watching the illuminated numbers fall with a ping. The Minotaur's tuba case flanked him like an armoured car. He looked old. We were all around nineteen or twenty but the Minotaur looked thirty-five. He had the uncompromising face of a French legionnaire.

'Gorgeous day,' I said

'Tell someone who cares.'

'Oh. Um . . . you're big, aren't you?' I said.

He leaned into my face. 'You would be too if you had to carry this thing around with you since you were seven years old.'

I stared, gulping.

'What are you looking at, for Christ's sake? Piss off back to your boyfriend.' Through the glass doors he searched for Phil, who was peeking from behind the collected works of Karl Stockhausen.

'Well, I was going to ask you to join the team, but, if you're going to be rude, I –'

'Join the *team*?' He chuckled. 'I wouldn't join your team of pussies if my life depended on it.'

He stepped into the lift, doors hissing as they began to close.

'He said you'd be too chicken-shit to stick your head in the scrum . . .'

Suddenly, a tuba case jammed between the lift doors. The Minotaur stood over me, blotting out all available light. Lifting me by the scruff of my black polo-neck, he drew me into his face. I could smell salt-and-vinegar chips on his breath.

'Who's the dead man who said that?'

(Sorry Marty!)

⌒

The next afternoon, I was strolling through the gardens on my way to training – frequently stopping to smell the smorgasbord of flora around me – when I bumped into Mike Harvey. I hadn't seen him since he'd played my sonata at the concert. He asked to join the Maulers. I was shocked. The finest pianist this country's produced since Woodward (certainly when it comes to the modern repertoire), Mike's fingers had been touched by the hand of God (whereas mine had been touched by the hand of Mr Bean). So I talked him out of it.

Vasari writes that when Michelangelo lost his temper with the Pope and was forced to retreat to Florence, Raphael had a peek at Michelangelo's work inside the Sistine Chapel. Dually inspired and crushed, he knew he would never rival the master's accomplishments. He decided to forge his own path. Miles Davis did much the same when confronted with the trumpeting gymnastics of Gillespie. To indulge in a sporting metaphor, the arts is replete with reserve-bench players who go on to eventually change the shape of the game.

I'd realised at an early age that I would never become the concert pianist my piano teacher, the wonderful Miss Strong, had longed for. This was a disappointment for both of us. When I was a gangly teenager, she'd even had a celebrated concert pianist come to her house to hear me play. While I played with passion and originality, I lacked the monk-like discipline required of the concert pianist. And, to her horror, I was improvising all the time. Bach sounded like Basie. I was destined to become a composer and jazz-pianist, not a Horowitz in thongs.

But we all knew Mike was something special. Had he broken a finger, it could have ended his career. And I would have had it hanging over my head for the rest of my life, making it difficult to wear a hat. As it stood, we already had the gifted Moscowitz in the team – Sir Richard's *wunderkind*. And Herringbone risked a stellar career with the Australian Opera whenever he so much as trained (one stray elbow to the larynx and he's singing arias like Tom Waits). So I suppose all of us risked something by playing, but none more than the instrumental majors. And they knew it. Some of the brass players refused to go into the scrum for fear of cracking a lip, raising Bernie's ire. (Marty asked to be moved from front-row to second-row for this very reason.) Take the embrasure for the French horn, for instance. It is notoriously intricate (the mouthpiece having both a deep and wide aperture). The slightest deviation in the lips can mean the difference between passing your degree, or failing it.

So I drew the line at one Michael Kieran Harvey.

With a dearth of players, rejecting Mike wasn't easy. Bernie was livid.

'Whaddya mean ya said "no"? I know a wicket-keeper whose fingers are like pretzels. He plays the guitar like fucken Neil Diamond.'

I jogged away with a smile, shrugging.

Training always kicked off with a lap of the gardens. I linked with the chain of panting musicians. With the game only six weeks away, we still didn't have enough players to field a team against Sydney University. I began to feel self-doubt. And who was I to lead them into battle? I cried at *La Boheme*. If it wasn't for Sol's anger therapy,

I wouldn't have *dreamed* of playing football. While Bernie screamed at us like a Hollywood drill-sergeant as we jogged, my tranquillisers rattled in a comforting 6/8 rhythm. He was irritated by our lassitude and ordered us to lap the gardens three times. Circuits complete, and doubled over and panting, I staggered over to our coach, who was chatting with Dad in the milky light of winter afternoon.

'Well, [*gasp*] have our chances [*wheeze*] improved?' I asked.

'Like you ever had any,' Bernie said.

I turned to Dad, always optimistic. 'We seem to be getting it together. Don't you agree, Dad?'

He winced.

Bernie shook his head. 'The string players are worried about their fingers. The brass players won't go into the scrum cosov their lips. It's a dead-set joke!'

'They have an important concert coming up,' I said. 'It's the Mahler.'

'I know, they've bloody invited me!'

'Are you going?'

'I wouldn't go if ya special guest vocalist was Slim Dusty.'

'Can't imagine him singing 'Song of the Earth'. He'd have to lose the hat,' said Phil, who joined us, eating a tub of low-fat yogurt.

'Youse at least need a big bastard to create some holes in the opposition so the string players can run some options.'

Licking the back of his spoon, Phil nodded to the camellias, 'Like him, you mean?'

In a vision reminiscent of a battle-weary Wellington spying Von Blücher, just as Napoleon unleashed the feared Old Guard, the-thing-with-the-tuba marched towards us, football boots the size of jet-skis hitched around his neck.

Bernie grabbed his hand. 'Well, g'day there, fella!' He turned to us. 'Where you been hidin this big bloke?'

'The back of the orchestra,' Phil said, polishing off the yogurt.

The Minotaur threw his tuba case down and sneered. 'Well, enough of the happy families. Where do you want me?'

'PROP FORWARD!' we said in unison.

'No problem,' he said, shooting daggers at Marty.

'Well, let's see ya punch up the ball, son,' Bernie said.

'With pleasure,' the Minotaur smiled, upturning the corner of his protuberant horn-player's lip.

The Minotaur ran the ball straight at poor Marty. As if King Minos had fallen into his own labyrinth, there was no escape. I bit my lip in suspense. Marty looked perplexed. The only option was to tackle the angry beast. We used to think of Marty as 'Big Marty', but next to the Minotaur he looked small and porky. Marty tried to tackle him around the chest. This was to prove an error in judgement. The Minotaur ran through Marty like a tank through a straw hut. (Stamping on his head for good measure.) Marty lay on the ground prostrate. He was dazed, patting his chest for cigarettes. I rushed over. I felt terrible. Bernie was jumping up and down with excitement. He shook hands with Dad like he'd accidentally discovered oil while digging a swimming pool in his backyard.

As Marty became lucid, the Minotaur stood over him. 'Who's chicken-shit now, bugle boy?'

Marty seemed confused. He was okay until he tried to walk. He was either doing the tango or the merengue, we couldn't tell.

We rallied around Marty as the Minotaur kicked the ball around the gardens with a Hannibal Lecter insouciance. He reminded me of a Rottweiler pup with a lamb bone. Bernie cocked his head and gave the Minotaur a loving smile, the sort of smile a mother reserves for her newborn.

We finally had our very own 'really big mean bastard'.

17

Saul in the past, Bernie

BERNIE WAS ADAMANT HE WASN'T attending the student concert. But something (or someone) changed his mind. I suspect I know who. The one person who always had Bernie's measure: his wife, Anne.

Brass-blonde, boobs and brashness, Anne Johns is one of my favourite people. Although she's bubbly and effusive, I've seen the buxom Anne scythe her husband with a remark worthy of Mae West. Married and divorced long before she met the golden-locked footballer whose star was very much in ascension, and unlike the other footballer's girlfriends and assorted groupies, Anne was streetwise. And while her meter-maid looks no doubt lured Bernie to the boudoir, her outrageous personality convinced him she was 'the one'.

I wasn't present for the next scene (and if I had been, it would have seemed a little kinky), so with the few throwaway remarks I've collected from Bernie over the years, here is another product from the fiction factory.

⌢

The bedroom is shrouded in darkness but for a tongue of moonlight that extends through a crack in the curtains and reaches Bernie, tossing and turning, tugging the sheets and generally disrupting Anne's sleep. He sighs theatrically.

'God! What *is* it, Bernie? I'm trying to bloody sleep!' she says, breaking the midnight quiet.

'Nothing. Go to sleep,' says Bernie.

Anne leans over and yanks a string that dangles from a lamp that is an electrified football. A matching lamp flanks the other side of the bed.

The room is painted in yellow light. On the walls moth-eaten framed football jerseys and greening brass trophies elbow sun-blanched photographs for room. Taking pride of place, a framed jockstrap. The scrawling handwriting reads, *With love and affection, Crusher Keith.*

'Nothing. Go to sleep, Anne,' Bernie says, turning off the lamp.

'Don't sulk, Bernie. It's just a game,' she says, scowling at the illuminated numbers on the 'Souths Will Never Say Die' memorial clock, presented to her husband at his testimonial dinner.

Bernie snaps on the lamp again. 'Just a game? Just a *game*? Ya don't play over a hundred and forty-five first-grade games, and represent ya country if it's "just a game" to ya, for Chrissake.'

'The Wallaby Tour was a long time ago, Bernie. Haven't you learned by now that it was always just a game? It's time to move on with your life. Look, if it's bothering you that much, maybe you should talk to Peter,' she says, dragging the red-and-green South Sydney doona over her chilled shoulder.

'You don't understand. He thinks his kid is some kinda athletic genius,' Bernie says. 'I just can't do it to him, Annie. Besides, I gave the bloke me word. And you know what that means: it's –'

'Yeah, yeah, I know . . . it's "etched in granite",' she says, squinting in the light.

'This football team has been a good distraction for the bloke. Stopped him moping about his other son and that. The bloke's never *been* so happy.'

Anne hugs him and nuzzles his neck. 'Bernie Johns, you're a big sensitive sap.'

'Ah, bullshit . . .'

'That's why those kids think so much of you. You're a lot like them. I think you were meant to coach this team.'

'Somehow the idea that I was put on earth to coach the Mozart Maulers is not all that comforting. I mean, I just don't understand where they're comin from.'

'Haven't they got a concert coming up or something?'

'Yeah, they think I'm actually going,' he says, chuckling.

'You should!'

'You *are* joking.'

'I've never been more serious in all my life.'

'What, sit through an hour of bloody Beethoven or something?'

'Try to understand them, Bernie. It'll be good for you. Expand your horizons.'

'You know . . . maybe you're right! Hey, will you come with me?'

'Are you kidding? I hate classical music.'

Anne snaps off the light.

18

Too Bizet to twig

CHATTING WITH LYDIA, STUNNING in her sixties, caper-green evening dress that she'd found at the trusty student boutique (otherwise known as St Vincent de Paul's), I spied one Bernie Johns. Dressed to the nines (well, low fours anyway), standing alone in the echoing foyer. He looked about as comfortable as a vegetarian in an abattoir on Offal Tuesday. Schools of concert-goers in evening dress darted in and around him. I was surprised. Bernie was the last person I'd expected to see. He'd gone to a lot of effort. He was in a tuxedo. Unfortunately, it was the tux bought for a slimmer version of himself in the 1970s; no doubt the one he wore to his wedding. It was a powder-blue affair with fat, paisley lapels. The trousers rode up around his ankles exposing tiny white socks that were flags of surrender. Some of the Maulers, in full orchestra drag, rushed up to greet him as if he were a visiting dignitary. Lydia and I wandered over.

'Hello, Bernie. I didn't think we'd see you here!' I said. 'Oh, sorry, this is my new girlfriend, Lydia.'

Lydia looked askance at me. I hadn't used the G-word as yet. (We had barely kissed!)

'Oh, *very* nice to meet ya, luv.' He turned to me. 'You bloody dark horse, captain.' (I think Bernie was under the impression I played for the other side.)

'Where are you sitting, Bernie?' said Moscowitz, sporting a silky black yarmulke.

'Yeah, we hope you have a good seat, Bernie. Meyer has the solo,' said Herringbone.

Our Hebrew half-back blushed.

Bernie looked at his ticket and shrugged. Big Marty took it and nodded, 'Great seat, Bernie.'

The Minotaur stomped past. I can't recall ever having seen the beast so animated.

'G'day, coach! Fancy seeing you here!' The bull dropped his tuba with a thud, shaking Bernie's hand.

'Well, well, big fella, you playin tonight, too?' Bernie asked.

'Someone's got to be the rudder for this ship of fools,' the Minatour sneered before checking his watch and marching off.

Bernie chuckled.

Suddenly, to my horror, *he* walked over. As usual he was the picture of sartorial elegance. He could well have come from a dinner with Prince Charles. It was, God forbid, Sir Richard! He pushed his way in. He smelt of expensive cologne and fine cigars. Or fine cologne and expensive cigars. Or was it cigars from Cologne incurring expensive fines? I can't recall. I was on tranquillisers. He lifted his large nose and cleared his throat. 'Well, isn't someone going to introduce me?'

'This is our new coach,' Pemberton said, without thinking.

Sir Richard tilted his silver head. 'I *beg* your pardon?'

Behind the Dean, Marty mouthed words to Preston: 'Huge Arafat's earring.' Or it may have been, 'You fucking idiot!' As quick as you like, Moscowitz feigned playing his violin behind Bernie. (We had never told Bernie the team was hush-hush. Didn't want to give him an excuse to leave.)

'Ah, strings! Excellent. And not a minute too soon! The eisteddfod's only weeks away. I was told you were in Florence till next month. Never mind.' The Dean outstretched a manicured hand. 'Richard Oberchain, Dean of the Conservatorium.'

Bernie pumped his arm, almost dislocating his shoulder. (As Sir Richard was conducting the orchestra, this was not his best move.) 'Bernie Johns. Pleased ta know ya, boss.'

Sir Richard reclaimed his knuckles. 'That's quite a grip, Johns. No chance of the baton slipping, eh?'

'Uh?'

'Bernie Johns? I'm afraid I've never heard of you,' Sir Richard said.

Bernie was offended. I felt the acid in my stomach.

Bernie threw a broken nose in the air. 'Well, I don't like to brag, but I was a bit of a player in me day.'

'Really?'

'Well, I guess not too many players have met Her Majesty, the Queen.'

'You've played in the UK?'

'Oh, sure, all over Europe, pal. Played with the best. Don't worry about that, boss.'

'Well, I say, I'm rather impressed!' Sir Richard nodded to us. 'Who would you say was the best player you ever worked with?'

I winced. Meyer mumbled something from the Old Testament. Marty fingered his cigarette packet. Pemberton closed his eyes and bit his lip.

'Oooh, gee, that's a tough one cause I played with so many talented blokes . . .' Bernie scratched his head. 'Gee . . . I'd have to say, Ella. Yeah, definitely Ella.'

'Fitzgerald?'

'No, Mark.'

'Ella? Can't say I've heard of an Ella. Ah, yes, now I remember, an Italian!'

'I always thought he was a Koori,' Bernie said to himself.

'I find it's always the Italians who have that certain something . . .' Sir Richard made a circle with his fine fingers. '. . . that certain *joie de vivre*. Wouldn't you agree?'

'Italians, eh? Well, you couldn't find a better player than Campese. Now that wog could really play!'

'Oh, eh, of course. Italian?'

'Oh, yeah, spaghetti-muncher for sure.'

Another Mauler walked past and waved to Bernie before rushing backstage. Bernie waved in reply.

'I see you're quite familiar with our students, then.'

'Oh, sure. I've been coaching them Thursday arvos for about six weeks now.'

'Really? How extraordinary! I wasn't aware of that. So you've seen them play as a group?' Sir Richard asked, smiling with delight.

'Oh, yeah.' Bernie leaned in. 'And let's be honest. They stink.'

'At *last*! Someone who agrees with me. They're terrible, aren't they? They need a lot of work to reach the finals.'

Preston covered his face.

'*Finals*? They gotta snowflake's chance in hell of reachin any finals, pal. I mean, that new tuba player goes okay, but the rest of them are bloody hopeless.'

'I couldn't agree with you more.'

'Problem is, they don't play with no feeling.'

'Exactly!' Sir Richard said, ignoring the double-negative. 'They play entirely without passion. I'm always telling them. And the string players . . .'

'Oh, Jesus, the *string* players! Let's be honest.' He leaned in and cupped his mouth. 'The string players play like a packer poofters.'

Sir Richard stepped back. 'Well, I wouldn't have put it quite that way, Johns.'

'You bloody well should, Dicky. That's the only language kids understand these days. I tell em all the time. They hate hearing it. They play a lot better afterwards but.'

Sir Richard patted Bernie on his granite-like shoulder. 'Well, I must say, it's been refreshing to meet you, Johns. I can see that you'll give them a shake up.'

Bernie whispered, 'Someone's gotta knock these pussies into shape.'

Sir Richard looked shocked and delighted in spite of himself. 'I couldn't have put it more succinctly myself. Enjoy the concert.'

'I'll try an stay awake.'

Sir Richard rolled his eyes. 'God, I know exactly what you mean. *Ciao.*'

'Yeah, nice ta meetcha, Dicky.'

Sir Richard, shaking his head and smiling, rushed backstage as the audience entered the auditorium in a torrent of tuxedos and ball gowns.

The team breathed a collective sigh of relief.

Bernie scanned our faces. 'Whasamatta with you blokes? Youse all look like you've seen a ghost!'

⌒

During the final movement, I tried to pick out Bernie via a pair of foldable opera glasses that I'd borrowed from the turkey-necked lady beside me. I scanned a row of seats that held elegantly dressed dignitaries before coming across Bernie, asleep, snoring, his mouth agape, a bag of potato chips spilled down the front of his powder-blue tux.

19

The devil and cake

AFTER MONTHS OF REHEARSAL, Lydia, Duncan and I were
ready for our own little concert. We had been rehearsing ever since
Lydia had agreed to do the show on our first date. We had secured a
venue: The Globe Theatre on Oxford Street. It resembled Shakespeare's spiritual home in name only (aside from the toilets, which
were Elizabethan in their plumbing). A seedy cellar that had once
been a punk venue (French's Nightclub), The Globe was an alternative theatre in the late 80s. Loads of burgeoning theatre companies
put on shows there. The title of our soirée was *The Castle of
Malcolm*. The title, like everything else in the show, had nothing to
do with the subject matter. The subject matter had nothing to do
with anything at all. In fact, we didn't really have any subject
matter to be honest. All in all, it was $7.50 worth of bullshit and
drivel (concession for students – who made up most of the audience).

The show consisted of Lydia, dressed in a black leotard and balaclava, dancing around the stage like Martha Graham on marijuana.
Tied to Lydia's balaclava were pieces of broken glass. This, Duncan
told us, was a representation of urban decay. It looked more like
a representation of a bungled hold-up.

The show began with Duncan and Lydia entombed in a plastic
membrane, which Duncan hacked open with a knife. He then
proceeded to recite the most angst-ridden, tedious student poetry since

Homer's post-adolescence. This literary pantomime was accompanied by yours truly playing abstract jazz on The Globe's rickety piano. My music was worse than Duncan's poetry. It was Lydia's task to make sense of all this with dance. The show laboured on for three painful hours. The audience bludgeoned us with indifference. In the early shows there was an intermission. As most of the audience never returned after the popcorn, we scrapped the intermission and locked the doors.

The only good thing about the show was the posters. These were designed and screen-printed by Cliff Campbell. The last time I ran into Cliff, he was an artist with Mambo. So you can take it as read that he had an emerging gift for pop art. I had known Cliff since I was fourteen. During one of my mother's fleeting homecomings, she shared an apartment that overlooked Elizabeth Bay. Mum's eccentric flatmate was Bunny, the ex-wife of one of this country's most esteemed poets. She was about Mum's age but had shacked up with Cliff (then a punk rocker). Bunny and Cliff would cook exotic dinners, accompanied by a squall of punk music. I would sit at a kitchen table doing my homework, watching them, wide-eyed. They'd talk wildly, challenging my every suburban attitude. It was a seminal period of my life. Bunny was the editor of a literary mag and piqued in me a lifelong passion for poetry, introducing me to many Australian poets and writers. Cliff turned me on to a pantheon of painters, sculptors and conceptual artists. And he possessed a smorgasbord of exotic vinyl: the Clash, The Residents, Thelonius Monk, Miles Davis and Penderecki.

At the time, Cliff was completing a group of papier-mâché sculptures called *The Pointers*. They were a paper'n'glue family that all pointed towards a 1950s black-and-white television. (Including the budgie.) I gleaned from this social satire that watching hours of mindless television was bad and that reading books was good. To this day, Bunny and Cliff have little idea what an influence they have had on my life.

On the final night, Bernie attended our avant-garde production (yes, we forced him to come), but things went awry. As the lights were inexorably raised like a Saharan dawn, Lydia and Duncan were presented on stage, immured in their plastic carapace. The audience leaned in anticipation, their faces reflected in the stage lights like the audience in a ballet by Degas. I began my abstract tinkling and musical bullshit, but something seemed wrong. Duncan started to hack away at the plastic but nothing happened. As we'd been doing the show for a week, the knife had become blunt. That night it wouldn't have cut through butter.

After a while the cell, fogging with breath, resembled a collapsed greenhouse. Concerned they would suffocate, I leapt from the piano, rushed backstage and returned with a pair of scissors. By that stage, Lydia (who'd had to be talked into doing the show in the first place), was standing in the clouding membrane with her arms folded, furious. Through the balaclava I could see her scowling at me. Meanwhile, Duncan was frantically hacking at the sheeting, *Psycho*-style, and turning blue. Then he slipped. He slashed Lydia in the leg, which, in retrospect, may have accounted for the audience sitting on the edge of their seats. (They all thought it was part of the show.) When our performers finally escaped through the hole I had cut, some fool actually clapped. Gasping, Duncan and Lydia finished the show in a spirit that would have made my mother clutch her breast with pride. Lydia danced and leapt around the stage leaving a trail of blood and glaring at me. Duncan quickly recited his poetry in panting breaths. I played the piano like Keith Jarrett on speed. The show came to an abrupt finish. There was the usual weary applause (which grew louder when the audience heard the doors being unchained). Bernie made for the exit with a current of relieved audience members, like a stunned salmon.

Lydia, *furious*, refused to do any more shows or have anything to do with me again.

Later that week I was sitting in orchestration class reading a copy of *Rugby League Week*, and desperately trying to fathom a way to patch things up with Lydia, when a Musicology student wearing a Byzantine smile tapped on the door. He handed a note to my lecturer, who shot me a look that said I was a condemned man. I was summoned to Sir Richard's office. Obviously not for brandy and cigars.

Phil whispered, 'Take that brown umbrella. I think it's just hit the fan.'

⌢

Sir Richard, Beelzebub in tweeds, opened the door and shooed me, chicken-like, into his gubernatorial chamber. Silently, he pointed to a seat. I was swallowed by an oversized leather armchair that would have been perfect for Orson Welles. It squeaked as I squirmed. He remained tacit. A grandfather clock ticked, a sentinel in the corner. I could hear the faint aviary sound of students practising their instruments in the surrounding rooms and gardens. Ignoring me, Sir Richard polished one of his collection of antique metronomes. Rows of the tiny wooden pyramids transformed the office into a museum model of the Valley of the Kings. He placed the timekeeper carefully back on the shelf and poured tea from a silver pot. He eyed me as a cat does a caged canary. I pulled at my collar. His resonant baritone ended the torture by silence.

'Tea?'

'Um . . . er . . . yes, no, er . . . okay . . . yes, please.'

He handed me an eggshell-thin cup and saucer. The Wedgwood china was so fine it tinkled in C sharp as I sat trembling, catching whiffs of furniture polish and bow rosin.

'Cake?'

'Thank you.'

This was to prove an error in judgment as, with nowhere to place the cup, I had enough to do simply balancing the saucer on my knee.

'I met a charming man the other evening,' he said in an oleaginous voice, pouring tea. 'After an initial misunderstanding, I'm recently informed he is the coach of our rugby *league* team.' He said the word 'league' as if spitting out an olive pit that had found its way into his martini.

'Um . . . well –'

'I enlightened my informant that this is impossible as the Board argued heatedly over a proposal to have a ping-pong table at the Conservatorium for fear of a musician breaking a finger.'

'It's just –'

'It seems that the man in that awful suit I met at last week's concert is somehow connected with it all and is being paid a "coaching fee" by the student body, in fact.'

'Well, there's a reason –'

'And I'm further informed that my music school has a match against Sydney *University* next month!'

'You see –'

He slammed his cup down with a clunk. 'Have you boys lost your *minds*?'

'Funny you should –'

'I *knew* I shouldn't have introduced Bartók in first year,' he said sotto voce. 'Something like this always happens.'

'It all started –'

'Now, don't misunderstand me. I'm not antipathetic to sport. Sugar? One lump or two?'

'Um . . . none, thank you.'

He dropped two cubes in my tea. They fell like ballast stones to the bottom of the cup.

'On the contrary, I was actively involved in sport at the Conservatorium in Vienna.' He extended a long index finger. 'I played chess! I was quite the player in my youth.' He suddenly became animated. 'Now, I'm quite prepared to schedule a chess match against Sydney University and –'

'It's not quite the same, Sir Richard,' I said, wincing.

'Why not? What on *earth* is the point of all this?'

I pondered for a moment. 'The only thing people care about in this country is sport. You know that. Arts funding is slashed year in, year out. What's the big deal if another musician joins the dole queue? Who cares if *we* break our fingers? It's not like Shane Warne breaking his spin finger. There would be a national outpouring of grief. There'd be a picture of his fat digit on the front page of every newspaper. The tabloids asking the nation to pray for his left pinky. Who cares what happens to us? We're artists.'

'So it's a political statement you're making then,' he said, sipping his tea and looking perplexed.

I shrugged. 'We just want to beat Sydney University.'

'I don't quite understand.'

'That's all right, neither do I.'

He got up and showed me to the door, shaking his head and tutting. 'I'm told that you don't stand a chance of even completing the game.'

'Well that "charming man in the awful suit" is at least going to help us *start* the game.'

He offered an unctuous smile. 'And you can rest assured that I will do everything in my power to prevent it. *Habetis bona deum,*' he said, closing the door on my face. (Have a nice day.)

Training was strained that day. I imagined Sir Richard, with his opera glasses, spying from his office. I hadn't seen Bernie since the performance at The Globe. I was keen to sound him out. I think he might have enjoyed the show because he had some probing questions about the text. I was jogging past when he pulled me aside.

'That dance show thingy?'

'Yeah?'

'Whatthefuckwasthatallabout?'

Sadly, I couldn't tell him. I rambled on, Duncan-like, with some student disquisition about the youth of today feeling disenfranchised and trying to find a voice amid the bleakness of urban desolation.

With the sagacity of the Dalai Lama with no neck, he said, 'To be honest, I though it was a crocker shit.'

We were extraordinarily crap that day. Bernie was clearly feeling the strain. I noticed he'd slapped a nicotine patch on his tongue. Even his eager assistant, my father, looked forlorn as we missed tackles and dropped balls with alarming regularity. I panted over to Dad and Bernie who stood with slumped shoulders, watching the circus.

Dad turned to Bernie. 'How are they shaping up, you reckon?'

'In a word: shithouse.'

'Well, that's an improvement anyway,' Dad said.

'Look at em, Pete. They tackle each other, help each other up and ask if they're okay and all that shit. It's not football; it's fucken ballroom-dancing.'

Dad sighed. 'What do we do, Bern?'

'Pete, ol mate, it's time to feed em to the Lions!'

20

Haydn from an old ghost

AS WE STEPPED OFF THE Conservatorium minibus, which was festooned with musical notes and symbols, and onto the slate-hard oval that was Snape Park, we met the other little team Bernie coached: the Maroubra Lions.

The Lions were part of the hard-nosed South Sydney Junior A-Grade League. The team was one of the feeder clubs for the professional side, the Rabbitohs – so-named after the men who sold rabbits (pre-myxomatosis) around the pubs in Redfern at the turn of last century. The Lions were sponsored by a local hotel (most rugby league teams are sponsored by pubs or brands of beer) and had 'The Sands Hotel' plastered in tall white letters across the front of their jerseys.

As the Lions ambled over, we held our breath. Even the Minotaur looked stressed. You see, these guys were the real deal. Many were Maoris and looked like bouncers who worked the doors of night-clubs patronised by bouncers. (As mentioned, Maroubra, like Bondi, is a beachside suburb popular with Sydney's Polynesian community.) Some of us considered getting back on the bus. But it had gone. Bernie introduced us.

'Okay, Maulers, here's the other little team I coach. Say hello to summer the boys. This is Chook, Changa, Boots, Corker, Melon, Cowboy, Jimmy, Brick, Rat and the big fella over there is

Peewee – don't annoy him and you'll be fine. You'll train with us tonight, have a light game and then we'll sink a few beers. Let's get to work.'

Peewee seems like a fictional contrivance, I know, but he was painfully real. If memory serves correctly, he was a six-foot-five, twenty-stone Polynesian prop-forward. To a clutch of weedy musos he was the Colossus of Rhodes squeezed into a red-and-green striped jersey. He politely asked if we were a local soccer team. (True!) It was with some awkwardness that I explained we were a rugby league team. Open-mouthed, he stared at me long enough to qualify as an out-take from a film by Ingmar Bergman.

Phil squealed into the car park in his lemon Volkswagen Beetle (with the rare oval-shaped back window). Racing over, he dropped a carton at our feet. He was giddy with excitement. Phil was sporting a Boy George-style kimono (fashionable at the time). The Lions looked at our manager like he was from Mars – or at least the Tokyo region of Mars.

'Thank God. They've arrived at last!' he said.

'What's fucken arrived?' Bernie said, looking askance at his Lions.

The Maulers ripped into the box like refugees. We held our brand-new jerseys to the light. Guinness-black and with the word 'Roland' in gold lettering across the front (Phil and I absurdly thought the colour black might intimidate Sydney Uni), they looked fabulous.

The Minotaur sneered. 'Roland?'

'Our new sponsor!' Phil said.

For those of you not musically inclined, Roland makes world-class electric pianos and keyboards. After being turned down for the umpteenth time by Pam, Treasurer of the Student Body, Phil and I went to see Roland. After quizzing us – making sure it wasn't someone in the company playing a practical joke – the munificent MD coughed up the sponsorship money. If that kind gentleman is reading this today, I'd suggest that it was the best $350 Roland ever spent publicising its company. Good karma for Roland! Anyway, Phil and I had been keeping the jerseys quiet in case they fell through.

Excitedly handing out matching socks and shorts, Phil hummed Schubert. Like Bernie, Marty seemed embarrassed by all the to-do in front of the Lions. Holding up a jersey, he growled in his Yorkshire machismo, 'Why not have fookin "Steinway" across the front and be done with it.'

The Lions seemed bemused. Bernie was delighted. Every team needs jerseys. And they didn't look half-bad, he thought. He held one up against the thin floodlit light, nodding. 'Roland? I think I drunk that beer on tour in France once.'

Moscowitz shouted. 'Mine's number seven! The half-back is always number seven.'

'I'm thirteen!' Herringbone sang.

'No, you're number nine,' Pemberton said.

'I'm sure it's thirteen.'

After checking corresponding numbers with respective positions (with help from the Lions), we slipped on our new jerseys, shorts and socks. We now had the full dress-up. We felt tall. (I had hitherto been training in an old jersey Bernie had given me. I still have it.)

Phil suddenly dropped his clipboard and bolted to the car. I tried to catch him but he was tearing out of the car park by the time I reached him. I was left in an eddy of dust. The roar of the Beetle descended the octave as it vanished into the quick dark of winter dusk.

I looked at the Lions, scanning their hard, sun-marked faces. The Maulers looked at each other, perplexed. What was the drama? With a shrug of the shoulders, I joined the training session that began, yes, you guessed it, with a goddamn lap of the oval.

'What was the matter with him?' Bernie said as I cantered past.

'Phil? I have no idea.'

After the breathless marathon around Snape Park, our first assignment was tackling. Bernie had set up a circuit of truck tyres. The idea was to tackle a tyre, roll away, then move on to the next one. Being a semi-professional club, the Lions had an entourage of trainers. Aside from Bernie's assistant coach, the raffish Johnny Ragland, the remaining cadre were players recovering from injury. So they screamed and cajoled us as we puffed and panted, tackled and stumbled our way around the circuit. Bernie wanted us to see a real training session. After all, Sydney University was a side that played every weekend and trained like a Roman legion. They had an Olympic-sized swimming pool, tackling machines and several gymnasiums. We had a pinball machine, a broken ping-pong table and a Steeden football with a slow leak.

In the middle of this chaos, a camera crew appeared. Bernie was horrified. A reporter from Channel 7's *Sportsworld* approached. The reporter was John Brady, a lovely guy and now the NRL's media liaison officer. It seemed *Sportsworld* had got wind of the impending game. Brady shoved a hairy microphone into Bernie's mortified face.

'So what's it like coaching the Mozart Maulers, Bernie?'

Bernie throttled me with a look. I ran off to tackle a tree or something as our coach was left awkwardly fielding questions. I secretly prayed to all the gods, including Allah, Krishna, Zeus, and the ghost of David Koresh, that Sir Richard wasn't a closet *Sportsworld* watcher. He would be furious that the match had become public knowledge. *Sportsworld* asked Bernie to carry on as normal. Bernie rolled his eyes at the word 'normal'.

After a concerto of manoeuvres and drills, we lined up against The Lions on the barren oval for a game. The Lions looked at us like their namesake: hungrily. I felt anxious. Meyer took a shot from his asthma spray. Marty broke wind. The Lions punted the ball. Lights, camera, action.

Now, we didn't play a game of full-contact football with the Lions for the simple reason that they would have put us into hospital.

Remember, they were virtually professional footballers. So we played a hybrid game of 'grab'. But don't worry, they let us know they were there. Try 'grabbing' Peewee at full speed. The only way to stop him that evening would have been with an urgent note from his mother. To even things out, Bernie eventually took Peewee off. Not that it mattered. They massacred us. But I remember it did help in coordinating things, stringing passes together under pressure and reconstructing the syntax of weak plays. We could see our game plan against Sydney Uni finally taking shape (i.e. avoid hospital for eighty minutes).

By then we'd picked up a couple of handy players. With the big day only weeks away, they were a gift from Orpheus: Quentin, hooker (bass clarinet); Charles, five-eighth (viola), who had played a handful of games before; our fullback, Harold, a bassoonist with Coke-bottle specs, who was so painfully shy his lenses were made from frosted glass; and Hamish (a classical guitarist). Hamish was important to yours truly because he was my inside centre. By then I had wisely abandoned the hooking role for the relative sanctuary of outside centre. So when the ball was finally passed down the line to Hamish and me, I relied on Hamish to run with it and not to pass the God-awful thing to me. I was prepared to run around and scream out the names of dead composers but viewed the ball as a ticking bomb.

On the wing was the lovely Casey (orchestral percussionist). A sallow youth with a shock of red hair, Casey had a smile that would melt chocolate. I liked Casey because next to him I looked well-built. Casey needed to make drastic changes to his diet by incorporating food.

The game was 'grab', so, if you didn't snatch the Lions quickly, they ran over you like road-kill. Bernie had instructed the Lions to rough us up, so this gave them carte blanche to crash into us.

By some cruel trick of fate, I found the ball between my long fingers. Before I had a chance to turn to Hamish and say, 'How dare you pass me the ball without prior written consent!' I was on my backside. The tackle was a shove more than anything so it didn't hurt. What hurt was falling to the ground! It was so unyielding. It would have been softer being tackled to the floor of St Paul's Cathedral. (I discovered that the centre of the oval was some sort of cricket pitch that was compacted solid from years of heavy rollers.) The sculptured lawn in front of Government House in the Botanic Gardens where we practised was a putting green compared with the grassless Snape Park.

The Lions' five-eighth, built like a limbed fortress, helped me to my feet before running off to make another tackle. Suddenly the colour drained from my face. I remembered Phil running to the car.

It was Jonno.

I stood numb, watching him canter around the oval. He was as adroit as ever, though years of gruelling rugby league had withered his looks (he'd left school to become a professional footballer). This one-time poster-boy of the Sperm Clinic now resembled a battle-weary soldier. My namesake's famous painting in the attic. His nose had been broken and re-broken so many times it looked like a potato that someone had trodden on. However, if he was big at school, he was now enormous. He possessed the shoulders of Atlas. His limbs, a series of rippling muscles.

I felt distressed. What would he do to me after the game? I told myself to be rational. To calm down. He wasn't going to suddenly give me a wedgie in the change room. He wasn't going to put glue in my hair. We were adults. And I now used gel. Taking deep breaths, and a Valium, I started to calm down. But I was left feeling dark. Jonno was the last person I wanted to see. I was a new being. I had reinvented myself. I had escaped that universe. Burned it from my mind with a blowtorch. I was now living in the inner-city, sneering and dressing in black, surrounded by bright young things who applauded personality and celebrated uniqueness. That underworld of cruel children existed only in my darkest dreams, dreams worthy of Poe.

⌒

No wonder Phil had bolted like a racehorse. He was terrified of Jonno. We both were. And Phil's crush on him had ended the day his Adonis had shown his true colours. (It must be said that Jonno had never bothered us again after that day. He'd made his point. And we'd had legions of new bullies to negotiate.) But Phil never forgave Jonno.

As I stood there contemplating this in a vivid playback, I saw Jonno watching. He was trying to place me. He had one eye on me and one eye on the play. It had never occurred to me that I would run into someone from school. After leaving, I seldom saw anyone from that horrid place again. Occasionally, I'd see them driving cabs or tipping rubble into skips on building sites, but I tended to look the other way and think about ice-cream. In hindsight, the odds seemed likely that I *would* meet someone from school. Let's face it: Bernie was coaching in my old stomping ground. I was only twenty. Many boys from school continued playing rugby or rugby league or both.

I was still reeling from meeting an old ghost when Bernie put an end to the slaughter. The score line resembled the national debt of Mexico by that stage anyway. And the Lions were tired after throwing us around like marionettes for an hour and needed to rest.

'Time for a few cleansing ales, boys!' Bernie said. The camera crew packed up their equipment in a series of silver cases. They left happy people. *Sportsworld* said they'd call Bernie when the piece was going to air. Bernie replied with a flat look.

⌒

The Lions were fabulous hosts. They'd actually organised a sausage sizzle for us. We were flabbergasted. We weren't expecting anything. As we chatted over the long shhhh of the onions, I avoided Jonno like cholera. He peeked at me from the barbecue as he chatted with Bernie and Johnny Ragland about next week's game. He still hadn't placed me. They had a couple of cases of beer (courtesy of their sponsor), which, among two football teams, 'didn't even touch the sides', as Dad says. (Dad was working that evening, by the way.) So it was decided to go back to their local and continue the libation. (This is why pubs sponsor football teams, I guess.) Marty was delighted. Moscowitz seemed stressed. He had his violin with him and it was a Stradivarius (not sure if the old master made it himself but it was precious nonetheless). Hard to imagine, I know, but Moscowitz's instrument was worth more than Bernie's house! (It was insured, but it was still not something you are careless with in a pub.) So it never left his person. He had to be talked into tackling without it.

With Jonno lurking around, I made excuses to leave. Bernie wouldn't hear of it.

'You're the bloody captain. You're the last to leave the pub, orright!'

I winced, glancing at Jonno.

21

I Pagliacci (the players) get well and truly rat-arsed

AS WE POURED THOUGH THE glass doors of the Sands Hotel en masse, four boozy punters sat comatosed beneath a row of televisions that blinked with various racing events. Betting slips lay scattered beneath them like leaves. A buxom, crooked-toothed barmaid leaned over the counter. Displaying a crevasse of cleavage, she perfunctorily syphoned beer into glass jugs. The sodden red beer-towel that compassed the length of the bar soon supported overflowing jugs of nut-brown ale.

The Maulers tried to get a round in but the Lions wouldn't allow us to put our hand in our pockets all night. Tricky when one of us needed to use a hanky.

Bernie collared me. 'What the fuck was that about with *Sportsworld* tonight?'

'I don't know, Bernie,' I said, as he shoved a frothing schooner into my hand.

'Jesus! I don't want to be back in the spotlight after all these years as the coach of a bunch of fucken violin players!'

'Must have been someone at Sydney Uni drumming up publicity for the team.'

Bernie clicked his fat fingers. 'Dave Barnes!'

'Dave who?'

'The Sydney Uni coach. Rubbing it in. Oh, I bet he's loving this.

Rotten bastard.'

'It's something different, I suppose,' I said, cringing.

'Something *different*? Listen, when I played, I had respect. It's very important to me, respect,' he said, draining his glass.

Hamish stuck his head into the conversation. 'Imagine how much respect you'll get when we beat Sydney Uni, Bernie!'

'Arr, you're not going on with that bullshit, too, are ya?'

'Are we a chance, Bernie?' I asked.

'Of course we are!' Hamish slurred, refilling his glass from a nearby jug.

'What *are* you blokes smokin?'

'You don't think we can beat them, Bern?' I said.

'*Beat* em? You beat em and I'll fair dinkum take piano lessons,' he said over his shoulder, jiggling his fly on the way to the toilets.

Hamish, glassy-eyed and full of bravado fuelled by amber nectar, patted me on the back. 'With us in the centres, Dorian, they don't stand a chance.'

'Oh, right,' I said, crashing back to earth.

Hamish, a great pal of Big Marty's, wandered over to him with a couple of beers. Marty was in his element, singing, and the life of the party. The Minotaur and Peewee were engaged in deep conversation – something about offensive tackling. At the end of the bar, Moscowitz, anchored to his violin, was chatting with the Lions' nuggety half-back.

I skulked off to drink on my own at the back bar, hiding from the inquisitive gaze of Jonno – who was putting two and two together and coming up with a wedgie. By that stage, we were drinking Depth Charges: schooners of beer with shot-glasses of some spirit sunk in them. I was stressed, so I drank a little quicker than is my custom. After a few Depth Charges and a Valium chaser, my tongue felt a little numb. I found it difficult to say the word 'kerfuffle' without drooling on my shoes.

Polishing off my fifth deep-sea explosion, I felt a weighty palm on my shoulder. Without looking I knew who it was. By that stage I was too pissed to care.

'Do we *know* each other, mate?' Jonno said. 'You see, I never forget a face.'

'Yeah, we went to school together,' I said through an upturned beer glass.

He cocked his tanned head. 'You sure?'

'Quite sure.' I jumped off the barstool and lay on the floor. 'Ow, stop kicking me, guys. You're breaking my ribs. I think I can hear a teacher coming. Arghh, fuck, that really hurt! I think I'm about to lose an eye . . .'

'Dorian!'

I jumped up. 'Also known as Bones, Arse-wipe, Poof and sometimes known under the little-used alias, That-Horrible-Prick-Who-Plays-the-Piano.'

'And the bloke in the black-dressing gown?'

'Phil.'

'I didn't recognise him,'

'He mostly wore a headlock at school.'

He chuckled. 'Yeah, I remember. Whatcha drinkin?' he said, his broken nose blanketing the natural resonance in the voice.

'Depth Charges.'

As Jonno waited for the order, I took a good look at him. Inclined to corpulence as a teen, he was quite heavy now, though much of it thew on thew. This muscle would turn to fat post-football. (A nerd's revenge!) And too much of our Australian sun will prematurely age you. There was now a haunted look about Jonno. The sea-blue eyes seemed paler. His lids, dark and sleepless. The bountiful sun-bleached locks, a barren paddock. As he handed me a fizzing beer, I could see something was on his mind.

'Look, I'm . . . sorry for punching you in the head that day,' he finally said.

'That's all right. The haemorrhaging has finally stopped and the specialist said the migraines should gradually disappear by the time I'm in my late fifties.'

'Oh, that's good news,' he nodded, sipping a beer. 'Why did Phil take off like that?' he asked in a melody of blunt notes.

'Because he was frightened of you.'

'Of *me*? Why?'

'Because you were a bully and an arsehole,' I said, fearless from beer.

'Come on. That was yonks ago. What did he think I was gunner do? Beat him up?'

'Why would we think any different? People like you made our lives hell. As if home-life wasn't traumatic enough, we had to then endure the bullying and infantile taunts day in, day out. There was no escape for people like Phil and me. It was a constant stress.'

'I never meant to hurt you that day.'

'It wasn't just the punch –'

'Come on. It was a tap –'

'Whatever. It was the degradation of it all. The way it made you constantly feel. Like a leper. Less human.'

Jonno seemed to be listening. Concerned almost. After some frowning deliberation he spoke.

'Mate, what can I say? I'm sorry. You do all sorts of stupid shit when you're a kid. Trying to fit in. Impressing others. Anyway, that's why I took off that day. So the others wouldn't lay into you. I had nothing against you or Phil. Look, will ya accept my apology?' He outstretched a camel-brown hand. 'Friends?'

I looked at his hand. I looked at mine. His was chunky and sinewy. Mine was long and thin, like a woman's. It was never engineered to be compressed into a fist and driven into someone's open face. For this, I had felt like a failure in adolescence, less of a man. Perhaps I was. I finally offered my hand. 'Okay. Friends.'

He smiled, shaking my hand and patting me paternally on the back. He took a sip of beer and wiped a trail of white scum from his cracked lips. 'You a professional musician?'

'Trying to be. What about you? Professional footballer?'

'That was the dream. Never happened, really.'

'Why?'

'Long story.'

'I'm not going anywhere.'

'Jeeze. Where do I start? Well, I got a contract with the Roosters (that's why his nickname was Chook, by the way). But I done all me AC joints.'

'That's shocking,' I said. (To this day, I have no idea what an AC joint is.)

'Put an end to the footy career. I just pick up glasses at the leagues club for a quid.'

'What about university? You used to be quite bright at school. I remember you getting a first in Science one year.'

'All I wanted to do was play footy but. Didn't take the school-work seriously. Goofed off. I was an idiot, to be honest. Then Mum got sick.'

As we sank beer after beer (Jonno on light, me on the 'submarine killers') he spoke in quiet tones about his career stagnation and his mother's lingering illness. I recall it was tricky hearing him against the cabaret of the pub (even from the back bar) but listened intently.

In his final year of school, Jonno was playing rugby for Randwick Rugby Union Club (he played league on Sundays with the Lions). He was a talented five-eighth and, before the advent of professionalism in rugby, Randwick did everything it could to keep him in union, bar a share portfolio and vintage wine cellar. Spotted by a talent scout, he was offered a contract with the Brisbane Broncos Rugby League Club and followed the same path as Bernie: into the cash cow that was rugby league. When his mother was diagnosed with a liver disease (brought on by alcoholism) he was forced to reject the contract to stay in Sydney. He was eventually signed to the (then Eastern Suburbs, now Sydney) Roosters. But the stress of his mother's deteriorating condition, and attention she required, dampened the fire needed to become an elite player. This, coupled with a string of unlucky injuries, saw him dropped to the splintered failure of the reserve bench. In the end, he never made the first-grade side. He said he was now playing on 'one leg' and only with the Lions for fun. With no career or interests outside sport, he'd become clinically depressed and was on medication for a while. The week I met him, he had just been offered a job as a prison guard in the neighbouring suburb of Long Bay, but had told them outright that he wouldn't shoot anyone going over the wall. He held an imaginary rifle to his shoulder, 'What am I going to do? Shoot a bloke?'

As Jonno's mother rotted in their pension flat, she ultimately lost control of her bowels. This was hard, he confessed. She became bitter. And drinking until almost the end, she would fire buckshot of abuse at him: he was a failure; he was a disappointment to her; he'd fucked up his life; he'd fucked up her life. She threw things at him: plates, cups, cutlery, a pair of scissors, cutting his scalp. On the ebb of these tirades, when she had screamed herself to exhaustion, he'd silently clean up the flotsam of her soul: her empty bottles, her cigarette packets, her medication, her vomit, her shit, and feel himself sinking. But something wonderful happened to impregnate this purgatory with at least some sort of meaning.

In the end, his mother couldn't hold anything down. On the drip, she became lucid. (Even as a boy he couldn't remember his mother sober.) Jonno met his mother for the first time. The farm girl who had married the boy next-door who'd died when he rolled his tractor. The farm girl who moved to the city with her baby and cleaned the houses of rich families in Vaucluse to make ends meet. The farm girl who bounced from one bad boyfriend to the next. The farm girl who discovered that life seemed to glow through the soft-focus lens of a vodka bottle.

In her final days, when she was unable to walk, Jonno would wheel her along the promenade of Maroubra beach. In the salty winter wind, they'd laugh and talk for hours. She spoke of the country; of the one-roomed schoolhouse; of Uncle Harvey's old MG that became a chicken coop; of the harvest; and the hot windless nights of summer. She spoke about his father for the first time. She said how proud he would have been of the son he never knew. Proud of the man he'd become. And that when she'd meet his father again, to begin their life over, she'd be sure to tell him so.

Jonno's voice cracked on the last word. He stared into his glass, eyes pooling with tears. I remained silent.

I can't tell you why Jonno felt compelled to divulge this. He wasn't drunk and it was painful for him. I almost got the feeling that he'd never told anyone before. Perhaps, like me, meeting someone from childhood stoked the embers of memory.

However, of one thing I was certain: I urgently needed to 'break the seal', as my father puts it (i.e. the first of many sorties to the pub's loo). I hadn't wanted to interrupt Jonno, so I was turning cross-eyed. Neil Armstrong never waited so long.

Like all men, I braced myself against the urinous smell and stepped up to the bunker of steel. I was aghast to find Cowboy slumped in the urinal. Plastered (as we all were by that stage), he was finding it difficult to get up, so I pulled him out. Getting to his feet, he wiped his trousers. A wet map of Africa remained on his left buttock. (No one had pissed on him or anything. They just wanted to see if he could do the breast-stroke, I guess.)

'Bloody, Guy!' he said.

'What guy?' I said.

He left with a handful of wet toilet paper to bomb the practical joker.

After taking the longest leak known to man, I wandered back to Jonno with the rolling gait of Magellan. It seemed someone was inconsiderately tipping the room from side to side. I thought about complaining to management. With a wobble, I sat back on my stool and we resumed our conversation. By then, something about Fords versus Holdens. My complete lack of knowledge about the motor industry was interrupted by someone's fat arm clamping like a nut-cracker around my head. This gorilla had me in a headlock and was jumping up and down, singing 'I want to rock and roll all night' made famous by that band of closet drag queens, Kiss. I looked up at Jonno.

'Dorian, meet Guy,' said Jonno.

I had never met this person before. He was a frightening, glassy-eyed, ten-year-old boy trapped in the body of a twenty-stone ex-footballer with no neck. Guy was, in fact, Bernie! Christened by the laconic Anne Johns, Guy started to peek from behind Bernie's bloodshot eyes after about seven-and-a-half schooners. By schooner ten, Guy had completely taken over and Bernie was nowhere to be found. Don't get me wrong, Guy wasn't a nasty person. Guy was simply the little boy who still wanted to rough it up with the lads, but was too old and battered to do so on the football field. Guy dragged me into the main bar. Everybody cheered. Marty, who by then had abandoned the glass to drink directly from the jug, blew a long raspberry. Still in a headlock, Guy hauled me to the front bar and casually ordered a beer. He was smoking. Guy was a heavy smoker. Jonno pulled up a stool beside him. I tried to speak.

'Bernie, um . . . that's kind of annoying, old mate,' I said, muffled by his chunky forearm.

'He can't hear you,' Jonno said over the circus of the bar. 'You have to call him Guy.'

'Ahem, Guy, I can't quite finish my beer,' I wheezed, his meaty arm bending my glasses.

Guy started singing a slurring rendition of either the Rolling Stones' 'Brown Sugar' or the national anthem of Kazakhstan.

'Guy must like you,' said Jonno, sipping his beer. 'He only does that if he likes you.'

'How pleasant,' I said, as Guy tapped the percussion adaptation of Rimsky-Korsakov's *Flight of the Bumblebee* with his mangled knuckles on my skull. Funnily enough, up until that point, Bernie had barely acknowledged my existence. If he wasn't yelling at me to try harder, he was calling me a girl. This was the first time in my life when bullying felt like endearment. 'Tell Guy I'm glad he likes me and that I'd be quite flattered if I wasn't about to pass out.' Guy's arm must have been getting sore, because he quickly changed arms. I took the breath of a drowning man. 'His wife must be delighted when he comes home,' I said, gasping.

'She locks Guy out of the house and waits for Bernie to come home,' said Jonno.

'Smart woman,' I choked.

Jonno laughed. 'Come on, Guy. Give it a rest.'

Guy let go. I collapsed to the floor. Guy grabbed Jonno's fingers. He started bending them back, smiling. Jonno coolly lit a cigarette with his free hand and spoke in kindergarten tones.

'Now, Guy, if you break Chook's fingers, Chooky won't be able to play on Sunday. It's a very important game, remember? There's a good boy. Put Chook's fingers back.'

Guy let them go and raced across the bar and tackled Peewee to the floor. Peewee looked up and sighed. 'I see Guy's arrived then.'

The room erupted as the Lions flopped on top of Guy. Someone poured a jug beer over him. Marty took his shoes, tied the laces together, and pitched them over a ceiling fan. They wheeled like a Dadaist's mobile. Two Lions grabbed Bernie's bantam offsider, Johnny Ragland, and snatched his toupee. It became a hairy Frisbee. The bar was transformed into a madhouse. I stood with my mouth open.

Jonno turned to me and sighed. 'Welcome to club football, Dorian.'

The room suddenly exploded with laughter. Wearing only his yarmulke and a smile, Moscowitz, darted stark naked through the front bar. He was performing that sacred, time-honoured, footballing ritual: 'The Dance of the Flaming Arseholes'. For the uninitiated, this dance involves sticking a long piece of toilet paper up your crack, lighting it, and running through the bar stark-bollock naked.

(Salome invented it when someone hid her veils on Herod's buck's night.) Moscowitz lapped the bar, rectum ablaze. I looked for his violin. It stood upturned in a nearby pot plant. Guy declared this blazing streak stupendous and climbed on a table, insisting the bar raise their glasses to the Mozart Maulers.

Herringbone scaled another table and began an aria from *I Pagliacci*. It was spectacular. The bar grew silent. His powerful tenor shook the shelves of glasses. At song's end, you could hear a pin drop. He finished to riotous applause. Then, quietly in a corner, Peewee sang 'Amazing Grace' in a sweet, high voice that belied his mass – so high it was almost castrato. It wasn't long before a couple of Polynesian team-mates joined him. Somerset Maugham describes Polynesian chorus (in one of those fabulous short stories he wrote while travelling the South Seas in the 1920s) as a kind of 'sour beauty'. That night I understood exactly what he meant. It's something in the intonation. It was simply beautiful.

The Maulers were moved to hear the big men sing so mellifluously. However, this impromptu soirée proved a soporific. We finished our drinks in quiet conversation and went home.

Guy, barefooted, decided to go for Chinese.

22

Twilight of the Gobs

I SAT IN SOL'S OFFICE NURSING a hangover that lasted nigh on three days. On the first day it hurt to play the note B flat. By the second, I couldn't go out in daylight without welding glasses and a black cape. By the third, aided by large doses of aspirin, I was feeling like my old self, although I did feel sexually aroused upon hearing the voice of Margaret Thatcher.

'What's in the dream diary this week?'

'God, it reads like Kafka,' I said.

'Let's hear it,' said Sol, lighting a Dunhill and reaching for his note pad.

'Well, I'm on a train. I'm travelling through the Scottish countryside on my way to a village called Fluff. God knows why. The conductor, who is Harpo Marx, asks for my ticket through coded honks of his horn. I hand him my ticket. But the ticket is a photo of Flaubert. He holds it, looks at me and mouths the word 'Emma', honks his horn, punches my ticket, and hands it back. I say to him, 'Does this train stop at Fluff?' He honks 'Yes' on his horn and I resume my seat next to my Uncle Charlie, who is dressed as Napoleon. Charlie passes me a sandwich made from the scores of Shostakovich's *Fragments from the Gadfly* and I eat it. What do you make of *that*?'

There was a long silence.

'Do you eat a lot of cheese before bedtime?' he said.

As Sol took notes and smoked himself to emphysema, the full horror of the previous night's events came back to me. As usual, I spoke in a long, Kerouac ramble – punctuated only by the clink of Sol's boxy lighter.

⌒

After the debacle at The Globe, Lydia wasn't returning my calls. By that stage the only way she would communicate with me at all was with naval signal flags from the roofs of tall buildings. Lydia was still angry with me for talking her into doing *The Castle of Malcolm* (despite her better judgement). Her friends who had come to the performance and met me after the show politely informed her that I was a lunatic and wondered what a gorgeous thing like Lydia would see in someone so painfully misanthropic as my good self. (The thought had crossed my mind.) Before I came on the scene, she had been dating a genial mechanic. Her friends said that if she went back to him, not only would she be happier, she would enjoy years of maintenance-free driving.

However, the more Lydia rejected me, the more anxious I became. I tried to play it cool at first. (No one likes 'needy'.) But in the end, my feigned nonchalance quickly deteriorated into 'needy'. What can I tell you? I was in love with her. I'd never met anyone like her before. She was so easy to talk with. So generous of spirit. So grounded. And we hadn't had a single disagreement since meeting – that is, until The Globe.

⌒

After we'd finished up at the Sands Hotel, and with a drunk's logic, I jumped a cab to Lydia's flat to 'set things right'. I was going to apologise for talking her into doing the show and for my general mental health (or lack thereof). Sadly, the plan was hatched at one a.m. and after enough depth charges to sink *The Nautilus*.

Lydia lived with her mother in a roomy flat in the manicured suburb of Northbridge – just on the other side of the harbour. At one-thirty, I fell out of the cab with a posy of broken flowers.

'Pssst!' I said, throwing a piece of gravel against her window.

No response.

I threw another and said, 'Pssst! Oi! Lydia!' Which may have came out as 'piss on Libya'.

Nothing.

I threw a larger stone. It broke the glass with a clink.

'Oh shit,' I said.

An angry head popped over the balcony. 'Go away!'

'Lydia, you look horrible. Do you have the flu?' I said, staggering over the flowerbed.

'Go away or I'll call the police.'

'You look terrible. You sure you're not sick?'

'This is Lydia's *mother*!' she said, in her sharp Dublin accent. 'Lydia doesn't want to see you. Go away.'

Great way to meet the future in-laws.

'Go inside, Mum. I'll handle this,' Lydia said before hanging her cherubic face over the balcony. 'Just what the hell are you doing, Dorian? It's nearly two o'clock in the morning!'

'Um . . . was that your mum? Nice lady,' I said wincing. Fluorescent lights winked in the surrounding apartments.

'Oh, you've made a *big* impression. Go home.'

'I've come to say I'm sorry about The Globe. I've brought you flowers. Eh . . . they may need a little tape.'

'As if the show wasn't humiliating enough. What's happened to your face?'

'Oh, I was tackling Chook or was it Changa? No it was Chook and then Changa . . . might have been Cowboy –'

'Football! I should have known. The whole thing's ridiculous. I thought I was going out with a composer!'

I tripped over a flowerpot. Another fluoro stuttered.

'Can I just ask you one thing?'

'*What?*'

'Um . . . can I use your loo?'

'Good *night*, Dorian!' She slammed the door. A piece of glass fell onto the balcony.

To further impress, I threw up on her letterbox.

⌢

Sol winced behind his clipboard.

'Does it look bad?' I asked.

'What do you think?'

'Tell me. Why do you shrinks always answer a question with a question?'

'Do we?'

'See, you did it again!' I said, holding my forehead and rifling through my pocket for aspirin.

'Did what?'

'There you go again: answering a question with a question.'

'Did I?'

'Yes.'

'Really?'

'Oh, forget it. Can I have a glass of water?'

'Would you like a glass of water?'

'God! It's like being on fucking *Sale of the Century*.'

As I'd had further emergency visits to casualty with hysterical anxiety, Sol suggested putting me into the psych unit at St Vincent's for a few days. He had a good reason. Sol's surgery, like most, was open from nine to five. I suffered from anxiety attacks mostly at night (although by then it was changing). So he had never seen one in the flesh. He wanted to stick me in the psych ward for a couple of weeks and have someone observe me. I was terrified; convinced they'd never let me out again. I was anxious and paranoid to the point of mania so I was never going to look at it logically. I told him flatly I wasn't going. This created some tension.

When I first met Sol, I'd make dry remarks about the attacks, perhaps a light pun about Jung, he'd chuckle, swipe my Medicare card, and I'd happily be on my way. But the stakes had been raised. The demons had begun to appear in daylight.

'What are you fearful about?' he asked.

'On a conscious level?' I asked this because when huddled in a corner in the foetal position, in the grip of intangible demons, there is no *conscious* reason to be fearful. An anxiety attack is, by nature, illogical. Your only escape is the womb of sleep. I thought for a while, unsure how to answer. 'Can't say exactly. Nothing on a conscious level. Though I fear the Democrats won't win the next election.'

'Why do you always feel the need to make jokes when you're stressed?'

'Something I've done since school. Humour feels like my only grip on sanity at times. Like Luther laughing and farting at the devil to weaken him. But then, German food tends to be gassy.'

He pulled out a prescription pad. 'What say I give you a stronger prescription?'

Now this floored me. Sol's strategy *ab initio* had been to avoid pills and tackle the demons head-on (pun unintended). I had faith in the football therapy. I didn't want new pills. Each capsule seemed like a brightly coloured coffin. But Sol reminded me to think of a tranquilliser as a safety net. He was simply suggesting a bigger net. I could see he was worried. I agreed to take them if things were unbearable (like every bloody night!).

He lit a fresh cigarette. 'What are you obsessing about?'

'Me, obsess?'

We both laughed. (He, a little longer than was polite, I thought.)

I sat there thinking. He sat there puffing.

'Well . . . ?' he asked, between tumours.

'How dare you interrupt me when I'm not speaking.'

He ashed.

'Haven't you got some X-rated ink blots we could look at?' I said. 'Like the one there on the wall. Now, I see anger, my school principal and Chinese food.'

'That's a painting by Miro.'

'He clearly needs therapy.'

'What's worrying you now?'

'Right now? Well, I'm worried about the game.'

'It's on in a couple of weeks, isn't it?'

'Yes. I'm shitting myself.'

He took notes. 'Why?'

I thought for a moment. 'I guess, I'm worried about falling apart in the game. Letting everyone down. The humiliation. I'm not worried about getting hurt, but I'm fearful that others will get hurt and I won't be there for them. You know, I'll be hiding behind the goal post or something.'

'What about the Nerds' Triangle?'

'I'd forgotten about that.'

Sol was referring to a dark episode that happened when I returned from New York. My mother still talks about the irony of it. I had been living in New York for six months and walking home late in the morning through some pretty scary neighbourhoods. I'd also been visiting musicians and painters in Alphabet City (then a veritable 1940s Dresden) and hanging out in jazz clubs and bars and worrying my mother sick. (You have to be 21 to drink in the States, but being tall, I got away with it at 18.) I had survived this only to return to Sydney to be jumped by four guys outside my old school.

I was walking home my then girlfriend, Giulietta (pre-Vespa). Giulietta was a gorgeous Italian and as unhinged as I was. We fought like seagulls. She didn't possess Lydia's tranquil Inland Sea that I so needed. Giulietta was a box of fireworks. This particular night we were sitting on the side of the road having our nightly argument, when a car pulled up. A huge guy got out: long hair, flannelette shirt, the whole western suburbs dress-up.

He asked for a light. I looked up, adjusted my glasses, and said I didn't have one. He started looking around like a bird (remember what that means?) and began casually gobbing on the pavement. His friends hopped out of the car and chatted and spat. They gobbed so much it became a Festival of Saliva. So here this guy was, chatting with me, spitting, looking over his shoulder, spitting, chatting. He seemed nice enough.

A second later I had his boot in my face. Perhaps he wanted me to light his boot with my teeth? Anyway, I was in the gutter when the others joined in to use me as a soccer ball. Big Dog crouched down to punch me in the head. I felt pain – in my face, my ribs, my spine. I felt blood trickle down the back of my throat. I looked up to see my old school, mocking me. It was saying, 'just when you thought you'd escaped, you little prick.' It prompted me to ask myself (which I later relayed to Sol): 'What is this suburb, some kind of Nerds' Bermuda Triangle?'

I cradled myself, foetus-like, from the blows and boots as best I could. They kept asking for my wallet. I would have gladly given it to them, but it was a little tricky as they were inconsiderately kicking me to death. Giulietta was screaming. As I became a tortoise, protecting myself and drifting off into the sanctuary of my imagination, Big Dog barked to his hounds.

'Get the bitch into the car!'

Two of them grabbed Giulietta by her beautiful long hair, which was the colour of dark chocolate, and dragged her to the car. As the remaining two were kicking and punching me, Big Dog's words echoed inside my head. *Get the bitch into the car, get the bitch into the car, get the bitch into the car.* I knew what that would mean for her. Out of the corner of my bleeding eye, I saw her terrified face as they tried to stuff her into the back seat, tearing at her skirt. While I was prepared to be beaten up, I couldn't live with myself if a girl I was with was gang-raped while I lay curled in the gutter like a snivelling coward. (I don't know if that was their intention, but I suspect they weren't taking her ice-skating.) I had to do something. So in a panic, I let out a bloodcurdling, high-pitched scream. Not a manly scream. It was more Julian Clary than John Wayne. It even stunned Giulietta. The long, diaphragmatic shriek startled the curs momentarily. I jumped to my feet. Everything was in slow motion. (Must have been the adrenaline, the police later said.) I remember the scene as a blur, my glasses smashed and twisted on the road. I heard Dad's voice in my head: *'If it's a mob, always go for the biggest one. Always go for the biggest one!'* (In his early twenties, Dad was jumped by a gang of toughs at Cabramatta station one night. He chinned the biggest one and the others bolted. Growing up in a migrant hostel meant, if under threat, you always got in the first punch.)

I stood nose to nose with Big Dog, circling. This scene obviously wasn't in Big Dog's action movie. He was apprehensive, confused. (He wasn't the only one. I was someone who'd elevated cowardice into a martial art.) I drew my fist behind my head and, with all my might, cracked him, plumb on the jaw. (A lucky punch.) I felt his knees buckle on the end of my fist. A horrible feeling. Years of avoiding physical confrontation by using my intellect and wit had boiled down to this. It felt awful, savage, Neanderthal. But it was the only thing to do. Pretty soon Big Dog, concussed and nursing his chin, was staggering and running around the Mini (yes, these heroes had stolen a Mini Cooper – hardly the ideal mobile phallus). As I chased him he howled at his pack to get back in the car. They released Giulietta and she fled like a rabbit. Little Dog, who obviously hadn't driven before, was trying to start the car in gear. I can still see the car leapfrogging along the street, with them screaming at each other like Keystone Cops (sorry, I know this is black), and Big

Dog orbiting the mini, while I, bloody-faced, peppered him with wild aeroplane swings, none of which connected. He finally shoved the novice driver from behind the wheel and got in, with me punching him in the side of the head through the driver's window as a small parting gift.

As Giulietta and I sat in the sandstone cottage of Coogee police station, with an indifferent sergeant who filled in forms while eating jelly-babies, I realised that night I'd discovered a new person buried within. Someone I'd never met before. A solitary resident. A reluctant brute.

I loathe confrontation. I've spent a lifetime avoiding it. However, the sad fact of life is that people take advantage of diplomacy on occasion. It wasn't very Buddhist of me to king-hit Big Dog that night, but if Churchill had been a lentil-eating Buddhist and not the cigar-smoking, whisky-drinking sot he was, we'd perhaps be eating pig snouts and sauerkraut right now.

It suddenly dawned on me. I turned to Sol, wide-eyed. 'Is this what this is all about? This football stuff? Am I trying to find the stranger who smacked that bully? Will this guy help me through all this madness? Is that what this fucking football is all about, Sol?'

Sol furiously took notes. 'Is that what you think?'

I looked at him flatly.

Prick.

23

Carmen, Bernie, it was only a joke!

Bernie copped a *lot* of stick over the Maulers; and Australians are uncompromising tormentors, the Spanish Inquisition in thongs. If they detect a weakness, they'll pick at it till it becomes gangrenous. Perhaps it's their way of toughening you up for the battle. When our European ancestors hunted bison with little more than spears and rocks, men needed to stand steadfast. If one panicked and fled, the herd could well charge the group. We don't hunt bison any more and this masculine rite of passage is superfluous, and only needed if you are a member of the Chippendales on a hen's night. But once the Maulers hit national television, there was nowhere for poor Bernie to hide. So again, largely from the fiction factory, and with the scantiest of facts, here is a snapshot of the raillery.

The Usual Suspects are gathered around the bar of The Dog. As Bernie returns from the bathroom, reefing traky-daks over his bulbous belly, the Suspects giggle, avoiding eye contact.

'What's the gag, fellas?'

Bernie sees the violin bow in his beer.

'Oh, *very* funny. Who told you packer low bastards?'

'We heard you got a concert coming up?' says Mulberry Cheeks. The bar splutters into their glasses.

'Okay, so now youse know. Ha ha bloody ha. I'm doing a favour for Pete, orright?'

Bernie's old team-mate and Sydney Uni coach, Dave Barnes, appears. (The procurer of the violin bow.) A man with an unsophisticated sense of humour, tickled by simple jokes.

Bernie turns crimson. 'What's *he* bloody doing here? Arr, this is a dead-set gee-up.'

'Now hang on,' says Dave. 'I'm told some of these boys can really play.'

Bernie agrees.

'Especially at weddings and bar mitzvahs.'

The bar explodes.

Bernie motions to leave. 'I'm bloody goin.'

'Don't listen to these ratbags, Bern. Have a schooey.' Mulberry Cheeks hands him a beer and an envelope. 'By the way, Pete dropped over the game plan for next Sunday.'

'Really?'

Bernie sets the beer on the bar and opens the envelope, theatrically shielding it from Dave Barnes.

It's an orchestral score from Mozart's *Marriage of Figaro*.

The bar becomes an opera of backslapping guffaws. Bernie has turned the colour of merlot.

He explodes. 'Oh, you're Mr Fucken Comedy, you are. At least these kids are havin a go. The only football you've ever touched, Gary, is the one hangin off ya rear-view mirror. And you know somethin? These kids have talent. That little halfback plays like Page-a-nini.'

'Didn't he play for the Bulldogs in '75?'

'He was a violinist, dickhead. He wrote *The Four Seasons*.'

'Really? I love *The Four Seasons*,' says Mulberry Cheeks, sincerely.

'Yeah?'

In a sweet falsetto, coupled with awkward dance steps and hand movements, Mulberry Cheeks sings, 'Walk like a man, talk like a man . . .'

Bernie storms out.

Dave Barnes calls after him. 'Carmen, Bern, where's ya sensor huma?'

⌒

Just when I thought I couldn't be more stressed, my mother called. Some fool had phoned her after watching *Sportsworld*. The charade of my 'little friendly game of football' was no more. Mother left a rambling dissertation on my answering machine (a one-act play composed of fourteen two-minute calls) about art, football, the price of a cup of coffee in Manhattan, the Dalai Lama, her broken heel, Thursday's audition, Frank's compacted wisdom tooth, with an epilogue insisting I drop out of the team *immediately*. I was instructed to call her at work that evening.

Mum was waiting tables at the J.P. Holy Horse Restaurant in New York. Like many restaurants in New York, 'Mrs Jays' employed struggling actors between jobs. However, this little bistro was hip enough to cash in on the idle talent. All the waiters performed.

The working apparel for the men was the tuxedo. The women also wore tuxedos, leotards, heels and fishnets. It was the Radio City chorus-girl look, with added ogle-factor. Waiters performed between orders with the house pianist. For a working-class girl from Cabramatta, it must have seemed an exciting place to work.

When I phoned, Mum was often in the midst of performing for customers. I'd hear her belting out 'My Way' or 'New York, New York', then rushing off to serve clam chowder before reaching the phone. Or another waiter would recite the soliloquy from *Hamlet* in the background, while tossing a caesar salad.

Mrs Jays was full of dreams and dreamers – most would go unfulfilled. These dreams must have seemed palpable at times, impregnating the wallpaper like the cigarette smoke and onions. Poor Mum worked there for years. During the day, she'd stand in line for auditions in the fat New York snow, every rejection another welt on her soul. At night, she'd serve lemon chicken and dream a little more. She'd given up so much to win she couldn't contemplate surrender.

If I called, and she had returned from another of those daylight wounds, she tried to be upbeat, but defeat permeated every other phrase. I could always hear it. Separation regardless, a child never forgets the many hues of its mother's voice. However, when I called Mum that evening she was happy. A call-back for a musical loomed. She was belting out a tune when I called.

'And now, the end is near . . .'

It was a surreal, aural landscape that trickled out of the receiver that evening: the melodramatic singing of show tunes, the clinking of cutlery, telephones bleating, the mélange of conversation, waiters barking orders at the kitchen, the Chinese chef, Mr Chang, spanking a bell and screaming in return.

Valerie, a fledgling actress from Arkansas, called Mum to the phone. 'Psst! Sheryl, it's your son from Arse-tralia.'

Mum pushed the time of the song, the pianist valiantly following her. The tune abruptly finished. There was some light applause. Someone belched. Mr Chang slapped his bell. Mum snatched the phone, breathless.

'Hi sweetie thanks for calling back but I'll have to be quick because Table 8 is giving me real grief you know they ordered the caesar and then said the lettuce wasn't fresh then they sent the sirloin back saying it was overcooked and now Mr Chang's furious and the maître d' is in a bad mood because he bombed out of a final call for *Chorus Line* and Lenny's home with the flu so I'm helping him with his tables and now they want me to do his act with Bernice at ten now tell me about this football madness and Sydney University.'

My mother is exhausting on coffee.

'Well, it's just –'

In the background a Brooklyn accent crooned 'All You Need is the Girl', punctuated by Mr Chang banging on his bell. (Didn't have a lot of time for the arts, Mr Chang.)

'Shewo [*ding ding*] pick up [*ding ding*] pick up. Taybor 8.'

'Just a minute, Mr Chang,' my mother said.

'Shewo, pick up [*ding ding*] going cold.'

'Darling-heart I don't have a lot of time so I'll be brief now you can't risk your career and your life's dream for a stupid game of football and don't tell me your father isn't behind this because I know he is so don't tell me he isn't okay but you must stop it immediately because one day you'll realise that beauty and enlightenment come to those who come from a point of despair did I tell you I'm up for *Guys and Dolls* by the way anyway but who turn that despair into beauty and capture that beauty in their work then have the ability to turn that work into something truly beautiful and that's when they find the real them and that's *just* what I discovered at the Matisse exhibition this week at The Met because it's like he was trying to find the hidden beauty in things or was it the beauty in hidden things I can't remember but anyway that's not the point what I'm really saying is –'

'[*Ding ding*] Shewo, pick up!'

'Be right there, Mr Chang. So that's what I mean about the search for beauty *God* it was inspiring anyway once you find that inner beauty you won't need pills or football or shrinks because –'

'Hey, Sheryl, do you know anything from *Cats,* honey?' a customer slurred.

'Not now, Ernie. I'm talking to my kid in Australia.'

'[*Ding ding*] Shewo, pick up! PICK UP!'

'In a minute, Mr Chang. So that's what you'll discover when you find the real you who is the you who you can't see now but the you who you will become can you believe these new shoes a week later and they still pinch anyway the you who becomes the ultimate you is the you who finds that inner beauty I'm talking about, *then* every-thing will fall into place because –'

'Sheryl, what about "Memory"? That's a nice toon, sweetie.'

'Give it a rest, Ernie. Give it a rest! Anyway, honey . . . you still there?'

By that stage I was smashing the receiver against my skull.

'Hello hello? Sweetie? Are you there . . . ?'

'Mum, I'm playing football at the behest of my psychiatrist. As a kind of anger therapy. It's not –'

'You *know* I detest violence I've always taught you to walk away look at the Dalai Lama and his struggle with the Maoists do you think he resorted to anger no way he just laughs at them you see it's like this sculptor friend of mine Charlie who's a manic depressive now Charlie created this beautiful piece entirely out of fish bones I'm not kidding he made the whole thing out of the leftovers of a steamed cod with black-bean sauce but this sculpture of Charlie's unfortunately reminded him of his ex-wife so he was in a real bind does he keep the piece and be reminded of her years of nagging or give in to this anger and destroy a thing of great beauty and perhaps a priceless work of art –'

I heard a blood curdling, high-pitched scream. 'SHEWO! [*ding, ding, ding, ding, ding*] PICK UP! PICK UP!'

'Right there, Mr Chang!'

'So what happened?' I asked.

'Huh?'

'To Charlie? The sculptor?'

'Oh, he ended up selling the piece to a Jewish banker from Queens now I can't remember the point to that story but I really hope our little chat has helped because I've got to go now love you petal bye.'

The phone went dead. But not before I tied it around my neck and jumped up and down.

24

How much more Strauss can I Handel?

I *HAD* HOPED TO TALK TO MY mother about Lydia and my ballooning anxiety but, although I've caricaturised her for comic effect (she's not *quite* that flaky), my mother was never much help. Mum was a bad listener. Whenever I needing nothing more than a sympathetic ear, she had a talent for relating everything to herself. Mum laboured under the misapprehension that this solipsism was helping me by equating her problems to mine. But it was simply another junction where we'd end up talking about her for twenty minutes till we arrived at the credits: 'Oh, this call must be costing you a fortune, petal! I better go.' Mum would then hang up in the sincere belief that she had helped me.

Funny how someone so intimate can be so distant. It took me a lifetime to realise that Mum (love her as I do) was never going to pilot me through my anxiety till she first laid rest to her own. On the other hand, Lydia was the Kofi Annan of listeners. She would listen with a sage-like taciturnity. For hours. And then say just the right thing, at just the right time. Those who had met her commented on a wisdom and maturity that belied her years. But Lydia wasn't returning my calls.

⌒

I was slumped in Film Composition/arranging class, head on desk, eyes mushroom-black, drooling on Bernstein's score for *On the*

Waterfront. I'd had another sleepless night. Although feeling low, this was actually my favourite class. My lecturer was Bill Motzing. Bill was a lovely man and had been a trombonist of note and had conducted just about every symphony orchestra in the country. He was then an esteemed film composer and eventually left for LA to score films (replaced by my old piano teacher, the unheralded genius that was the late Roger Frampton).

Bill had noticed my swelling depression and asked if studies were getting me down (they *had* been slipping by then). I was about to disgorge my soul, spill the beans about the team, about Lydia, about my mother, about anything from the anarchist treatises of Michail Bakunin to the dangers of hormone replacement therapy, when a student with a pimples-by-Pollock face handed him a note. The student stole that all-too-familiar glance at me. I was summoned to The Tower. Phil made the sign of the cross, lit a candle and said something in Latin.

⌢

Sir Richard ushered me into his office. I sat in my usual chair, which was designed to make you feel small. I did. He sat listening to Brahms, humming along completely out of tune. Stephen Hawking sang better. (You'd be surprised how many first-class musicians can't hold a tune.)

He peeked through the blinds. 'Let's go for a stroll. I have some scores to drop off for the Verdi tonight.'

Grabbing his Panama and stuffing scores into a soft leather satchel, we emerged into bright winter sunshine. This was a relief because I felt intimidated in his dark office and the walk made conversation less interrogative – all part of the strategy. We ambled across the rolling lawn and down to Farm Cove, tracing the biscuit-yellow sandstone wall to Bennelong Point. The low wall, an unending rusk. Floating canopies of gum leaves nudged it as we walked.

He indicated a flower. 'The magnolias this year are simply glorious, are they not?'

'Yes.'

He had quite a bounding step for an old man. The stride of achievement. I suppose he had accomplished a lot in his career: child protégé; stellar career as a concert musician in London; now head of the most prestigious music school in the country. Why wouldn't he stride? The arts had rewarded his dedication as happens to but a few.

'How long have you been at the Conservatorium?' he asked.

'Not long.'

'I see.'

He tipped his hat to an elderly lady. 'Glorious day, madam!

The blushing dame, twin set and pearls, nodded.

'Your piece for the concert showed promise . . .'

'Really?'

'. . . for warmed-over Messiaen.'

Warmed-over *Messiaen*? The nerve! But listening to it today, the old bastard was dead right.

'Who performed the piece?' he asked.

'Michael Kieran Harvey.'

He stopped in his tracks. 'Dear *God*, please tell me he's not in this horrid football team.'

'No,' I said, feeling relief at having dissuaded him from joining.

He admired a fig tree. 'What sculptor could ever hope to create anything so magnificent?'

We kept walking, with me trailing poodle-like. Sunlight fell on the harbour like crushed rhinestones. I looked across the harbour to Northbridge and felt a pang.

'I have written to the Dean of Sydney University asking him to put a stop to this game.'

'You're kidding? What did he say?'

He pulled out a pair of half-moon specs from a hard leather case.

Balancing them on the end of his nose, he took out a note and opened it. 'It reads, and I quote: *They are all over eighteen and may do as they please. It will do the little darlings some good to be smashed around the park.* End quote. Lacks poetry, but one gets the general idea.' He folded his reading glasses back into the case and, like an exclamation mark, snapped it shut. He delicately folded the note (as if it were a handwritten poem by Wordsworth) into the pocket of his Italian-linen shirt.

Dear reader, I should point out that there was much competition between the Con and the Sydney Uni music department at the time. Sydney Uni has a fabulous music department and an impressive staff, including Peter Sculthorpe, our most celebrated composer. But as most students auditioned for the Con, Sydney Uni often played 'second fiddle' (*groan*) to the Con. Seeing a spark of something in my work (which failed to ever ignite), Peter had suggested I audition for Sydney Uni. In the end, I decided to audition for the Con as I was able to combine jazz subjects. I also wanted to study piano under Mike Nock.

'Do you plan a career in composition?' Sir Richard asked.

'I'd like to one day write opera.'

We stopped at the steps of the breathtaking Sydney Opera House. It stood before us like a giant crouching swan.

'You know, it's a small world, the world of opera. Tiny. Like a village, one might say.' He tapped his long nose. 'Everyone knows everyone.'

'Are you threatening me, Sir Richard?'

'Magnificent building, isn't it? The zenith of a composer's aspirations.' He bounded up the steps and out of sight.

⌒

Later that afternoon I was in class for all of ten minutes when another note was handed to the lecturer. Graham Hair, who took us for counterpoint, shot me a deadpan look. 'Another message for the Duke.'

'I'm sorry about all this.'

'Sir Richard must have prepared the gallows,' Phil whispered.

But it wasn't Sir Richard. It was Bernie. He was at some bar. You can always hear when someone's calling from a bar. A universal sound bite.

'What's up, Bernie? The note said it was urgent.'

'Mate, I need ya to have a look at this. Can you come down?'

'I'm in class, but okay. What's the matter, Bern?'

'I just want you to see this. Do you know the Sydney Uni Oval Bar?'

'Sure.'

'See ya in twenty minutes.' [click]

It was all very Raymond Chandler. I jumped on the Vespa and made my way to Sydney University.

The Oval Bar is a unique watering hole. An amalgam of athleticism and Anglophilia, there's a queer Etonian/RSL Club atmosphere. Framed sepia pics of Old Boys with broom-bristle moustaches and tasselled caps glare from walls. Ancient footballs, like the shrivelled scrotums of rhinos, sit in illuminated glass cabinets. I noticed yellowing pictures of muscled women holding rowing sculls above their heads like caryatids. Encircling shelves held a veritable Aladdin's cave of trophies that glinted in the soft light of the sagging westerly sun. This miscellany of sporting achievement was pitted against 1970s concrete and glass, poker machines and juke boxes.

It suddenly dawned on me that this university took its sport *very* seriously. No doubt this was the subtle point Bernie was making as he cleared his throat and pointed to the gallery of trophies and shields. However, the coup de grâce awaited outside. As he pushed a wet glass of beer into my hand, we made our way to the balcony that overlooked Oval #1: the oval where we would play the following Sunday. Sydney University's sporting empyrean.

The oval, transformed into a grid of bright orange cones, was a boot-camp of footballers. A collegial agoge. The players ran a fugue of intertwining drills that dazzled the eye. There were tackle-bags, scrum machines, coaches, trainers, assistants, statisticians. The team looked capable of taking out the Sandinistas, let alone kicking the shit out of a group of concert musicians. Bernie turned to me.

'You sure you wanna go through with this, Café Boy?' (A nickname Bernie calls me to this day.) 'This won't be no joke, you know. These boys are gunner hurt youse.'

Although I'd seen Uni play before (which was stressful enough), I had not seen them train before. As they ran their multifarious drills and plays, I felt stressed. They didn't look as menacing as the Maroubra Lions, they simply resembled a platoon of well-drilled soldiers. And they all looked incredibly fit! In comparison, we could have been a pub darts team. I took some deep breaths and thought for a while.

'You know, Bernie, in Periclean Greece, about 400 B.C., there were two dynasties that fought for control of the eastern Mediterranean: the Spartans and the Athenians. The Spartans were a dull bunch. Like these guys, they existed for war. Each male citizen, from birth, was forced to become a soldier. They made time for little else. The Athenians, on the other hand, encouraged the arts, science, freedom of thought. They formed a democracy. They laid the foundations for the life we know today. But, in terms of warfare, they were no match for the Spartans. After the Persians destroyed their city, the Athenians, with incredible daring, took to the sea in boats. By default, they became expert seamen and built a superior navy. When they eventually returned to their city, they built a wall out of its ruins. This fortified the city – and did not please the Spartans. This meant, with their powerful navy, they might *just* be able to defend themselves against the Spartan warrior race.

'When the Spartans eventually declared war on their democratic neighbours, laying waste the surrounding countryside, the Athenians fought bravely from behind their walls. Whenever they faced the Spartans on the battlefield, however, they were slaughtered. But in a dazzling fluke – during the battle for the island of Sphacteria – the Athenians *actually* defeated the Spartans! We're talking the same folks who fought to the death against the Persians at the battle of Thermoply. No one had expected such a victory. It was unprecedented in western history. It was against all odds. The Spartans had never lost a battle, had never surrendered, such was their awesome reputation as warriors. Anyway, after about twenty-seven years of fighting and relentless siege, the Spartans were ultimately victorious. But, Bernie, there was that *one* time in history when the artists *actually* defeated the jocks . . .'

Bernie threw his hands in the air, 'What have all these wogs got to do with football?'

I sighed. 'We're going to give it our best shot, Bernie. What can I say?'

'Fair enough,' he said, into his beer glass.

The Sydney Uni coach spotted us hovering on the balcony. 'Hey, Bernie!'

One by one, the players stopped, a giant machine grinding to a halt. Bernie hid behind a pot plant. (This only made things worse in my opinion.)

'Hey, there's the conductor!' Barnes said. 'Spyin on us, coach?'

The players fell about laughing.

'See you next Sunday!' he said. 'We need the tackle practice!'

Bernie slid inside.

'Don't forget to bring your baton!' Barnes said.

I walked inside and closed the door, muffling the laughter. We walked up to the bar, shoulders slumped.

'Same again?' I asked.

'Yeah,' Bernie said flatly. 'Now, youse won't bottle out on me, will ya? I mean, if no one turns up, it'll be embarrassing . . .'

'We'll be there, Bernie. We won't let you down.'

Bernie finished his drink and skulked off. I had an early gig that evening and it wasn't worth going home again. So I had a couple of beers on my own at the bar. A pretty girl, chatting with her student friends, reminded me of Lydia. Fuelled with amber courage, I called Lydia from the bar. Dialling her number, I prayed that her mother wouldn't pick up. (She had been monitoring the phone like the Gestapo.)

'Hello?' Lydia answered.

I played it cool.

'Lydia oh thank God I've been trying to reach you how have you been I've been wanting to talk about the other night look I'm sorry about your letterbox but I think I must have eaten something in fact I think it may have been pork and you know the Jews knew something when they warned their people off pork but look I know The Globe was a disaster but Duncan God that guy is a laugh you know the other day he said to me anyway what I wanted to say is well yes I really need to tell you . . . hello hello?'

The phone went dead.

25

The Valkyrie with the Harley and tattoos

SATURDAY NIGHT WAS THE EVE of the match. I was sitting at the bar (arranging peanuts into an orderly pattern) in a little jazz club where I used to play called The Real Old Café. It's now some God-awful den infested with poker machines and a DJ. I worked there a lot when it was a jazz club. This was when jazz was 'in' for about five minutes in the late eighties. By the time my trio started to pull good crowds, it was 'out' again.

I was on a set-break when a guy in a shiny suit eyeballed me from the end of the bar. I thought little of it and returned to my peanuts. The bass player and drummer were outside having a scoobie so I was on my own. (Big Marty was going to sit-in that night but didn't show for some reason.) I haven't smoked dope in years – not since my very first attack (and *never* since). As I battled to keep anxiety attacks at bay, a puff of weed would have instantly turned me into the Ringling Brothers Circus or, at best, a twenty-four-piece starter set of silverware with matching salt-and-pepper shakers.

Phil bolted down the stairs with the news. He had his violin case with him. He mostly used it as a kind of purse. And it was Phil's prop to get into any music venue for zip. With the right body language they'd assume he was sitting-in with the band. (Try it sometime. But never use a piano-accordion case or risk being beaten up by the band at the door.) Phil confronted me with the grim news.

We'd lost yet *another* Mauler. Sir Richard had been on the phone, spooking all the players, saying the Con's insurance policy did not cover spinal injuries. Cunning old bastard. It wasn't hard to spook them. We were all shitting ourselves. So at the eleventh hour we lost key players. I won't embarrass them by naming them in this book.*
Losing our five-eighth sounded the death knell. I turned to Phil.

'Phil, I'm begging you. You *have* to play.'

'Sorry, Dorian. I like my face the way it is. Are you going to call it off or shall I?'

'I'll do it. Never know, I might think of something at the last minute.'

Phil drained his wine and left for his gig. He was playing in a string quartet for some society wedding in Kirribilli. He promised to call later to see if I'd come up with any ideas. (I did: move to the remote and windswept island of St Helena.)

My biggest anxiety was telling Dad. He'd be bitterly disappointed. Dad loved the team. He liked the camaraderie of it all and thought it good for me. However, I did feel a sense of relief that the match would be cancelled. But I also felt remorse: that we would be giving in to the knockers who said we'd never go through with the game. However, if I was stressed about telling Dad, I *dreaded* telling Bernie. What would Guy have to say about it? I felt a headlock approaching. Perhaps Bernie would feel relieved. I mean, he never wanted to coach us in the first place, I reasoned. This cheered me up – so did the Valium I swallowed with a mouthful of beer.

As I sat thinking, the ageing guy in the shining suit, a conglomerate of fashion extremes, approached. He was one of those people with absolutely no sense of style whatsoever but had a library of fashion magazines at home. He had to be one of two people: an aspiring politician trying to win the youth vote, or an ageing record executive.

*Roger, James, Charles and Terrence.

He shoved a card in my hand that read: 'A&R Manager, Delta Records.' (One of the 'big six' multinational record labels at the time.) He said my 'manager' had sent him my demo tape, and he liked what he heard. Delta wanted to sign me. My jaw landed on the end of his side-buckled, zebra-striped pointy shoes. He asked me to walk him to the door. He wasn't a smoker and hated sitting in the canopy of smoke that clung to the low ceiling.

He irritably cleared his throat. 'This place is a shit hole, but I love it. I love artists.'

'I didn't know you guys liked jazz?'

'Are you kidding? We love jazz. Love it love it love it,' he said, looking at his watch.

Apparently, someone had told him jazz was the 'new black'.

'Yeah, love the piano. My kid plays the piano,' he said, hailing a cab. 'I'm in London all next week with Adam Ant. Now, there's a guy who'll go the distance! Anyway, call me Monday week.' He looked around. 'Love this place. *Groovy*,' he said, in the kind of way your grandfather would say 'radical'.

I stood in the doorway, staring at the card. Mad Jake, the club's bouncer, bade him goodnight. Mad Jake was congenial to anyone in a suit in case it happened to be the mystery owner. Rumour had it that the owner was a radio personality (dispossessed of one), but no one really quite knew who.

A party of drunken revellers arrived at the door. Jake extracted their money. Lydia suddenly appeared behind them. My heart vaulted against my breastbone. However, I *did* play it cool this time. I suppose I'd resigned myself that it was over. Shame. I was *so* fond of her. I'd emerged from childhood finding it hard to trust women. But I trusted this girl with my life. We seemed to click.

She looked beautiful in the wan moonlight that streaked the city streets behind her. The intoxicating potpourri of her scent – perfume, hairspray, talc, deodorant, moisturiser – had me thinking I was standing at the Gates of Paradise. It sounds trite to say I felt an ache in my heart, but the poets had it dead right: nothing aches like unrequited love.

'I called Phil. He's told me everything,' she said, running her fingers through her shock of chestnut curls. 'What will you do? Call it off?'

'Probably,' I said.

She handed me a petal of paper. 'Look, this is my brother's number. He was a star player in high school. You can use a ring-in, can't you?'

'You mean somebody from outside the Con?'

'It's allowed, isn't it?'

'I don't know if "allowed" is the operative word but we could get away with it, which is almost the same thing. What position did he play?'

'Something called . . . five-eighth.'

'Excellent!'

'Oh, and he used to play drums with the navy band.'

'A musician as well? Perfect!'

'Not a musician who's about to be signed to Delta Records.'

'So *you're* my manager. Wow! Thanks for sending them my tape. That was sweet.' (Lydia really *did* send them my demo.)

'You'll *have* to pull out now. My brother can take your place.'

'No, I'm going to play if I can.'

She folded her pretty white arms that were dotted with moles like chocolate drops. A speckled beauty.

'Lyd, I can't explain, but it just feels that everything in my life boils down to this game. Sounds crazy, I know. But, remember, I am crazy. I have a certificate and these pills.'

She laughed. I'd miss that laugh. 'Dorian, look, the reason I've come down tonight is . . . I've come to say goodbye. I didn't want to end it screaming at you from my balcony at two in the morning.'

'It was one-thirty.'

'Whatever.'

'Look, I know I've made an arse of things these past months, Lyd, but don't give up on me just yet. Take a chance.'

Here eyes widened. 'Take a chance? Take a *chance*? I almost suffocated in a plastic cocoon, was stabbed in the leg by a crazed poet, only to dance around a stage like a drunken idiot in a pool of my own blood, while my dancing friends sat in the audience, giggling. And you're asking me to take a *chance*? I don't need any more chances in my life. I want surety. And you can't offer me that, Dorian.'

'I understand. I'm hardly the catch of the century.'

This was her cue to insert, *Oh, I wouldn't put it quite like that*.

There was an awkward silence. A car honked its horn. The doorman belched.

'Oh, I almost forgot!' I handed her a cassette. (I'd been carrying it around just in case I ran into her again.) 'I wrote a song for you. It's called *Lydia's Waltz*. Might record it one day. Thanks to you.'

'Oh . . . um . . . thank you.' This really threw her. It's awful when people give you gifts as you're dumping them.

'You know if this was a Hollywood movie, you'd go home and listen to it, realise your mistake, and fall madly in love with me.'

'Life's not a movie, Dorian. Goodbye.' She kissed me on the cheek and walked off.

'Thanks for being there for me all these months,' I yelled.

I watched her disappear into George Street and out of my life. I felt myself sinking.

'Pretty girl,' Mad Jake said, lighting up a cigarette and arching his back, cat-like.

'Very,' I sighed.

'Who was the guy in the suit?' Jake asked, pulling at his collar.

'He wasn't the owner,' I said flatly.

'Thank God. I was reading the bloody paper when he walked in.'

I liked Mad Jake. He was an ex-bikie with an art gallery of tattoos, several missing teeth and a night owl's tan but he was a nice cat.

We were interrupted by three drunks who tried to sneak past. He stopped all three with one hand.

'Ten dollar cover charge tonight, fellas.'

'Ten bucks?' one slurred. 'Who's playing?'

'Dorian Mode,' Jake said.

'Who the fuck's that?'

'A man of unparalleled genius and charm,' I said.

Jake chuckled.

'Drink my piss,' one of the drunks said, racing past us. Jake chased him, deftly weaving in and out of the patrons, eventually tackling him to the floor. He then picked up the interloper, dragged him outside and threw him into the legs of his swaying cronies. Fortunately the guy wasn't hurt. Jake was in a good mood that evening.

'Now, piss off before I get cranky. Gawn, on ya bike!' he said.

The three scurried off like mice.

'Where did you learn to tackle like that?'

'I used to play professionally.'

'Football?'

'Yeah.'

I suddenly heard Wagner's Valkyrie motif in my head. 'You're joking?' (A cunning plan began taking shape.)

'Straight up,' he said, lighting up a smoke. He lifted the sleeve of his jacket. 'Look!' He showed me one of his tattoos. It was a picture of someone putting an axe through the head of a Hare Krishna. (I don't expect you to believe me but Jake *really* did have this tattoo.) I leaned in to read the inscription in the dim light.

'*Kill Krishna?* What can that possibly mean except bad karma?'

'No, not that one, ya goose. *That* one!' With a blackened fingernail he pointed to a picture of a jet. 'I played footy for the best club in Australia. Twenty-three professional games.'

'*The Bombers?* What kind of rugby league team is that?'

'Rugby league?' He leaned in. 'Aussie Rules. I played Aussie Rules, mate.'

My non-sporting and overseas readers are suddenly wondering if I'm still on tranquillisers. Briefly, Aussie Rules is a fabulous game played originally in the southern states of Australia (it's since evolved into a booming national competition). It is a bastardised game of Gaelic football designed by people who felt Gaelic football wasn't nasty enough. They say that 'rugby is a game for thugs played by gentlemen', 'rugby league is a game for gentlemen played by thugs' and 'Aussie Rules is a game for thugs played by thugs'. And that 'the banjo is played by people with no sense of moral dignity'. For sheer bone on bone contract, rugby league is the toughest sport by a long chalk, but AFL (Aussie Rules) is a very rough game in its own way. And at the time was marred by all-in-brawls and melees. It's mainly played by very tall guys who punt the ball to each other over great distances. So punting and catching or 'marking' the ball (as it's known) is a feature of the game. Jake was what was called a ruckman. Apparently, Jake was so menacing on the field that his career was cut short by the governing body that oversees the game. Too unstable for AFL – and not morally bankrupt enough for the Catholic priesthood – he moved to Sydney and started managing punk bands, working on the door of their gigs.

I scratched my head. 'Aussie Rules? But that's a completely different game.'

'From fucken what?'

'Never mind. What are you doing tomorrow?'

I had to get back to the bandstand, so I quickly filled him in. I told him if anyone asked, he played the banjo.

26

Requiem

AS I ARRIVED AT SYDNEY UNI, rivulets of people made their way to the oval. Some were from the Con, others from Uni. To my horror, a crowd was building. I idled on the scooter, watching. A group of girls I recognised from the Con skipped past, arm in arm. A long-haired boy in oversized trousers growled past on a skateboard. I guess a lot of people watch *Sportsworld*. I felt a cramp in my stomach. One stellar wit had made a banner that read: 'Mozart's Requiem.' I dropped my wrist on the accelerator, blew past him and sneered. Not only were the Uni crowd here to see us get our heads kicked in, so too were our own folk.

I'd had a bad night and little sleep. In my predawn torpor, I took sleeping pills (an idiocy I practise still). So I slept like Rip Van Winkle for a couple of hours until Phil called (five times before I eventually picked up) asking exactly where the hell I was.

Yawning, I guided the Vespa through the crowd, continually replaying the final scene with Lydia in my head. Should've said this. Should've said that. What if I'd said this? What if I'd done that?

I walked into the ringing Velázquez grey visitors' locker room (that was designed to make visiting teams feel about as welcome as Cortés in Mexico) with plum-black eyes. Bernie greeted me with his usual tact.

'Ya look like shit. How ya sposed to play today? You're the

fucken captain, for Chrissake!' He walked off, shaking his head, pacing.

I staggered over to Phil. My eyelids felt like stone. 'Have the replacements turned up?'

'Looks like they're no shows. All we have is what you see before you. Oh, and him.' Phil pointed to a life-size cardboard cut-out of Wally Lewis wearing a paper party hat. (Someone had brought it along as a replacement player. Droll.) Unless we were playing eleven players, and a cardboard cut-out of Quentin Crisp, we were screwed.

'Never mind,' I said, rubbing my eyes.

'You look awful,' he said.

'Cheers.'

I looked around. Marty and the Minotaur were sneaking slugs from a hip flask. Moscowitz was sucking on his asthma spray. Harold was engaged in emergency plumbing with his usual nose-bleeds. Herringbone and Pemberton were staring at the floor. Others were peeking out the window at the Uni players arriving, saying things like, 'Look at the size of that one. I'd hate to tackle him. Perhaps he's playing with another team.'

It cut a grim scene.

'We don't have enough players. What are you going to do?' Phil whispered.

'No choice. I'll have to call it off.' Funny, he almost looked disappointed. 'Well, what choice do I have?' I whispered.

'Of course. Of course. Will you break the news to Bernie or shall I?'

'I'll break the news to Bernie.' While Guy breaks my fingers, I thought.

Bernie was still pacing. He was a mosaic of nicotine patches. If he had smoked a cigar it would have induced an instant coronary. However, this didn't stop him cajoling Marty for a Marlborough Light. Bernie walked outside to smoke it. Brushing past him at the door, with a pair of boots laced around his neck, was a stocky, balding guy who resembled our cut-out of Wally Lewis. He looked at us. We looked at him.

'Oh, home-team dressing-room's next door, man,' I said.

'You Dorian?' he asked, looking me up and down.

'Yes.'

'I'm Andrew. Lydia's brother.' He outstretched a hirsute hand, glancing around.

'I didn't think you'd come,' I said. (He had travelled from Nowra – three hours by train – to be at the game.)

'So where's the team?' he asked, confused.

Unfortunately, everyone heard him say this. The room grew silent.

'But . . . you said it was against Sydney Uni . . .'

More silence.

He mouthed the words 'Noah's Ark' or it could well have been 'Holy Fuck'.

'Listen, when you meet our coach, you play the drums, right? You played the drums, yeah?'

'With the navy band. Not very well. I moved to signals after six months.'

'Don't worry. Just remember, if anyone asks, you play the drums – *anyone*!'

'Got it.'

Bernie returned with a lung of cigarette smoke, expelling it with a sigh.

'Bern, we've lost a couple of players through . . . er . . . syphilis . . .'

'Really?'

'But we have a replacement. This is Andrew.'

Bernie looked impressed because Andrew – unlike the rest of us – actually looked like a footballer. You know, all chest and no neck.

'Well ya look fit. Where do you play?' Bernie asked.

Andrew looked at me. 'Um . . . mainly jazz clubs on the South Coast . . .'

'No, what position . . . never mind. You look like you've played before. Would I be right?'

'I've played before.'

'Reckon you could play five-eight?'

'I can play five-four. Or six-eight. Although, I'm better avoiding contrapuntal time signatures.'

Bernie threw his fat arms in the air. 'Jesus! Look, do ya reckon you could organise these blokes? Feed the ball to the backs and that?'

'You mean like a drummer feeding rhythm to the band?' he said, twinkle in his eye.

'Yeah, yeah, yeah, like a bloody band.' Bernie hadn't got much sleep, either.

Our conversation was drowned by the aural flatulence of a Harley Davidson. Mad Jake, looking like Chopper Read's nastier cousin, made his entrance. He was muffed in headphones, cranked so loud they would have induced bleeding from the eardrums of Beethoven. He wore a faded red-and-black AFL jersey under a grazed motorcycle jacket. I was relieved he wasn't in T-shirt *sans* jacket. Jake's inky frescos would have given the game away. He peeled his wraparound sunglasses and surveyed the room.

'Arr, you're fucken joking,' he said to me.

'Here's the other replacement, Bernie,' I said.

The team were dually impressed and horrified.

Bernie became animated. 'Well, well, where ya been hidin this mean-lookin fella?'

'With the banjos,' said Phil dryly.

'Ever played rugby league before, son?'

He shook his closely cropped head. 'Nup.'

Bernie looked defeated.

'You should see him tackle at the jazz club, Bern. No one gets past him,' I said.

Bernie screwed up his face. 'Huh?'

Mad Jake drew a menacing smile, exposing several missing teeth. 'Don't sweat it, pal. If these nancies can play, I can play.'

'That's the spirit, son. Smile at em. At least you'll scare em.' He shooed us to the benches. 'Now everyone take a pew. I wanna have a serious talk with youse.'

Cocking his head to allow his sombrero through the door, Dad entered, carrying a portable deckchair and an esky full of beer. An old Kodak camera was draped around his neck. He removed his sombrero and sat next to me.

'This it?' he asked.

'Afraid so.'

'What happened to –?'

'They bottled.'

'And –?'

'Same.'

'Are you telling me –'

'Had to wash his hair.'

Dad dropped his head and fingered his sombrero. He looked stressed. Something else was on his mind.

Bernie paced as he spoke. 'Now I want youse all to stick to the pattern. None of youse are to deviate from the pattern for a second. Now, where's our half-back!'

Moscowitz jumped in his seat.

'Now, what's the pattern? Tell us.'

Moscowitz was stressed. I could hear a tremolo in his larynx. 'We run the play from left to right. Once we've got them bunched, we run the play the other way.'

'Right! Otherwise no holes will open up for us to run into and that.'

Moscowitz bolted to the toilets. The strangled sound of vomiting echoed, filling us with confidence.

'Now I know some of youse are a bit nervous today . . .' Bernie said.

More sounds of vomiting.

'Some more than others.'

'Yeah, I always feel this way before the Penderecki violin con-certo,' Moscowitz called from the toilet.

'Yeah, same feelin, I guess,' Bernie said.

Moscowitz staggered back in, lozenge-green. We looked at each other, nauseous with dread.

Some of the other fathers (who had to see it with their own eyes to believe it) crept in. Bernie, conscious of an audience, dipped into his bag of inspirational clichés and speeches. As none of us had much played before he could recycle old sermons. He surveyed the anxious players and their fathers.

'Now, half of Sydney's out there today and believe me, I know it's intimidating.' He walked around the locker-room like Patton. 'You don't want to make a mistake. Don't want to make a goose of yer-self. But it's good to have butterflies. I seen plentya professional footy blokes spew before a big game.'

'Really?' Moscowitz asked.

'Sure.'

'Straight up?' I asked (no pun intended).

'I remember me first rugby test. Before I moved to league. Lotta people said I shouldn't have been picked over such and such. You know, the usual media bullshit. Said the whole Wallaby squad was shit. Worst side ever picked, they reckoned. Press said we didn't have Buckley's of winning a single game on tour. But that first game, when we run out onto Murrayfield, we all looked at each other in our gold jerseys, shivering in the fucken snow and that, and felt proud. When they played our national anthem, well . . . blokes cried, I don't mind tellin ya. We all looked at each other and *knew*.' A dramatic pause. 'We knew we would die for each other that day. The whole country had written us off! But someone forgot to tell fifteen blokes freezing their arses off in Scotland. We were there to win. To die, if need be . . .' Bernie yelled, finger pointing to the ceiling.

We sat, open-mouthed.

'And let me tell you, that this buncha no-hopers smashed those Scotch bastards all over the paddock.' He raised his voice, almost screaming. 'So never let *no one* write you off before a game!' His speech was so stirring we were starting to believe we were a chance. He dropped his voice to a low, sombre note. 'Where would this country be if we let blokes write us off? When youse run out there today, I want youse to think about ya forefathers. Blokes who've allowed you to live the life of freedom you have today. Great warriors! Like them Greek blokes Dorian and I was talking about the other day, the Ethereals and the Spatulas!'

The Maulers looked confused.

'I want you to think about them blokes in Gallipoli. Them blokes in water-filled trenches on the Somme and that. Think of them forty-thousand horsemen who charged the machine guns at Beersheba with nothing but bayonets and a shitload of guts. They were blokes just like you. They'd never been in a battle before. They were farmers and shearers and bushmen and that. Just blokes who happened to own horses. Blokes having a go. Blokes havin a fucken dig . . .'

I don't know if it was the lingering pills or lack of sleep but the locker room suddenly became a giant trench. *Plumes of smoke drifted across the room. Foul-smelling cordite tickled my nostrils. The faint sound of shellfire in the distance. Someone cleaned the end of his flute as if it were a rifle . . .*

'But those blokes weren't fighting for the officers or the government or the Queen. They were fighting for their mates. Isn't this what this is all about, today? Mates? I broke me bloody leg in that game at Murrayfield. What did I care? It broke for me mates. For –'

Bernie's speech, which would have rivaled the soliloquy from *Henry V* but for punctuating gas brought on by a dodgy burrito, was interrupted by a slow handclap from the back of the locker-room. It was the opposition coach.

'Very nice speech, coach. But did you tell em how you actually broke it?'

'Shut up, Barnesy.'

'Broke it slipping when he came out of the dressing room at half-time. How do I know? Because I played alongside him in the game.'

'Still dirty on me for not passing ya the ball against the French. Aren't ya, Dave?'

Barnes became red in the face. 'I could have bloody scored and tied the series!'

'Blanco had you covered and you know it.'

'Bullshit.'

'Fact,' Bernie said, looking around and nodding.

'Anyway, boys, Bernie could play a bit in his day. I'll give him that. But coaching is about leadership. Tactics.' He tapped his head. 'Brains.'

Bernie smiled sourly. 'We'll go orright. Don't worry yourself, Dave.'

'I hope these boys aren't worried about their fingers.'

We looked at each other like inmates on death row.

'Don't listen to him, boys. This is what they call "gamesmanship" in the trade. Bernie tore a $50 note from his wallet. 'I got an avocado here, Barnesy. Why not put your money where ya overworked mouth is?'

'You're not *serious*?'

Bernie placed a fleshy arm around the Sydney Uni coach. 'Let us step outside to negotiate terms.'

The rival coaches spoke in muffled voices before Bernie returned, alone, and addressed us in reverent tones.

'Okay, I admit, I did break me leg comin out of the locker-room at half-time. The floor was an ice rink. Someone had polished the bastard within an inch of its life. Sabotage, the press called it. But that first half, I played the game of me life. A year later I was signed to Souths to play rugby league. For big money, too! The game was a turning point in me life. But, like I said, we were all new blokes. Nervous. And the bloke who had the spew was Barnesy, I don't mind tellin ya. But he went orright, too. We all did. It was our big concert, if ya like. We *had* to perform. After the media had put the slipper into us, there'd be no second chance. So we were all nervous. And lookin around here today, I'm reminded of them same blokes.'

Phil rolled his eyes.

'Blokes who "didn't stand a chance". Blokes that were "no hopers". But youse have just as much chance of winning this game as Uni. That's what's great about football: when the whistle blows, it's anyone's day. Now, that fifty bucks was to show youse how much I believe in youse all. So I want to hear a big, bloodcurdling team cheer. Orright? One . . . two . . . three . . .'

'MOOOOOZART MAAAAUUUUULERS!' we screamed.

'Now run out there and *take* this game!' Bernie screamed.

The Maulers tore out of the locker-room and onto the field like Agamemnon and his men attacking the walls of Troy for the first time. Several fathers had formed a gauntlet outside the door, slapping our backs as we took the field. I was last in line. Dad was talking with Bernie as the final Mauler squeezed through the door.

Dad winced. 'That was confident dropping an avocado on the boys, Bern.'

'Barnesy gave me three to one that they'd beat us by at least sixty points. I figured, what the hell, they're only on the field for eighty minutes.'

'Oh.'

27

Going for baroque

WE STOOD ON THE SUN-DRENCHED field, our hearts inflated by Bernie's speech. The crowd was swelling by the minute. Scanning the sideline, I saw Bernie's wife, Anne, and my stepmother, Patsy, laying out wine and cheese on a chequered picnic blanket. I spotted the boozers from The Dog. They made a beeline for the balcony of the Oval Bar, sloshed already. Even some of the Maroubra Lions had turned up. They shouted at us from the sideline. 'Lock up the ball-carrier!' 'Don't forget to spread out across the field!' 'Tackle the man, not the ball!' 'Peanuts are fattening!' 'Existentialism is nothing more than an inexorable, meaningless descent into nihilism!'

Sol had turned up. He was chain-smoking and pacing up and down the sideline in his crumpled suit, speckled with cigarette burns, a half-carton of Dunhills protruded from his jacket pocket like a house brick. The crowd was dotted with faces from our alma mater. Cassandra played the melody from Chopin's funeral dirge on her violin; not much appreciated by us. Seemed some were there to support us; others, to see us dismembered to music.

Then, our world changed. Someone unleashed the Spartans. We cowered in their vast shadow. The crowd became silent, reverent. With an aura that was golden, they took their familiar positions on the battlefield. They possessed the nobility of Hector, the cunning of Odysseus, the stamina of Achilles. They stood proudly at the zenith of masculine evolution. They were: Sydney University. We were: screwed.

Resplendent in their crisp blue-and-gold jerseys, they ran through their warm-ups and stretches with the confidence of champions. As they hadn't lost a single game all year, why would they act any different? They seemed nonchalant.

I don't expect you to believe me, but this really *did* happen: Tom Burge (currently Head of Brass at the National University in Canberra) suddenly vomited on his boots. This shocked us. Luckily, the opposition didn't notice the impromptu barf. In fact, they didn't notice *us*. We expected them to eye us like ravenous wolves. Nothing could be further from the truth. Just another day at the office for Uni. It didn't occur to us that simply because *we* had thought about the match every minute of the day, they had. We had never played before. They played every weekend; some of them every weekend for years.

Hearing them chatting in the back line about late afternoon movie sessions, I squinted in the distance. I was behind the try line. It's not recommended you play football in glasses (I didn't own contact lenses then) so their back line was a blurring paper-cut-out of figures that stretched from sideline to sideline. With a bit of luck they wouldn't put a ball over me. I was so short-sighted I would have tackled the sun. I moved closer to the enemy position.

Uni's five-eighth yawned, picked his nose and spat. What is it with sports stars and their disregard of social mores? Even on television. If they're not gobbing on the grass, they're scratching their balls. Musicians can't do that – not unless you're Ozzy Osbourne or Dame Joan Sutherland.

What struck me the most was their composure. The coach was on the sidelines reading the newspaper, for God's sake. These guys deemed the result a fait accompli. This really pissed me off.

One of the drunks from The Dog bellowed from the balcony, cradling an overflowing schooner. 'What have you got for us today, music boys? Anything by Elton John?'

The crowd detonated a chuckle. One of the Lions, Jonno, in fact, looked up and told him to 'shut up and give em a go'. Jonno gave me a friendly wave. I waved back. Then I noticed my fingers and was jolted by a current of panic. I tried not to think about the record contract.

The referee, lab-white jersey with matching knee-high socks, strutted onto the field. He was a genial, balding man in his early fifties. We waited for Uni to kick off.

Mysteriously, I was called to the halfway line. Phil (on the sideline) and I looked at each other and shrugged. I looked at Marty and he shrugged. What could be the problem? Jonno boomed from the sideline.

'The coin toss! They need you for the coin toss, captain.'

Of course! I gave him the thumbs up and ran like Mr Bean to centre field.

I stood opposite the Uni captain, who seemed nice enough. He towered over me. The referee glared at us, addressing us in schoolmaster tones.

'Now, this is a friendly. I want a clean game.' He turned to the Uni captain, an impregnable citadel of muscle. (And I kid you not, my opposite *number*.) 'If I see any player involved in a head-high tackle, knees in the tackle, eye-gouging, I'll send him off.'

'What's eye-gouging?' I asked.

'Huh?'

'Eye-gouging. What is it?'

'Um, well it's when someone digs their finger into your eye-socket to gouge your eye out,' the official said, fingering his chrome whistle.

I pondered.

'Well, on the upside, sunglasses would be 50 per cent off.'

The Uni captain looked at the referee, who looked at him, who looked at me. The ref continued, 'Now, when I say "Held" the tackle is completed . . .'

If I say 'Help!' does that count for anything? I thought.

'If I see anyone throwing a punch, I'll send em off. Got it?'

We nodded. (God, I hope they weren't planning to punch us. I hadn't thought of that.)

The ref turned to me, 'Heads or tails?'

'Oh, I'm easy.'

'No, you have to choose.'

'Oh . . . um, heads,' I said, shrugging.

The coin fell into the sunlit fingers of grass. We leaned over to find it as if it was a vital fragment of Mesopotamian pottery.

'Heads it is,' the ref said, stooping. 'Which way do you want to run?'

The quickest way home, I said but it came out as, 'Oh . . . I don't know. You decide.'

'No, no, you have to choose,' he said. 'You're the captain.'

'Which way would *you* run?' Figured he'd know.

'Eh . . . no one's ever asked me before. Eh . . . well, the wind is blowing from the south so I'd run from left to right for this half or perhaps you should have the breeze in the second half, but if the wind changes you've lost all advantage, no, run with the breeze while you have it. You never know, it could change in the second half.'

'Are you expecting late wind?'

The Uni captain stood grinding his teeth.

'I'd run from left to right,' the kindly official said.

'Sounds cool,' I said. 'Cheers.'

'Does the Conservatorium want to kick off?'

I turned to the Sydney Uni captain, who by then had cracked a molar. 'What would you do, if you were me?'

He snatched the ball. 'We'll kick off for Christ's sake!'

'Now shake hands,' the ref said.

We did. His hand became a winepress.

'And remember, I want a clean game!' the ref added.

We returned to our respective teams, the Uni captain shaking his head and tutting.

'What was that all about? Is everything okay?' Pemberton asked with tremolo.

'Yeah, I was just chatting to the ref. He's a nice cat.'

The referee blew a long descending/ascending scale on his whistle. The Uni captain punted the ball.

My stomach dropped.

Game on.

28

The magic fluke

THE BALL DRIBBLED TO OUR FEET. We all stood there looking at it as if it was the severed head of Charles the First. Sydney Uni charged like a herd of bison. I looked at Moscowitz, who was closest. He looked at me. I looked at Phil on the sideline. Phil looked at Moscowitz. Moscowitz looked at Bernie. I looked at Bernie. Bernie looked at me. We all looked at Bernie. Sydney Uni sharpened in my focus. Bernie, red in the face, screamed.

'Don't just stand there lookin at it! Someone pick up the pill and run with it!'

Meyer's father, who looked slightly more Jewish than a rabbi, yelled at his trembling son, 'Run, Meyer! Run like the wind!'

With the courage of David and the physique of Woody Allen, Moscowitz, clad in a leather helmet (he refused to play without his yarmulke), picked up the football and charged up field, screaming. 'Come on, boys, over the trenches! Aaahhh!'

We followed up-field, screaming like men possessed, towards the wall of flesh that descended upon us like a blue-and-gold tsunami. The crowd went up as one. They came down just as quickly. Moscowitz was smashed by three Uni players in an ugly gang-tackle. It shook the very earth beneath us. Even Bernie winced. What can I tell you? They absolutely creamed him.

Before being tackled, Moscowitz was heard to mumble, 'Sweet Moses!'

Poor guy. They were still finding pieces of him in Melbourne a week later. He lay beneath the Uni forwards as if under The Palace of the Philistines, post-Samson. As the opposition lazily removed their heavy frames from his limp person, there was a hush around the oval. A bird chirped. So inanimate was our noble Hebrew ball-carrier that the referee blew three staccato blasts on his whistle, stopping play. He rushed over. Meyer lay on the ground like a foetus in a leather helmet. This *really* freaked us out. The Uni players resumed their positions and chatted about the weather as we crowded around the corpse of Moscowitz wondering what the hell to do. This was only the *first* tackle!

Moscowitz's father started arguing with one of the touch judges (sideline judges, for those not au fait with rugby league). He was throwing his hands in the air – at one point invoking the Torah. Bernie ran on with his extensive medical kit: a bottle of water. Dad trailed him as assistant surgeon. Bernie poured the bottle of water over our halfback. Perhaps it was from Lourdes? He tapped him on the bottom and whispered paternally in his bloodied ear, 'Come on, champ. On your feet.'

To his credit, Moscowitz drunkenly got to his feet and played the ball. Herringbone tentatively positioned himself in dummy-half. Shell-shocked by Moscowitz's poleaxing, he threw a dreadful pass that nearly resulted in a turnover. Fortunately, Marty smothered it with his ample girth. Mad Jake laughed. He looked bored.

Marty got up to play the ball, but not before getting a 'facial' from the Uni forwards. Seemed this was their modus operandi with each tackle. As Marty got to his feet, he swore at the opposing second-rower, who was grinning like a South American dictator. We all stood in a bunch, not really having any plan of attack. You could have thrown a blanket over us. (Perhaps we could have hidden under it till the game was over.) This was in stark contrast to Sydney University who were evenly spread across the field like a row of poplars.

Bernie screamed from the sideline, 'Spread out for Chrissakes! Spread out!'

Tackle after tackle, Uni drove us back. By the fourth tackle we were back-pedalling faster than Howard on Medicare.

'Stick to the bloody pattern! For Chrissake, stick to the bloody pattern!' Bernie screamed. Problem was, none of us could *remember* the pattern! An Islamic arabesque? A Highland tartan from the McDougal clan? We were in a panic.

Without taking his eyes off the newspaper, Dave Barnes chuckled with hubris.

In a flash of brilliance, Lydia's brother positioned himself in dummy-half on the last tackle. Knowing the opposition would think we'd kick, he hoodwinked them. Feigning a pass, he chipped, regathered and shot up field like a greyhound. One of the Uni players tried to tackle him, but Andrew palmed him away like Luke Skywalker.

Their playmaker screamed. 'Someone tackle him for *Christ's Sake*!'

If it were not for a superb covering tackle from their full-back, Andrew would have actually *scored*. This was a seminal moment in the game.

I looked over at Dave Barnes, who had suddenly dropped his newspaper, mouth agape. We bolted up field and scrambled in offence. Bernie tore up the sideline. The panting ref restarted the tackle count. Moscowitz, back on deck as half-back and growing in confidence, threw an elegant pass that was equal in technique to the bowing of Paganini. A rampaging Minotaur cradled the ball. The snorting beast, drunk on the smell of his enemy's blood, charged at the wall of Uni forwards. They dropped off him like flies. Incredibly, we found ourselves inches from their try line! We looked at each other wide-eyed. This wasn't in our movie. We had to pinch ourselves.

Sydney Uni scrambled in defence. They were screaming at each other and pointing to holes in their defensive line. It was queer to watch. Half the university's music department (including their

Dean) were there to see Uni rub our musical noses in it. But one didn't attend the Colosseum to watch the Christians beat up on the lions. The Uni military machine was in disarray. Forwards were in the backs. Backs were in the forwards. Their nuggety hooker (the Little General, we dubbed him) rallied his stunned troops. The shocked crowd screamed in counterpoint.

Bernie screached. 'Don't just stand there admirin the bloke. Support im!'

We strung together a daisy chain of passes that impressed even us! (Thankfully stopping short of yours truly.) Amazingly, no one dropped the ball as was our custom in training.

Bernie jumped up and down, yelling. 'Stick to the pattern! Stick to the pattern! Stick to the pattern!'

At last we remembered what the pattern was! We moved play from left to right and along their defensive line as per Bernie's instructions.

Mad Jake, suddenly interested, politely called for the ball in a toothless howl, 'Give me the ball, fool!'

Moscowitz fired a bullet pass to Jake, who, similar to the Minotaur, delighted in running directly into the Uni players rather than around them. Howling like a stoned banshee, he crashed into them headfirst and was tackled only centimetres from their line. Jake was horrible to tackle. He was all elbows and knees. About three Uni players went down trying to ground him: clutching eyes, cheekbones, groins. It must be said that Jake really rattled Uni. In the end, no one enjoyed tackling him. He was one angry, toothless thrashing machine. One of the Uni players gave him the usual facial as Jake wriggled to his feet. Not familiar with the northern code of football, Jake deemed this illegal and threw a wild punch (which mercifully missed). The referee charged in and told him to settle. Perhaps somewhere in the wilds of Tasmania and away from all human contact. One of the Uni tacklers, who stood opposite, looked numb with shock.

I shook my head. 'Never piss off a banjo player.'

He nodded, wide-eyed.

Roughing up Mad Jake was an error in judgment. A better strategy would have been to give him the ball with a posy of flowers and a thoughtful handwritten note.

Dave Barnes frantically screamed coded plays from the sideline. 'I want to see an X-ray defensive pattern. I want a six-three combo. Grassy, Grassy! For Christ sake, tell Bosco I want the Ringo Formation. Tell him the Ringo Formation!'

There were so many secret messages and codes, at one stage we thought the Beatles were reforming. At least Bernie's no-frills football was easily digested, designed for simple musicians: run from left to right, bunch them up, wait for holes to appear in the defence, slip through and tackle the crap out of them.

A sneering Jake played the ball between his long legs. Moscowitz faked a pass, slipped through the legs of a groping forward and . . . yes . . . it is true . . . we did . . . we actually *scored*!

There was hush around the oval. No one had predicted it. Phil and I gaped at each other from across the field. Even the referee looked surprised. He glanced at his touch judges, who returned smiling nods of approval. Then we heard the sweetest notes known to man. Prettier than a Gershwin melody. Savoured more than a motif by Debussy. It was the blessed sound of a referee's whistle blowing four points on the scoreboard.

The crowd exploded. Bernie and Dad were shaking hands like prospectors who'd hit the mother lode. Sol lit two cigarettes. My flatmate, Duncan, held a bust of Mozart aloft in one hand, a flagon of cheap sherry in the other. The Lions tore out of the grandstand and rushed to the sidelines.

Bernie's snowy-haired son, who was the ball-boy, gathered the ball for Moscowitz as he lined up the kick for the extra two points. He presented it to our half-back like the crown of a vanquished king. The crowd bellowed a madrigal of instructions.

'Take your time, mate. Don't rush it,' the Lions' kicker said, tearing onto the field with a bucket of kicking sand (this was pre-tees).

Moscowitz painstakingly moulded a patty of sand, then placed the ball on it like a jeweller setting a priceless stone into a ring.

We ran back to our line, ecstatic. Bernie rushed onto the field. He was more animated than Bugs Bunny. He passed around water bottles, from which we drank as if we had just crossed the Sahara on rollerblades. We were panting, but not overly puffed at that stage. Bernie was giddy with delight. It was infectious. He spoke at the speed of light.

'You guys are goin *unreal*! I can't fucken believe it. Watch their playmaker but. The hooker. Watch that bloke like a hawk. He's the leader. He's the General – not the captain, forget im.'

With flick-pass speed, he turned to Marty and the Minotaur. 'I want youse two to run at him at every opportunity. Got it? Directly at im. Whenever you get the ball. I want that bloke tackled outer the game. Now, where's that banjo player? Listen, big fella.' He chuckled. 'Don't throw any punches, pal. We can't afford to lose a single player. Unlike them, we got no reserves. They got squads of em. Captain? *Captain*? Where's fucken Café Boy?'

I was hiding behind the Minotaur, hoping he wouldn't notice me.

'Over ere,' he said, towing me by the jersey. 'Are you in this fucken game or what?' he whispered. 'Go looking for the ball. Ya can't just wait for the pill to be delivered to ya by limo. You're the bloody captain. Show some leadership, for Chrissake!'

I hid my face.

Bernie ran off with his water bottles and yelled over his shoulder, 'Remember. Stick to the pattern!'

I squinted at Moscowitz downfield. The kick was on a tricky angle. Roughly ten metres to the side of the posts. He stood for an age before kicking it. Moses on the edge of the Red Sea. Moscowitz, the perfectionist he was, practised his kicks after training with the exactitude of a neurosurgeon. Needless to say, he didn't let us down.

The ball sailed effortlessly through the oversized 'H' (that I always said stood for 'Hide!'). It was a textbook kick. The crowd erupted. Moscowitz's father ran up and down the sidelines, clutching his black hat and jumping in the air, his long black coat parachuting behind.

The Uni players stood like the lost legion of Varus. They were shell-shocked, confused. Out of the corner of my eye, I saw someone I guessed was the University Dean. He was steaming towards Dave Barnes. I couldn't tell what he was saying but in the words of Cicero about Antony, 'He seemed to be spewing rather than speaking.'

Then the most exquisite portrait appeared. It rivalled the beauty of Matisse, the subtlety of Rembrandt, the daring of Chagall. It was a weathered scoreboard that read: SYDNEY UNIVERSITY 0 VISITORS 6.

Catching the eye of Dave Barnes, Bernie placed a $50 note between his teeth and performed a teasing dance. (The same thing Shylock did to Antonio, pissed, outside a pub in Venice.) The Uni coach glared at him. Dad and Phil's dad were clutching their sides and howling at Bernie. Phil plucked his violin from its case and started playing Queen's 'We Will Rock You'. The crowd sang in discordant chorus. Moscowitz raced back to our huddle wide-eyed with excitement. One of the clearest memories I have of the game is his astonished face. I still see it. He looked wild, like an escaped convict.

'We can beat these guys!' he said. 'We can actually *beat* these guys! They're not so tough!'

We pondered this. We had only ever planned to complete the game with our internal organs intact, not actually win it – even though we joked we would. This reverie was interrupted by the referee blowing time back on. (Moscowitz had taken so painfully long with the kick, the clock was stopped.)

I looked over at Dad. He shook his fist and smiled as much as to say, *Come on, mate, get stuck in.* It's true, I was holding back. But why? There simply wasn't time to be scared. I was in a battle: survive or perish. I was tentative because I didn't want to let my friends down. Didn't want to drop the ball or miss a tackle. That's why I moved to outside centre. The name sounded auxiliary. Anyway, it turned out that my involvement in proceedings would be decided for me. Matched in the forwards, Uni tested our back line.

Moscowitz booted the ball down field. Uni's wiry full-back ran it back at our enveloping line. The poor guy was poleaxed by Jake, Marty and the Minotaur in a tackle that would later be referred to as 'the revenge of Moscowitz'. The full-back didn't move. An inanimate mound of flesh. To his credit, he finally got up and gingerly played the ball between his legs. The ball was fed to the Uni backs. A current of adrenaline ran though our backline. This was it. Then the unexpected: they punted the ball early in the tackle count. We were waiting for them to do this on the sixth tackle, as one is supposed to do in rugby league. To my horror, the ball made a beeline right for me. A pig-skinned guided missile. I squinted at the sky, which was white with midday heat. The wobbling orb grew larger as it fell, comet-like, to terra firma. I steadied myself beneath it. I told myself I could catch it. Uni charged downfield. The Maulers were screaming at me to catch it. Bernie was screaming. Dad was screaming. The Lions were screaming. Duncan was screaming – only not at me, but at Sol who, in the excitement, had walked into him with his cigarette. I saw the Uni captain bearing down on me. I looked at him. I looked at the sky. Gone. No, there it was. The Uni captain charged like a hoplite as he drew closer. Don't look at him, look at the ball. Stand your ground. Don't take your eyes off the ball. Stand firm. Stand firm. I visualised my hands being three times their size. I imagined them cradling the ball as a mother does her newborn. I chanted: *You can do it, you can do it.* The ball suddenly came hurtling out of the sun. Growing larger. It fell like the Hindenburg. Impossibly, it seemed to gain velocity the closer it came. Then I knew. It was mine. I owned it.

Then I dropped it. As clean as a spud.

The crowd groaned.

One of the drunks from The Dog cackled from the balcony.

Luckily, Hamish, my centre partner, dived on the spillage. He looked up at me, frowning. The panting umpire ran downfield and blew his whistle.

Scrum.

I looked over at Dad with drooping shoulders. My worst fears had been realised. I'd made an arse of myself. I'd let Dad down. I'd let the team down. I'd let Bernie down. Some captain! Dad simply smiled and shrugged. I returned to the drifting school of backs.

The boys packed into the scrum. Rugby league scrums aren't contested in the way they are in rugby union so the ball seemed out before it was in.

The bantam Uni half-back sniped around the blind side of the scrum. With Hamish bearing down on him, he pitched the ball to the Uni captain. Deducing I was a weak link, he ran right at me.

Dad bellowed from the sideline, 'Tackle him, son!'

Seeing nothing but me and four points before him, he ran flat out at my person. I stood like a roo in a spotlight. I somehow *had* to tackle him. His piston-like knees blurred. I'd have to take him around the chest. No, like Bernie says, without legs he's going nowhere.

As I was contemplating all this, screaming and running around from the far side of the scrum, like a half-starved Japanese soldier, was Mad Jake. As I crouched to feebly take out the leader's legs, Jake nailed him – almost breaking him in two, and forcing him to fumble the ball. It dribbled behind. Uni's winger bellied on it.

Jake got up and stood over the bruised captain. 'Sorry, mate, members only,' he said, turning to me with a twinkle in his eye.

The Uni captain looked perplexed.

Jake smiled through missing teeth. (He even looked like a banjo player!) He wore no mouthguard; there was no need. His dental work must have unnerved the opposition.

'Cheers, Jake,' I said.

'That's okay. I hate that guy.'

'Which guy? The captain?'

'Huh?

'Which guy do you hate, Jake?'

'All of em!' he said.

The winger played the ball and passed to the Sydney Uni captain, who had one eye on Jake and one eye on me.

'Tackle him,' Dad hooted.

I dived for his ankles, which were spinning like the prop of a Cessna. I collected his boot in my face. With the aplomb of Fred Astaire, he danced around my feeble lunge and scored in the corner. The crowd – now on our side – moaned.

Dave Barnes returned to his newspaper. Life was back to normal. It had just been a bad dream. Dad's shoulders drooped. Cassandra revived the goddamn funeral dirge. The Maulers dropped their heads.

Bernie ran onto the field, pulling me aside. He placed two heavy arms on my shoulders and looked me squarely in the face.

'Look at me. Look at me. Now, a lot of people are depending on you today, Café Boy. Do you know that? Look, I know ya worried about making mistakes an that, but I just wanna see you havin a fucken dig. That's all I ask. The reason you copped some shoe in that tackle is that you went in half-baked. That's how blokes get hurt in football. Goin in half-cocked. Worried about injuries an that. You won't feel nuthin if you give 110 per cent. [Why do people say that?] Now, I want to see ya hurl yourself at them Uni blokes like a fucken missile. Come on, let's see ya put them ridiculous shoulder pads to use.'

They were ridiculous. Most of the Maulers didn't wear shoulder pads, but I had purchased a costly pair that sat beneath my jersey like a three-seater sofa.

'Doesn't matter if it's crap. They just wanna see you have a go. Lift the team. It'll be like a ripple in a lake that will turn into a tidal wave.'

'You can't have a tidal wave in a lake, Bernie.'

'Can't you?'

'It would be unusual.'

'Oh.'

'Just how big is this lake?'

'Jesus! Look, what I'm sayin is, it'll have an effect on em, the entire team. Trust me. So come on . . . have a fucken dig. Make your old man's day, for Chrissake.'

Bernie walked over and circled the forlorn Maulers, whispering pearls of wisdom to each player like Obi-Wan Kenobi with a semi-arthritic hip.

Uni converted the try with a stellar kick from the sideline and darted back upfield.

Bernie jogged to the sideline. 'Come on boys, heads up!' he said, water bottles splashing about him.

After Bernie's consonant-starved entreaty, I decided it was, in fact, time to 'have a dig'.

Uni – capitalising on their momentum – instantly kicked the ball deep into our half. The horrid thing dribbled to my feet. I took a deep breath. I looked at the blue wall moving downfield. This was it. I picked up the God-awful thing, closed my eyes and ran into them as hard as I possibly could. The crowd roared. Three Uni forwards, who had possibly eaten granite for breakfast, kindly met me at the three-quarter line. They hammered me senseless. However, I managed to keep secure the ball. I was unable to see daylight beneath them as they lay across me. They were heavy as stones. I drowned in their smell: sweat, garlic, lineament, b.o., apple-scented shampoo, grass, the rusk smell of their collective breath. In no other activity, aside from sex, Greco-Roman wrestling or peak hour, are you this close to another human being.

And you know something? Bernie was right. It didn't hurt. What I failed to read in the small print, however, was that the next day I would be unable to walk, or eat anything but mashed bananas. But at the moment of impact, I didn't feel the tackle. From that moment, I went in to each play '110 per cent'. (God, I hate even writing it.) And, as Bernie predicted, it lifted the team. It was a crap hit-up, but it didn't matter. If we were going to win this, everyone had to give his all.

I looked over at Dad, who punched his fist in the air. Phil gave me a stealthy thumbs-up. Duncan thumped his man-boobs.

On the sixth tackle, Andrew punted the ball spectacularly high. Uni's lock steadied himself beneath the rifling leather. Mad Jake and the Minotaur closed in. Out of the corner of his eye the Uni player lost his nerve and took a peek at them, dropping the ball. Harold, our blind winger (yes, someone with poorer eyesight than mine!), fell on it. The Little General dropped an elbow on the bridge of our winger's nose, smashing it like an egg. It may have been accidental but it looked suspect. Blood splattered over Harold's boots as if he'd lost his grip on a bottle of shiraz. There was some push and shove between Mauler and Uni players. We were livid. You'd have to be Ray Charles to have missed it. I ran in.

'Are you all right, Harold?' I asked, gently slapping his face.

Harold nodded but smiled at me as if I was a character from a Lewis Carroll novel. He had to come off. We were not happy. One of the Maulers was shoved to the turf in the ensuing melée.

It was a red rag to a bull. Mad Jake ran in and started throwing them. What can I say? Jake lived to fight. His fists fell on anyone in proximity – including some of our own players.

I pulled at his jumper. 'Calm down, Jake. We can't afford to lose you, man.'

Bernie screamed at the referee, who had missed the rhinal peccadillo. He did, however, see the mess that was Harold's face. No doubt he took this into account with regard to Jake's rampant fisticuffs. The crowd booed and hissed the Little General as if he were the villain in a nineteenth-century melodrama. Harold was helped, cadaver-like, to his feet.

Bernie charged onto the field and rushed the whistleblower. 'Are you *blind*, sir? That was a blatant late tackle. I've never seen anything like it in all my *life*! He should be sent off, for Chrissake!'

Cornering the referee Bernie half-heartedly threw some 'magic water' over the wobbling Harold, who was shouldered from the field by Duncan and Jonno. (Jonno was now Bernie's de facto assistant coach.) Bernie fed me water by pouring it down my shorts. 'Why is that bloke still on the field, for Chrissake? Just tell me that!'

Not prepared to surrender the slightest advantage, Dave Barnes rushed onto the field. A pair of designer sunglasses bobbed around his suntanned neck. 'And what about this maniac,' screamed Barnes, pointing at Jake. 'What fucken instrument does he play?'

'The banjo,' Bernie said.

'Bullshit!' said Barnes.

Bernie turned his back on him and pursued the bewildered official, hound-like. 'Why is that bloke still on the field, for Chrissake?'

The Little General hid his face. Bernie was *desperate* to take him out of the game.

'Stop tryin to intimidate the referee, Bernie. You were always doing that as a player and now you're doing it as a bloody *coach*,' Barnes said.

'He's got to go!' said Bernie.

Barnes threw his hands in the air. 'I don't believe this!'

'Now listen here. I'll referee this –' the official said.

Bernie turned to Barnes. 'You've never gotten over that bloody French game, have you, Dave?'

The Uni coach's voice climbed in pitch, 'I could have tied the *series*, for Chrissake!'

'I've got the fucken video at home, Dave. Blanco had you covered!' Bernie said, throwing his hands about.

They were shouting an inch from each other's face. By then, Bernie had turned the colour of his True Blue Chemicals work shirt. We didn't know what to do. I thought they were going to start throwing them. The drunks cheered them on from the balcony. Sol yelled from the sidelines something about 'repressed hostility being nothing more than latent inferiority'.

Bernie got as close to Barnes as you can get without exchanging bodily fluids. Fearing the worst, Dad ran on to drag Bernie off. Sombrero catching the wind.

'I've got two hundred that says we'll win this!' Bernie said, shuffling through his wallet.

'You *are* joking. That's the easiest money I've ever made.'

The referee finally lost it, throwing down his whistle in disgust. He pointed to the sideline. 'You two! Off my field! *Now!* I don't want to see either of you again for the rest of the game – even with water!'

Dave stormed off with his nose in the air, but not before snatching the cash from Bernie's sausage-like fingers.

'I want the same odds!' Bernie screamed, Dad towing him to the opposing sideline.

The referee sighed, shook his head and blew a penalty.

Moscowitz took the free kick. He took his usual forty minutes, which infuriated the Uni players. As he eventually took his three measured steps, with two giant steps to the side, he looked up at the posts as if they were the Gates of Jericho. Holding his right arm up for balance in a salute that would have horrified his grandfather, he leaned into the kick. The drunks razzed him. But focus was a 'gimme' with Moscowitz. He was a concert violinist. He had the concentration of Alan Turing. The ball swan-dived over the black dot.

The crowd exploded. We were back in the lead. Catching Dave's eye, Bernie indicated the scoreboard like a game-show assistant. Barnes scowled.

Sydney Uni put the ball high overhead. Like a goddamn homing pigeon with a bomb tied to its foot, it found me. (Perhaps, from all my squinting, they'd fathomed I was short-sighted.) Again I tried to pick it out against the midday sun. This time it was hopeless; I couldn't pick it out at all. Pluto was clearer. To make things worse, out of the corner of my eye, I saw Mad Jake running towards me like a maniac. What is he doing this time? Is he about to tackle me? I was in a panic. A phalanx of Uni players bore down on me. From my flank, Jake raced towards me like a bee-stung rhino. I didn't know which way to look. I tried to steady myself. I looked into the sky, which had become a blurring nondescript smear of orange suffused with white: a Rothko canvas. Jake suddenly scaled my back like Edmund Hillary on amphetamines, plucking the ball from the air: an eagle snatching a sparrow. He fell to earth with the ball as the Uni forwards reached him.

He turned to me. 'Not a bad mark, eh?'

'Thanks, Jake, I just couldn't see a bloody thing.'

The referee blew a long sigh on his whistle.

Half-time.

29

Intermission

AS THE BRUISED, SWEAT-STREAKED combatants limped to their respective dressing-rooms, Dad and I stood gaping at the scoreboard, which incredibly read: SYDNEY UNIVERSITY 6 VISITORS 8.

The half-time score was never to read like this. We felt if Uni were only ahead by twenty or so points, we were not shamed. But this? What did it all mean? Was it an evil portent? A harbinger of impending doom? Was Sydney Uni about to be consumed by locusts? Was the Con about to be levelled by earthquake? Was Danni Minogue making another comeback?

The Uni Dean brawled with Dave Barnes before storming off. (To be ever the bridesmaid in music was one thing, to be catching a bouquet of jockstraps was quite another.) Purple with rage and fretting for his career, Dave Barnes marched to the home-team locker-room like Caesar discovering his legionaries had not defeated the Gauls, but instead exchanged exciting new recipes for pastries.

Dad made his way to the locker-room – but not before savouring the scoreboard one last time. Phil's dad ran off to find ice for dear Harold's re-modelled snout. Sir Richard would be livid to see the state of his bassoonist's face at concert practice the following Monday. We later discovered that Sir Richard had planted a spy in the crowd, with instructions to call him with fifteen-minute updates. Our fretting Dean was terrified that his fine musicians, and in particular, his principal violinist and future star of the world stage, would injure themselves for the impending eisteddfod. However, Sir Richard was so astounded to hear that his students were leading Uni at half-time, he tore out of the Con in his silver Bentley and raced to the field, almost skittling a string quartet in the driveway.

As the last Mauler was swallowed into the gut of the booming locker-room. A carnival of cheers greeted each one. What a contrast to the funereal atmosphere pre-kick-off. Friends, relatives and a multitude of well-wishers joined the weary players. (Everyone loves a winner!) After my final double-blink at the scoreboard, I too made my way to the bowels of the grandstand (where the locker-rooms were situated). I spied Bernie and Jonno puffing on a cigarette and giggling at an open window. Bernie motioned me over. I asked what was up. He drew a chubby finger to his lips. It seemed they were eavesdropping on the opposition. Cocking an ear to the window, I heard Dave Barnes address his troops. The metallic crash of a steel chair pealed as it was thrown across the locker-room.

'They're a team of fucken *violinists*, for Christ's Sake! You blokes are dead-set fucken joking. People out there are laughing at you. Laughing at me. Laughing at this university . . .'

Bernie and Jonno erupted with hissing giggles, their eyes glazed with tears.

'What's going on with that banjo player?' one of the Uni players asked.

Bernie and Jonno held each other and shook.

'How do *I* fucken know?' Barnes screamed. 'I don't believe this . . . Look, I don't care if the third trombone player's insulted your auntie. They're a bunch of fucken concert musicians, for Christ's Sake!'

I left Bernie and Jonno writhing like eels. Elbowing past the crowd at the door of the locker-room, well-wishers – including Sol – patted me on the back. (I hadn't experienced this much back patting since breastfeeding days.)

The hard midday light softened with cigarette smoke. It was tricky finding a seat. There must have been well over fifty people in the room. A high-pitched medley of excited voices bounced off the concrete and tiles. It resonates in my mind today. The briny smell of sport hung in the air as I squeezed past Duncan to find a seat next to Hamish. Lions were everywhere with advice. The Minotaur engaged in an animated conversation with Peewee. Some of the other Lions were talking with our forwards about offensive scrums. The Lions' stringy full-back, Melon, was coaching our full-back, aping catching a high ball. Dad waved across the room. He was in a serious tactical discussion with Moscowitz's father. A battle of the hats.

Thrilled by our effort in the first half, we knew it was a long forty minutes to victory. The atmosphere was excited but tense. Bernie and Jonno arrived, their faces sweaty from laughter. Bernie was beside himself, jumping up and down with each syllable.

'I don't fucken believe you blokes! You're goin fantastic! Where's that new drummer? Mate, those plays were straight outa the coachin manual. And where's the big fella . . . our banjo man . . . ?'

Jake grunted from the corner, smoking, and drinking from a tall bottle of tequila.

'Mate, you took that high ball like a bloody wedge-tailed eagle. Should be playin for the Swans, mate! I'm so proud of all of ya . . .' Bernie noticed the broadening pall of gloom. 'Whasamatta? Youse look like ya couldn't get a root in a whorehouse.'

Marty pointed to Harold, who was balancing a bag of frozen peas on his nose. (While Phil's dad went for ice, the canteen lady came to the rescue.) 'We've got no winger. And no reserves, remember?'

'They'll open us up like a tin can,' Herringbone said in his ringing tenor.

'Perhaps we should forfeit,' Harold said mutely, through the peas.

Silence engulfed the room.

'I was praying it wouldn't come to this . . .' a voice rumbled from the back of the locker-room. Phil stood on the bench and opened his violin case. He pulled out a decrepit pair of football boots and held them in the air like Excalibur. 'My father has kept them since I last played. Hides in his garage and polishes them every Mardi Gras, feeling depressed. Anyway, I know I'm going to regret this . . . but where do you want me to play?' (Somewhere an angel in a sequined cassock got its wings.)

A cheer broke, flashing a smile on Phil's terrified face. (I know you won't believe me, but despite his better judgement, Phil *did* play in the second half.)

'That's it, pal, always stand behind your mates,' Bernie said.

'Especially when they're naked,' Phil mumbled.

'Now, everyone take a pew. We need to have a little chat, because this next forty minutes will be the most important forty minutes of ya lives.'

Maulers shuffled to find a seat. Phil was handed Harold's blood-mottled jersey. With the tips of two fingers, he took it like a bag filled with turds. Parents and onlookers stood piously against the wall. Bernie waited for a dramatic silence – a conductor waiting to lift his baton.

'Now, boys, I don't want youse to be under no illusions,' he said softly. 'We took em by surprise that half. It can happen in football. But expect a *very* different Sydney Uni this half. Make no bones about it. It's gunner get pretty fucken rough out there. The game really starts in this half. You'll have to dig deeper than ever before. We can't afford no mistakes. And remember, we have to . . .'

'STICK TO THE PATTERN!' we chorused.

The room chuckled.

Bernie drew a warm smile, a smile I had not seen before. He looked as if he actually liked us.

'Yep, that's right. We must stick to the pattern. But, more importantly, we must stick by each other. Stick by ya mates. Cause, as I said before kick-off, we've all become mates.'

We looked at each other and nodded.

'So now I'm asking youse, as a mate, to stick to the pattern,' Bernie continued. 'But, as I said, it's gunner get rough out there. You'll panic. You'll wanna abandon the pattern. You'll wanna play every man for himself. But youse can't lose ya rag. Youse can't panic. Youse can't get angry.' He turned to Mad Jake. 'And that means none of youse.' He returned to the team. 'Cause that's *just* what they want. They want to rattle ya. So they'll sledge ya. They'll gouge ya. They'll drop knees into ya . . .' There was a pregnant pause. 'They'll tread on ya hands.'

Some of us instinctively looked at our fingers. Phil turned the colour of sour milk. Moscowitz took an almighty gasp of Ventolin, now a permanent snorkel in his mouth. Marty lit two cigarettes and passed one to the Minotaur. I stole a glance at Dad. He looked stressed. Bernie paced.

'They'll pull out all the stops. Understand this: they've got nuthin to gain and everything to lose. They'll come outer that locker-room ready to eat meat. But I wanna see you blokes give it to em ten-fold. They won't expect that. I wanna see blokes throwin emselves at the opposition. I wanna see you blokes bash em. Everyone has to dig deep. Deeper than you've ever dug in ya lives. If each man doesn't give 110 per cent –'

In corduroy and tweeds, Sir Richard made his way into the airless room.

'G'day, boss!' said Bernie. 'Didn't think we'd see *you* ere!'

'What, and miss our inaugural victory?' Sir Richard said as dead-pan as you like.

The room cheered. Bernie slapped him on the back, almost dis-lodging an eyeball. 'On ya, pal!'

Sir Richard found a corner. He looked odd sitting on a locker-room bench; like Prince Charles on a barstool.

Bernie theatrically looked around the room. 'Now, let me just say this.' He shook his fist slowly. 'If you blokes win this, you'll never

forget this day for the rest of ya lives. I know I bloody won't! He sig-
naled me. 'The captain will now give us his half-time speech.'

I looked at Jonno and shrugged. Half-time speech? That wasn't in
the program notes.

Jonno motioned me over and whispered. 'Just speak from the
heart, mate.'

I stood thinking of what in God's name to say to the assembly of
bruised faces before me. There was an uncomfortable silence.

'Well, um . . . it's like Bernie says,' I said. 'Mates.' I paused.
'I mean, I've always known why *I'm* playing football, but I've never
known why *you're* all playing football. I suppose I've been too
frightened to ask, in case you had some kind of epiphany and left en
masse.' There was a brace of chuckles. 'But . . . I think that's what
this has been all about, hasn't it? Mates? When we first came
together, everyone was bitching with everybody else. But now . . .
well, people are putting their careers on the line for each other.'

Maulers nodded.

'I think what we've really discovered is "mateship". It's a new
feeling. Let's be honest, the arts offer few opportunities. Rewards
only the elite. We're more like competitors than colleagues at times.
There are no *real* mates at the Con. Plenty of egos. Plenty of people
sniping behind your back. Not too many people ready to give up
everything for one another. And isn't that we're doing today?
Putting ourselves on the line for each other? And it's had a ripple
effect through the entire Conservatorium. Even the *orchestra* is
sounding better!'

Sir Richard nodded.

'I see this game as an opera. It's long. It's exhausting. It's Wagner's
bloody *Ring*. So we mustn't play as a group of soloists. We must
play as a team. As a series of tight sections. If Bernie has taught us
anything over these past months, it's teamwork.'

Sir Richard shot a smile at Bernie.

'But in the first minutes of the game, nerves got the better of us.

We ignored the conductor's notes. Uni drove us into the dirt. If we do this in the second half, we're sunk. We *must* stick to Bernie's pattern, or not only will we lose the game, we may get very hurt. Make no mistake: we're in a battle. We need to be there for each other. Backing each other up. Supporting each other. Christ, even Phil's supporting us. And I *know*, for a fact, he's shitting himself.'

Phil nodded with slapstick effect. The room cackled.

'We each need to give, dare I say it, 110 per cent.' I rolled my eyes. Murmurs of agreement.

'Not only for yourself, but for each other. For your "mate". Anyway, I know Bernie was being a mate when Dad talked him into coaching us.'

Bernie dropped his head.

'But he didn't let his old mate down. And we won't let Bernie down.' I paused. 'Look, I don't know if we can win today. But I'm not going to die wondering. As inept as I am, I'm going out there to give it my best shot.'

I took Bernie's hand.

'On a personal note, I'd like to take this opportunity to thank Bernie. I know, for one, I'm a better human being for having met him. He's a beautiful cat.' I caught Phil's eye. 'Bernie, the team has a little something for you.'

We presented Bernie with a stunning bouquet of flowers. Phil selected them personally. (I told Phil to buy wine!) Bernie stood dumbfounded. I gave him a hug. Our poet laureate Duncan stood on a bench and recited his football poem. Each member of the team lined up to exit and hug our coach, who stood rigid, clutching his bouquet.

Sir Richard examined the flowers on his way out. 'Oh, I simply *adore* irises.'

Bernie, dazed, staggered out of the locker room holding his gift. The Maulers charged onto the field. Uni took to the field like ravenous beasts. The Uni coach and Bernie walked to the sideline together. Bernie looked at Dave, who looked at Bernie, who tossed the flowers to Jonno.

'Mind these, mate.' He turned to Barnes. 'Wife's anniversary.'

The coaches resumed their positions on the opposing sidelines. Dad waved me over. I followed him back into the vacuum of the locker-room. He removed his sombrero.

'What's up, Dad?'

He pulled tape from his pocket and bandaged my hands, mummy-like.

'What's going on? How am I going to catch the ball?'

Dad smiled and shook his head. 'Let's face it. For a footballer, you make a fucken good musician.'

'True,' I said. He looked stressed. 'Something's on your mind, Dad. What's wrong?'

He sat down. 'Your mother called. She told me about the record contract.'

'Oh,' I said, sitting next to him.

'Like Bernie said, things are going to get nasty out there. Maybe you should sit this half out. I mean . . . it's only a game of football.'

'Can you repeat that?'

'What?'

I looked into his face. 'You know, Dad, I've been waiting all my life to hear those words.'

'Well, there I've said it. Should've said it years ago. Should've said a lot of things years ago. To you. Your brother . . .'

'Dad, I can't let my mates down, now. It wouldn't be right.'

He walked around the room, gently tapping the lockers. 'I don't know why I like footy. I spose I've always thought it teaches ya good lessons in life.' He turned to me. 'I think ya just learned one of em today.

I kissed him on the forehead and ran onto the field.

'Stay safe out there,' he chuckled. 'Ya silly prick!'

⌒

I joined the other Maulers. We stood like troops awaiting the signal to go over the top. Phil trembled on my wing. I could hear his jewellery rattling. His father called out, demanding to know just what the hell he was doing on the field. Jonno enlightened him. Open-mouthed, he flopped to his seat and asked for a small glass of sherry.

'Dorian. Dorian! Where do I stand?' Phil said.

'I don't know . . . anywhere. You're playing on the wing. So near the sideline.'

'Dorian. Dorian!'

'What?'

'What do I do after that?'

'Just a little theatre, Phil. Look like you mean business. And, whatever you do, don't drop the ball.' (The pot calling the kettle etc.)

'Dorian. Dorian!'

'Yes, what is it Phil?'

'What if someone runs at me?'

'I don't know. Fall in front of them. Trip them up.'

'Dorian. Psst. Dorian.'

'*What* Phil?'

'My father is watching. I don't want to embarrass him.'

'Don't worry. He'll be in good company.'

'Dorian!'

'Jesus. *What* Phil?'

There was a tremor in his voice. 'Don't pass me the ball unless it's an emergency.'

The referee, looking to both flanks, raised an arm and blew his whistle.

'Phil, this *is* an emergency!'

30

Cadenza

THERE WAS A NOTICEABLE difference in the opposition. Uni had injected fresh troops, markedly superior from those who played the first half. This prompted Bernie to turn to Sir Richard and say, 'Where did those guys come from? The fucken Bat Cave?'

I know for a *fact* that Uni fielded some serious replacements, because roughly ten years later my trio was playing at the Tilbury Hotel in Woolloomooloo when a towering guy approached the bandstand.

'You won't remember me, but I captained Sydney University's football team against you some years ago,' he said.

It was fabulous to meet my old adversary. On my break, he kindly bought me a beer and we found a corner to reminisce. He helped me fill some white-noise within the game. He said that after that first-half shock, Uni fielded its crack troops, one of whom was an ex-professional who actually played a handful of games for the Balmain Tigers! (Glad I didn't know at the time. I would have crapped myself.) He said that their coach was adamant that his team was not about to go down to an orchestra.

⌒

Fresh troops regardless, the crowd was wholly on our side. This was to prove a factor. One of the endearing qualities of my fellow countrymen is that they will always support the underdog (at the expense of their national side at times). The crowd realised it was about to witness something remarkable. So they booed and hissed Uni as if they were Beelzebub's Thirteen. Even the drunks from The Dog stopped goading us. We had a quasi home-ground advantage! Almost every spectator – including the Sydney Uni students and the stunned visiting English Combined University Rugby League team (billeted by the students) – was willing the Sydney Conservatorium of Music to victory.

As the leather egg pitched high overhead, Uni played with new resolve. Right from the first tackle they turned up the aggression like a flame under a tepid pot. A smog of testosterone clung to the air. You could smell it. Taste it in the back of your mouth.

Uni's plan was to rattle Mad Jake and have him taken out of the game. So they sledged him, gouged him, dropped knees into him, said cruel things about the banjo. It wasn't only Jake they bashed: we all copped it. Just as Bernie had predicted, they roughed us up, big time. Nevertheless, we took it on the chin. We were there to win, not whine. However, Jake was on the receiving end of most of it. He reacted badly each time. The ref continually warned him not to throw punches, till Bernie finally pulled him from the field for a few minutes to take a few deep breaths (leaving us a man short). Amazingly, with the ghosts of Byron and Shelley at his heels, Duncan (still in his slippers!) snatched Jake's jersey and staggered on in his stead. By that stage, he was too pissed to play and was more a liability than an asset. Yet he made a couple of crunching tackles and filled a hole in our line. He also quoted Keats at their five-eighth, causing him to fumble at the antiquated syntax.

It was obvious that Duncan had to come off. So Mad Jake, who under Bernie's instructions was deep breathing and practising tai chi on the sideline, retuned to the front line. He immediately charged up the ball with his usual mania. They targeted him instantly. It must be said that the Uni players had plenty of intestinal fortitude. It seemed they'd rather end up with a broken jaw, thereby having Jake sent off, than suffer the ignominy of defeat. Jake came up swinging every time.

Launching myself again and again at the Uni line, I eventually suffered a concussion. When I became lucid I found myself on my back with Jonno shouting instructions, drops of salty sweat stinging my grazed face. (Bernie was still in exile.)

'Bernie wants all forwards to run at the Little General. He wants two men to a tackle and no dropped balls. Tell Marty to play on the opposite side of the ruck. He wants Casey to switch with Phil on the wing. If the ball's in our half, he wants only four tackles, a kick, then a *big* chase. Come on, mate, on your feet. Have you got it? Have you got all that? Look at me. Look at me. Have you got that?'

I nodded. Groggy, I wasn't sure which way was up. I got up and fell over again. I got up and ran over to the team, as if dodging a bee, and, in a long unintelligible slur, screamed at the Maulers.

'Bernie wants all the forwards to behave in general. Don't grab your balls. Phil is a bitch. He wants Marty to fuck Casey from the opposite side. He wants four drinks and a chaser!'

The team stared at me.

No, that can't be right. 'I don't know. Just stick to the fucking pattern!' I ran off to make a tackle, spitting out blades of grass.

☺

It wasn't long before we had the ball deep in Uni's half. Jake crashed into their line, but not before someone felled him and several other tacklers dropped on him like parachutists. Then the Little General stamped on Jake's fingers. This was the straw that broke the tattooed camel's back. Jake got to his feet. He threw the ball down and king-hit the lock-forward (who had little to do with anything), dropping him like a sack of doorknobs. The referee blew the pea out of his whistle.

It was too much for our coach. Defying the referee's edict, Bernie bolted onto the field with his props (i.e. water bottles) pleading our case.

'Did you see that, sir? That player deliberately jumped on our man's fingers!' Bernie said over his shoulder, swabbing Jake's fingers with a sponge.

'Yes, I did see that,' said the referee, glaring at the General.

'This bloke plays the banjo! He's got a concert in Alabama next week. The fucken . . . world banjo finals,' Bernie was desperate. We couldn't afford to lose a single player.

Dave Barnes sprinted onto the field, he too with his water bottles. He also spoke over his shoulder, feeding water to his thirsty chicks. 'He should be sent off! Banjo finals or no bloody banjo finals. The guy's a dead-set lunatic!'

The referee agreed and, looking at Jake, pointed to the sideline.

'I'm takin him off now, anyway. I'll have to have his hand in ice,' Bernie said, sulking off with a seething Jake. 'Country music will never be the same again!' he said over his shoulder.

We were now a player down. Uni's plan had succeeded.

The frazzled official called the two captains and the Little General aside for a serious chat.

'Look, this man is a professional musician,' the exasperated ref said. 'There's no need to resort to those sort of tactics.'

'Tactics? The guy's a bloody lunatic!' The General turned to me. 'Every tackle, he gets up throwing them!'

'Country music has that effect on you after a while,' I said.

'If I see either team playing foul, I'll call this game off! Do you hear me?' said the ref. 'Do you hear me?'

We nodded like chastised schoolboys.

The ref blew time back on.

⌒

With their endless supply of fresh players, us a player short, and the Little General playing like Andrew bloody Johns on speed, Uni scored in quick succession. It was remarkable how a single player could have such an effect on a team. We were way behind. Despite the crowd bellowing encouragement till they were hoarse, Uni belted us from one side of the park to the other. Uni seemed as unstoppable as time. They unleashed a veritable blitzkrieg of football against us. We were under constant assault from all flanks. We were exhausted. After Uni scored again, we sought welcome respite behind our try line. The kicker negotiated the kick. Buckled over, none of us could siphon enough air. I saw Bernie and Jonno stealing glances at the Little General and speaking conspiratorially. 'He's got to go,' Bernie said. Jonno nodded.

Got to go? Go where? I thought. To the loo? Late-night shopping? To wash his hair?

After the next couple of plays, as if by magic, Jonno appeared beside me in a black and gold Maulers jersey. (Turned out he wore the same sized boots as Harold.) Jonno must have been on the field for all but five minutes, so we got away with it. You see, Jonno looked about as much like a concert musician as Yehudi Menuhin looked like Sylvester Stallone's personal trainer. What can I say? Jonno was a semi-professional footballer. The guy had neck muscles on his neck muscles.

'What are *you* doing here?' I asked, getting up from a tackle, covered in dirt.

'Just a bitta housekeeping,' Jonno said.

I screwed up my face. 'Housekeeping?'

It would have been less than a minute before he made 'that tackle' – the tackle that turned the game. As Jonno waited patiently in the back line, he reminded me of a Bengal tiger stalking a straggling bearer. As soon as the Little General had the ball, Jonno's eyes lit up. I looked at Bernie who looked at the General and then back at Jonno.

As usual, the General was running with the ball in two hands, directing players and pointing to holes in our defence like goddamn Peter Sterling. He managed to get an elegant ball away to his five-eighth (fortunately, Andrew was on him like a hound) before Jonno launched himself at the General, cutting him in two and knocking him out cold! What can I tell you? Jonno absolutely *creamed* this guy. The General slumped in a heap like a bag of old clothes. Play moved across field without anyone noticing. With sci-fi speed Bernie switched Jonno with Hamish. I saw he gave Jonno a gentle congratulatory tap on the backside. Finally the ref spotted the booted cadaver in centre-field. He blew play to an abeyance. The General hadn't moved an eyelash. Tutankhamen was more animate. The little playmaker was stretchered from the arena and a fresh warrior took his stead.

⌢

I wasn't happy about the tackle. I felt we were stooping to their level. We didn't want to win that way. It wasn't a gentleman's tackle. It was late. It was suspect. It was fucking brilliant!

Bernie said to me in the pub after the game, 'First rule of battle: nice guys come last,' then burped and walked off. With the Little General removed from the battlefield, we had a chance. It was all we needed. Uni was now a rudderless ship. Our 'pattern' had them quickly bunched and it wasn't long before we scored a couple of quick tries (none by the author, sadly). Moscowitz's precise goal kicks put us back in the lead. Everyone's spirits lifted – even Phil had a couple of sniping runs down the wing. We were proud of him. (His father was beside himself.) And when Phil ran, Carl Lewis couldn't run him down.

Despite being driven back for the first part of the second half, not one of us let Bernie down. And, as Bernie says to this very day, 'Blokes were dead-set launching themselves at blokes.'

With no one holding their safety in the slightest regard on both sides, the ground shook with tackles. The diminutive Moscowitz smashed ten bells out of the Uni lock-forward. Hamish and I crunched the five-eighth in a kamikaze two-man tackle, forcing him out of the play for several vital minutes. I saw the Minotaur head-butt the opposing prop-forward as he locked, cog-like, into a now heavily contested scrum. It was no holds barred, no quarter offered or taken. At the closing stages, blood leached from almost every player. Noses, ears, mouths, eyes. And every second tackle was a scuffle as people fought for the slightest advantage. Despite having no fresh troops, and ignoring the ever-changing guard of Uni storm troopers who ran at us like missiles, we were beating a team that was supposed to lick us by eighty points. It was the most intense, protracted experience of my life – for many of us, no doubt.

As we played to exhaustion, clutching for breath at times, spitting blood at others, the little square of university turf became the oval at the gates of Hades. We played as if for our very souls. I can still hear the Lions screaming at us; Bernie screaming at us; Dave Barnes and his staff screaming at Uni; Uni screaming at each other; the Maulers screaming at me; me screaming out the names of the impressionists. In the closing minutes of the game, we were penned by an unintelligible wall of noise – a miasma of hoarse screams and cheers. It was incredible. It was like walking directly into an orchestral score by Hans Henze, where every instrument in the orchestra is shouting at you simultaneously – the ear unable to lock on to a single motif.

Dad, however, was silent, looking into the heavens with clasped palms, a pocket of sunlight catching his pleading face: an El Greco portrait.

At 24 points to Uni's 20, and with less than a minute to go, we held them a metre from our line. A Uni try would have tied the game. A try and a converted goal kick would have won it for the university. They threw everything at us with Teutonic determination. We defended a torrent of never-ending sallies.

In a breathless denouement, we held Uni for twelve gut-wrenching tackles. Dad says, to this day, that he thought our line would buckle at any moment.

Now, as a writer, you go out of your way to avoid cheesy, happy endings – unless, that is, you are writing a memoir. Then it is most desirous to have one. In my semi-concussed stupor – and I kid you not – I heard the voice of Aphrodite, screaming from the sidelines.

'Tackle, Dorian! Time's almost up on the clock.'

It was Lydia. She waved the cassette and blew me a kiss.

As the Sydney Uni captain made a last, desperate attempt to crash through our back line, Hamish and I drove him back with all our remaining strength. It was hard. We were spent. But so was he. As he inched towards our line, Phil ran in and drove his shoulder into the Uni captain forcing him to the earth, a millimetre from our line. Then we heard an angel's shriek:

The referee blowing full-time on his whistle.

The Sydney Conservatorium of Music had beaten the University of Sydney: 24 points to 20.

We had won the game.

Coda

I STILL CAN'T BELIEVE WE WON that day. We challenged other universities that year and never won another game. In fact, they gave us a real touch-up, to be honest. Word had got out; they were ready for us. But that inaugural victory stays with me like a favourite chord. I rate it as my finest achievement. I note the Greek dramatist, Aeschylus, in writing his own epitaph, completely ignored his eighty odd plays and mentions only the courage he displayed against the Persians at the Battle of Marathon. I don't know, must be a guy thing.

After the game we went back to Sydney Uni's local watering hole, the Forest Lodge Hotel in Glebe (not the Oval bar). It must be said that the Uni boys were gracious losers and gentlemen to the last. Even the Little General (who had regained consciousness) bought us rounds of drinks. I recall the Uni players wearing team T-shirts sporting a caricature of a man's face that, if you looked closely enough, was an assembly of a penis and testicles. We thought it droll. After ten schooners it was hysterical. In fact, two flies crawling up the wall had us howling. By then we were pissed and giddy with delight. It was infectious. Even the Uni boys were begrudgingly pleased for us, alcohol anaesthetising the pain of defeat.

I still see the bar in my mind: Lydia and I are kissing madly; Herringbone is singing arias; Marty is humming, fleecing a poker machine, a palisade of beers along the top; Meyer and his father are dancing; Phil and Hamish are lobbing peanuts at each other, laughing like loons; various Maulers are reliving game highlights; Bernie and Dave Barnes are arm in arm, singing. And my father? Dad is in the corner with a quiet beer and a smile on his face that later has to be surgically removed.

⌒

It's sad, but people move on in life. I don't much know what became of the Maulers. Many of them joined various orchestras and ensembles and matured into extraordinary artists. I recently received an email from Big Marty. Now married and living in the Channel Islands, he runs a little music school with his wife.

My centre partner, Hamish (aka Peter Donaghy), who I ran into five years ago at the Ritz Carlton Hotel when I had my trio there, became an accountant. He married his sweetheart, Michelle, a vocalist from the Con, now a high-school music teacher.

Most of the others I have not seen or heard from since. Although I think of them often.

In a Sophoclean turn of events, Duncan became a homeless person. It seemed that while I clung to sanity by my fingernails, Duncan blew away his like someone cheerfully blowing a kiss to a departing loved one. So if you are accosted by a derelict quoting Browning, be kind.

In 1995, Sol (aka Dr. Gregory Berry) penned a landmark book entitled *Dream Analysis – Thinking Beyond Jung*. In my attempts to track him down for the purposes of this book (Osama bin Laden is easier to find!) a former colleague of his remarked that he still fields calls from Greg's old patients, claiming he saved them by getting them off medication with his unique and insightful analysis. And by simply giving them hope. He is still smoking.

The wonderful Phil is a composite. He is my best friend at school and my best friend at the Conservatorium (who were so similar they could have been the same person).

Sir Richard is a fiction.

And me? Well, I eventually signed my record deal (and no, it didn't all happen on the eve of the game). I had a nervous breakdown on tour in Adelaide (Adelaide can have that effect on people). I lost my contract some months later. I *so* wish to tell you that I was instantly cured at the blow of the referee's whistle, but it took many long and painful years before I fully recovered. I survived this Dark Age solely with the love of one very special person: my wife.

It's funny where life leads you. After years of depression, few gigs and two new mouths to feed, out of the blue one day, I said to my wife, 'I've decided to become a writer. It means we won't have any money for about seven years but I'll feel a lot better about myself and that's the main thing.' There was a silence. She agreed. (For a moment I thought she was about to say, 'Have you thought about getting a *job*?')

These days, I live on the coast and spend my time writing, practising the piano and playing little gigs with my trio here and there (nothing earth-shattering). I am currently head of the Jazz Department of the Central Coast Conservatorium of Music (a part-time gig). When I'm not writing or playing the piano, I am beach-fishing. It's my passion. I spend thousands of solitary hours staring into the waves, accompanied only by my healed friend: my imagination.

I have a wonderful life.

As I write this final chapter, my beautiful wife brings me a cup of tea. Tea leaves wheel in the cup. She says this means we will soon come into money. She's been saying this for years. We're still broke. For seventeen years, her unyielding love has been a harbour in which I have been able to seek shelter, before making the necessary repairs to again venture out to sea. She places the cup beside me with a clink.

'Thanks, Lydia,' I say.

She kisses me softly on the neck, 'Nearly finished?'

'I'm writing the final chapter.'

She scowls. 'You haven't made fun of my mother, have you?'

'Of course not,' I lie.

'Do you think people will like it?'

'I don't know. It's dark in places.'

'What is life but darkness and light?'

'You're a wise old broad. Do people ever tell you that?'

'Constantly.' She peeks through the blinds of my studio. 'Have a look at your two sons.'

I see my eleven-year-old kicking a football around the backyard. He is a veritable try-scoring machine for his little team, the Terrigal Trojans. (I hope the irony of the name is not lost on you. Hey, how many eleven-year-olds can say they've read Homer?) His side was the only Terrigal team to win their grand final this year. When, under lights at Gosford stadium, he scored a length-of-the-field try in the dying minutes of the game, they say his grandfather's cheering could be heard in Venezuela. When I watch him play, he astounds me – he has the concentration of a concert pianist. Who knows? He may become a footballer of note one day. He clearly has a natural talent (forcing me to recently ask Lydia for a paternity test).

Then I spot my gorgeous, eccentric nine-year-old. A boy destined for greatness, he amazes Lydia and me with his incredible courage: the courage to be himself. Resplendent in lime-green shorts, neon-blue gumboots and yellow washing-up gloves, he has collapsed on the grass, exhausted after looking for butterflies all afternoon. He is supine, staring at the clouds, watching the way they inch across the sky, daydreaming. He'll do this for hours.

No paternity test needed.

It saddens me to say that Lydia never danced again after 'The Globe Fiasco'. (She still has the scar on her leg where silly Duncan snipped her with the knife.) I don't know why she stopped dancing. She says the children have become her living artworks (a concept my mother struggles to come to grips with on occasion). However, sometimes I return home to find the furniture slightly askew. She's been at it again: dancing in secret. I've never seen it, but in my mind the living room is transformed into the stage of Covent Garden. She is showered with bouquets and deafened by thunderous applause. I *so* wish she still danced. Whenever I see the furniture rearranged, I feel a pang.

Bernie still works as a salesman for True Blue Chemicals, a great little company run by a group of ex-football players. Recently, from a private box, Bernie, Dad, Anne and Patsy watched Bernie's youngest son play his initial first-grade game for the South Sydney Rabbitohs (the team I have supported ever since playing football) in the final round of the season. He scored his inaugural try for the team on the bell. I don't think Bernie will mind me telling you that he shed a tear. (Dad did too, caught up in the moment.) It was a proud day for the Johns family. Bernie's elder son (our ball boy, if you remember) plays for Randwick (as does my brother-in-law) and is a star player for the state team: the Waratahs. He is sheer electricity on the field and will soon represent his country. My sons and I love watching him play. I imagine Bernie played much the same in his day, *sans* twenty stone.

And Dad? I can't honestly say that Dad and I instantly formed a relationship from a single game of football, but it seemed an appropriate metaphor all the same. When I was a boy my father was a stranger to me. I only met him when I started playing football and drinking in pubs. But my father is a babushka doll. Each schooner reveals another doll. Only by stepping into Dad's universe was I able to meet the final doll.

I've forgiven both Dad and Mum for my turbulent entry into the world. They were only kids. And at some stage you have to let go of the past to find a future. I've discovered you can have a great relationship with your parents if, in the end, it boils down to one thing: your love for them is greater than your anger. Lydia taught me that by loving your parents unconditionally, you are able to move on with life. I wasn't able to rewrite my childhood, but through love and empathy, I was able to edit my adulthood.

Aside from Lydia, Dad is my best mate. We spend a lot of time together. He loves fishing. A man, he says, can learn a lot about life from fishing. I suppose Dad remains the same: a man of simple pleasures. Every Friday afternoon, you'll find him at the Randwick Rugby Club (not so much at the Dog, these days) with his boozy pals. He'll sink a thousand schooners then be magically transported to his front door by 'The Beer Scooter' (i.e. he has no idea how he got home). He'll wake up disoriented and contorted on the lounge at three in the morning with an empty wine bottle and half a kebab in his pocket. The next day, he will sit in his office and work for ten hours. (How does he do it? God, I'd be sick for a week!) I guess it's true people don't change, but I have noticed that they grow. Dad has grown. And the boys and I love him (and Mum) with an intensity that burns like the sun.

My mother and I have a better relationship these days, too. It must be said that Mum has worked hard at it. I love her for it. I would not today be an artist without her constant support and guidance. She's a better listener these days, too, and calls regularly. We are closer than we have ever been. She realises she missed out on a lot. But at the time, she was a facsimile of my own neuroses. It was hard for her to travel any other road than the one she ultimately chose.

Dad is still tough to impress with artistic achievements. A little while back, I called him with the news that my agent had signed my first novel, *A Café in Venice*, to the biggest publishing house in Europe.

Dad said, 'Yeah, great,' but he had even *better* news! He had managed to hire a boat for our impending fishing trip for the full three days! This meant that we could 'get on the piss' the entire time without returning the boat each day. 'What a bloody coup!' he added.

I laughed. Years ago I would have been horribly wounded. I must have blinked and grown up. Somehow I knew that career achievements will fade, but when he's gone, I'll think about that fishing trip for the rest of my life.

Dad enjoys his grandchildren. He finally has his football hero. The other day I mentioned that the boys are excelling in the arts. I said his youngest grandson is developing into a fine pianist and his elder grandson had just won a state-wide short story competition. To which he replied, as quick as you like, 'Who cares? He's going to play for Randwick! Maybe Souths.'

We looked at each other and exploded with laughter. I think we realised he sounded like a character from this book.

⌒

I don't care if my boys become athletes or artists. Both, I've discovered, are not dissimilar. To be successful, each requires a modicum of natural talent, hard work and just a pinch of luck. However, of one thing I'm certain. Whatever my boys *do* become in life, I hope we remain mates – whatever the balance sheet, if you've achieved that, you've done something right as a father. Though, if I'm honest, I hope they have *some* interest in the arts. While the athlete has the ability to inspire feelings of triumph and conquest, the artist will forever bring light to the dark corners of the heart.

Surprise in Jumper

Reading about *The Mozart Maulers* ("No Con job – its students really could play . . . footy", *Herald*, July 26) brought back all the horrible memories of that day. I can assure Dorian Mode that the people who played for Sydney University on that day have not forgotten about it.

Indeed, when old uni team-mates gather around, it is this cursed game more than any (including winning a premiership) that gets talked about. How jokes soon turned to puzzlement, to bewilderment, to shock and to, alas, a loss.

I'm not sure who was playing with the trombone up their jumper but it remains to this day the only time I have been knocked unconscious in a game. I suggest when the match is shown in the movie, it could be accompanied by the *1812 Overture*. Good luck to all involved.

Danny White,
Earlwood
July 27

A CAFÉ IN VENICE

DORIAN MODE

Quirky and neurotic, Gordon B. Shoesmith is a 30-something jazz musician seeing his twelfth psychiatrist in as many years. He increasingly discovers that there is a conflict between his artist's idealism and the hard reality of Life, fuelled by his ambitious journalist girlfriend, Jenny, and her disapproving parents.

Gordon finds himself on an improvised, medicated roller-coaster ride of self-discovery that drags him from cockroach-infested, inner-city anonymity to mercurial artistic success, to the cynical world of advertising. He's finally tossed onto the road that leads to a cafe, run by Joe, a middle-aged, Palestinian Elvis impersonator, in the desert town of Venice, South Australia.

A Cafe in Venice is a surreal, comic insight into the personal fulfilment we aspire to in a mad, intransigent world.

A GIRL, A SMOCK AND A SIMPLE PLAN

CHRIS DAFFEY

'Julian Crowler was a large child. Not large enough to be considered fat, but fat enough to be considered large. At five feet and three inches, he towered above your average sixth grader and represented the kind of shambling, slow-witted menace that no primary school could be without . . . In a poll conducted at the beginning of grade six, Julian Crowler was voted the second most frightening sight in the playground. Julian Crowler eating a meat pie was voted first.'

This hilarious novel takes us down memory lane to grade six primary school – to the games we played and the friendships we formed. To weirdo teachers, schoolyard scuffles and scary moments outside the Principal's office. It's also the story of a crush, and one boy's quest to win over a girl called Jenny.